"I ca

"God help me, I love you," Anthony said. "But I can't live my life when all my men are dead. Every minute I spend in this house, guilt eats at me. Every second I spend with you, I feel ashamed that I came home when all the others came home in body bags."

Kristen gently took his face into her two hands. "You've been given more time than your men, that's all," she said. "Shutting yourself off from living life in the time you've been given hurts everyone, including me and Amy. We *need* you to be part of our lives. It's your responsibility—your obligation—to live, Anthony. You were a hero to your men. You can't let them down now."

Anthony couldn't see past the blur of his tears, so he pulled Kristen into his arms. The ice inside him receded a little. And the guilt began to ease its stranglehold on his heart....

Dear Readers,

Marriages are so often challenging. But marriages between military members are even more demanding than most. Long separations, dramatically different experiences and the trauma of war can thwart even the most loving couple. Add the responsibility of a child to the mix and the difficulties may seem insurmountable. But sometimes love conquers all.

Major Anthony Garitano and Major Kristen Clark have more than their fair share of obstacles to overcome. His deployment to a harsh land far away from her duty station has taken its toll. War has changed him. And motherhood has changed her. But when the two reunite, joining forces to save their daughter from a revenge-seeking terrorist, they rediscover the power of love.

I hope you enjoy this story of two officers who refuse to let their dedication to the military overwhelm their dedication to each other.

Elizabeth Ashtree

www.elizabethashtree.com
eashtree@aol.com

A Marriage of Majors
Elizabeth Ashtree

TORONTO • NEW YORK • LONDON
AMSTERDAM • PARIS • SYDNEY • HAMBURG
STOCKHOLM • ATHENS • TOKYO • MILAN • MADRID
PRAGUE • WARSAW • BUDAPEST • AUCKLAND

ISBN 0-373-71216-2

A MARRIAGE OF MAJORS

Copyright © 2004 by Randi Elizabeth DuFresne.

www.eHarlequin.com

Printed in U.S.A.

To my husband, for reminding me every day
that laughter is the glue that holds a marriage together.
To my sisters for their help with the medical aspects of this
book. And to all our children, for teaching us that the
true challenge of motherhood is letting go.

Books by Elizabeth Ashtree

HARLEQUIN SUPERROMANCE
828—AN OFFICER AND A HERO
1036—THE COLONEL AND THE KID
1089—A CAPTAIN'S HONOR

Don't miss any of our special offers. Write to us at the
following address for information on our newest releases.

Harlequin Reader Service
U.S.: 3010 Walden Ave., P.O. Box 1325, Buffalo, NY 14269
Canadian: P.O. Box 609, Fort Erie, Ont. L2A 5X3

PROLOGUE

MAJOR ANTHONY GARITANO stepped forward and surveyed the captives. There were twenty-six of them kneeling on the hard, dry earth with their hands clasped behind their heads—just the way he'd told them to. Dust swirled around them, and the hot, parched wind danced with their loose clothing and the dangling ends of their turbans. The prisoners were tired, hungry, thirsty and defeated. Anthony took no pleasure in their misery. Yet this successful capture brought him and his team of Army Rangers one step closer to leaving this hellhole for some much-needed R and R. One more series of caves to clear out, then they'd be heading home.

For a split second, his mind drifted to thoughts of his wife and the daughter he'd not yet met. But then his training kicked in and he shook his head, forcing himself back to the moment. This was a dangerous place and he couldn't afford to lose his concentration.

"Where's that truck, JJ?" he said as he touched the activation button on the communication device at his throat.

"Four miles south, moving at a snail's pace, sir."

"It'll be dark before we can turn over the prisoners to the relief soldiers. Weasel, give these people some water."

"Yes, sir," came the instant reply into Anthony's earphone from Sergeant Walter Grim, better known as

Weasel due to his ability to squeeze himself through the most unlikely openings. After a pause, Weasel's voice squawked over the radio again. "Which people, sir?"

Anthony looked up, spotted the Sergeant among the others across the clearing, and glared at him. "The prisoners, Sergeant."

"Yes, sir. Right away." Weasel took two steps toward the canteens. Then a shrill cry split the air, halting him in midstride.

Instantly on high alert, Anthony snapped his attention back to the captives. One had raised his face to the sky and delivered the battle cry. Out of the corner of his eye, Anthony could see that Master Sergeant "Scopes" Spiro already had his fifty-five-millimeter weapon raised to his shoulder with a bead on the disruptive prisoner's forehead. But then an answering cry resounded through the superheated afternoon air, turning Anthony's blood cold. This other voice echoed down from the high ground to the left.

Everything happened at once then. Scopes raised his sight up into the rocky hills from which the second cry had come, but he also backed up rapidly until he was behind the remains of a crumbling mortar hut. Training kicked in and the other members of the team also went to ground, hitting the dirt behind gear and outcroppings until they were invisible from the high ground. All except Anthony. He simply went down on one knee, making himself a smaller target as he raised his M-4 to his shoulder and scanned the area through the weapon's sight. He would rather be shot at than let a single one of these terrorist scum escape.

Thank God for Kevlar vests, he thought as he coolly inched his focus across the landscape searching for the target. An abrupt *vip* slashed the air—a rifle shot whizzed past his head and a chunk of dry earth leaped upward, just a few feet past him. Anthony didn't flinch. His life, and the lives of his men, depended on his steadfastness.

A flash of light reflected off something angular. He aimed, squeezed the trigger, absorbed the recoil into his shoulder, and aimed again. What appeared at this distance to be a Russian-made AK-47 rifle completed a couple of somersaults and hit the ground near a large boulder. Bingo! Anthony's single bullet had taken out at least one enemy weapon.

"Watch out, Scopes! Tiger's gonna steal your job," someone said in hushed tones, using Anthony's nickname.

"Cut the chatter," Anthony ordered quietly as he watched the Russian rifle slide down the slope a few feet before it lodged in a crag. One rifle out of commission, but Anthony had no way of knowing whether the target had other weapons.

Apparently not, if he could tell anything from the string of Arabic, French and English curses that rained down on them, all in the same voice. A single figure scurried backward and up in a desperate attempt to escape. Three of his men—JJ, McCool, and Billy—ran toward the target, leaping rocks and scurrying up the hillside faster than most men could run on flat pavement.

"Scopes, take out a leg or something," Anthony ordered his sharpshooter.

"Our guys keep drifting into my sight, sir. You want I should try and take a shot anyway?" Scopes said through the tiny speaker lodged in Anthony's ear.

"No. Only if you get a clean bead," Anthony said, frustration lashing at his insides.

One of the prisoners lifted himself off one knee and

before another blink of an eye, Anthony had him sighted along the short barrel of his M-4. "Down!" he ordered with a gesture. The man complied instantly, but now Anthony needed to remain focused on the prisoners, lest one of them make another attempt to escape.

"Target's out of range," Scopes declared. "Sorry, sir."

"Cover the prisoners," Anthony ordered. And the instant he heard the dull click-clack of his shooter shifting the position of his weapon to sight on the kneeling men, Anthony lowered his own rifle and ran full speed up the hill himself.

He stopped in his tracks ten yards into his mad dash when he saw the target turn and leap atop a wide rock. Hands raised into the air, the man gave his battle cry again. There seemed to be something wrong with his right hand, but the only truly important fact was that there were no other weapons in it.

"I am Taaoun," the man cried in surprisingly good English. Then he added, "I will hunt you down and kill you. Your children will die, too. I will wipe your stink from the earth. I will find you, Garitano, you vile American follower of Satan." His dark beard and gray turban made his English words and American accent seem completely wrong. Some quirk of the hills made them echo down to the Army Rangers with perfect clarity despite the distance. "Do you hear me, Garitano? I will kill you!" Then the gunman jumped backward and disappeared from sight behind the rock.

Less than a minute later, JJ scrambled to the spot. The radio brought his words to Anthony's ear a nanosecond before the wind did. "There's an opening here. We'll need Weasel to follow him down this hole."

"Weasel, get up there," Anthony said into his mike.

"McCool, go back down and help Scopes retain control of the prisoners." Major Anthony Garitano, newly marked for death by a terrorist who spoke perfect English, continued up the slope.

"Sir, come have a look at this," said Billy Brinewater. The young Lieutenant had been the first to dub Anthony Sir Tony the Tiger.

Anthony veered left toward where Billy stood looking down at the ground. A few paces more and the pair of them stood shoulder to shoulder, gazing at something in the dirt. "What the hell is that?" Anthony asked.

"Looks like he gave us the finger," Billy answered with a smirk. And as soon as he put a name to the bloodied thing tilted on the edge of a slab of stone, the image clarified in Anthony's mind. It was, indeed, a finger. A trigger finger, to be more precise.

"Bag it," Anthony said. "What else is here?" He scanned the area where the target had been hiding.

"The AK-47 is down there a piece," Billy said. "And behind the rock here we've got a pair of binoculars."

Anthony's desert boots crunched on the gravel as he stepped around to take a look. "They explain how he knows my name, at least." He glanced down at his last name, sewn over the right pocket of his tan desert camouflage uniform.

"He's missing a finger now, so he won't be hard to spot," Billy observed.

"He'll wear gloves," Anthony said as he perused the area. "At least that's what I'd do."

"I hadn't thought of that."

"That's why you're a Lieutenant and I'm a major. Just don't let me forget to write down what the guy called himself. Tatooine or something."

"Tatooine is the planet in *Star Wars* where Anakin

Skywalker was born. The guy said he was Taaoun, whatever the hell that means.''

"Just send all this stuff with the boys in the truck," Anthony said. "They can figure out what they want to do about Taaoun. We have our next mission to complete.''

But not even Weasel could figure out which way the target had gone inside the warren of tunnels. After three hours, Anthony called off the search. The truck came, a rare hot meal was served, the prisoners and evidence were taken away.

Every man felt the downward drag of disappointment that the target had managed to escape them. But they were due twenty miles north by daybreak and Anthony needed to get his team moving. They packed and hoisted their gear onto their capable shoulders.

"Move out!" Anthony called to his men. As he marched beside them, he thought again of his wife waiting for him at home. He ached to turn in the opposite direction, to make his way to base camp, and from there to any form of transportation that would bring him to Kristen and baby Amy. Instead, he trudged forward, doggedly pursuing the enemy, performing his duty as his country had asked of him.

Twenty miles down the road, he and his men gave their country everything they had to give—and then some.

CHAPTER ONE

KRISTEN STOOD UNDER the cloudless sky on the tarmac of the U.S. Army airfield in Wiesbaden, Germany, waiting for her husband to disembark. The plane stood in front of her, but the hatch had yet to open. With every passing minute, her eighteen-month-old daughter grew fussier. When busy little hands began to pull on Kristen's uniform epaulettes, apparently attempting to rip the embroidered gold leaf of a major off her shoulder, she put Amy down and tried to redirect her daughter's attention with her car keys.

So much for looking nice for this reunion with her husband after a year and a half apart. The crisply ironed uniform shirt she'd donned in the morning was now wrinkled and damp in places. She doubted her black necktie had remained straight after all the jostling she'd done in the last half hour, but she didn't dare let her attention drift long enough to check.

She pasted a smile on her lips. Hoping. She'd been told of his extensive injuries and about his depression, disorientation and occasional bouts of delusion. The man who had never known defeat would take longer than others to adjust to its bitter taste, she'd been told. So she'd spent hours and hours working with the on-post psychologist to map out the best plan to aid Anthony's emotional recovery. But how could she really be ready for him? His face had been torn up so badly that it would require more plastic surgery once he recovered some strength. He'd lost a few yards of intestines, though they'd been able to piece him back together once he'd been transported to Kabul from wherever in Afghanistan he'd been at the time of the explosion.

Kristen wanted to weep just thinking about it. But tears wouldn't do the tough Major Anthony Garitano a bit of good. Her proud warrior husband would hate being on the receiving end of even the tiniest bit of pity. For that reason, she'd forced herself to keep from rushing to him in the Afghanistan hospital. And her duties at the U.S. Army airfield here in Germany left little room for sitting helplessly at his bedside. Better to stay home with Amy, better to remain at her duty station, better to pray for his recovery in private so no one—least of all Anthony—would see her tears.

Finally, the hatch at the side of the airplane swooshed open. The darkness beyond the door drew her focus as she fumbled for a better hold on her daughter's hand. "Daddy's coming," she bent down and whispered to her. "Look, Amy. Daddy's coming."

That got Amy's attention. She'd heard a great deal about her daddy and she'd even started kissing his photograph goodnight after her bedtime story. "Da Da?" she queried as she looked with a creased brow toward the yawning, empty opening in the plane. She pointed her chubby finger toward the door and waited. Anticipation, the stepsister of dread, uncoiled within Kristen's heart and began to pound against its walls as they waited.

At last, a figure appeared.

She'd expected a wheelchair, so when a man stepped out into the light, she let out her pent-up breath. This could not be Anthony. Not this man, who lacked her husband's six-foot-three-inch height and muscled breadth. Slowly, he walked the few feet to the railing of the ramp and scanned the area.

He could *not* be her husband—and yet there was Anthony's dark, wavy hair. Moving slowly closer, towing a resistant Amy, Kristen saw the dark, deep-set eyes, the stubborn jaw, the sensuous mouth. She looked at Anthony's face—thinner, paler and with a long, jagged scar running from his temple to his throat and another, less obvious one from the bridge of his nose across his cheek—and she felt a deep sadness.

She had tried so hard to prepare herself. But reality made a direct hit to her solar plexus and she could hardly breathe. This Anthony—whose desert camouflage uniform hung loosely on his frame—this Anthony was not anything like the man she'd married.

Neither was she the same woman with whom he'd exchanged vows, she reminded herself. So much time had passed, so much had happened to them independently. They were strangers to one other. Complete strangers.

And yet…and yet…her husband had come home. Alive. So many had not. Against all odds, Anthony had escaped the deadly explosion with his lungs still drawing breath and his heart still beating. Barely.

Suddenly the tears she choked back were tears of joy. She needed to touch him, reassure herself that he lived and breathed by holding him close. Pulling Amy behind her, she strode toward him, never taking her gaze away from his ravaged, unsmiling face.

HE WOULD RECOGNIZE HER SMILE hidden among a thousand others. And there she was, waiting for him. Smiling at him. He stared, hungry for the sight of her. He wanted to hold her—needed to feel her arms around him. Wishing he could hurry, but knowing he'd fall on his face if he tried, he began the long descent along the handicap ramp, determined to greet her on his own two feet.

The doctors had wanted him in a wheelchair. To shut them up, he'd agreed to one—right up until the moment the hatch had opened. Then he'd risen from the chair and walked—or, more accurately, shuffled—toward the opening before the medics could block his way.

As she neared the plane and the gap between them contracted, he noticed more than Kristen's smile. She'd cut off her beautiful hair and she'd lost the delightful fullness to her face that had been there when they'd last seen each other. She'd been pregnant then. Now, her skin was tanned, her flesh lean and taut, her eyes more serious and penetrating. But her smile glowed as brightly.

With his throat closing and his breath catching, fighting to suppress the emotions clawing at his heart, he looked down at his feet and made them move one in front of the other. The ramp stretched before him, easy to negotiate in a wheelchair, but seemingly endless as he forced his shaky legs into obedience. First the ramp sloped right, then left. After more steps than he'd have believed himself capable of, he found himself in the home stretch leading to the pavement resting over friendly German soil.

The exertion produced dampness on his brow that he longed to wipe away. But he had no spare energy with which to lift his hand. Only a month ago, he'd walked twenty miles with a seventy-pound pack without difficulty. Now, a few yards were a strain. His pride demanded that he not let that strain show.

Ruthlessly, he reminded himself that he had no right

to pride. He had no right to this feeling of pressurized relief and joy that welled inside him as he approached his wife. He'd failed his men. There would be no happy endings for them. And as he began to remember, his vision blurred and his hearing dulled. The horrible memories filled his mind, blotting out everything else.

"Anthony," he heard her say in that silky, sultry voice of hers. And the terrible images disappeared as his gaze refocused on her face, not two feet from where he'd come to a stop near the end of the ramp. A crease marred the smoothness between her brows, telegraphing her concern. But her eyes were hopeful.

"Kristen," he rasped past the lingering effects of the various tubes that had scraped down his throat while he'd been in the hospital. She looked so different. Just as pretty, with eyes as frank and honest as ever. But he hardly knew her. And she sure as hell didn't know him anymore.

Too much time and tragedy had made them strangers. To be honest, they'd never known each other all that well to begin with. Now he was a broken man. A shell of what he used to be. Scarred and damaged and soulless.

They would divorce soon. He knew that. While he was in the hospital, his mind had wandered over the subject and had come to this inevitable conclusion. They might try for a while. Kristen would insist on trying. But then they would end their marriage. Because he could never measure up to the man he had been. And she deserved better.

Perhaps he should simply tell her that he'd had time to look at things from every angle and that divorce was inevitable. He could save her the time she would otherwise invest in trying to heal him. If he could persuade her to give in to the only possible conclusion, he'd be free to crawl into a deep hole somewhere and let the darkness smother him.

Not yet, an inner voice pleaded. Don't tell her yet. Just take these few hours to be with her—maybe a few days—to make certain she'll be okay on her own and to store up memories as sustenance for the future. Bleak, bleak future…

Heaviness began to consume him. His insides suddenly felt weighted and there seemed to be no point in doing anything at all. He stood there without moving as seconds stretched by. Inside his mind, the voice of the fighter he'd once been screamed for him to take her into his embrace and kiss her breathless—which is what he would have done before his world had been shredded beyond all recognition on that last rocky hillside in Afghanistan. Yes, kissing her would be wonderful after spending so much time away. But he couldn't seem to make the effort.

"I'm so glad you're home," she said. And then, there it was again. Her smile. Her warm, honest, reassuring smile. Slightly forced, he felt sure, but as bright and beautiful as ever. She beamed at him and opened her arms invitingly.

Somehow, his legs carried him into her embrace. His arms found their way around her slim torso. His head fell to her shoulder, partly from bone-deep weariness and partly to hide the stinging tears that filled his eyes. Warmth spread through him, chasing away the cold, blank weight that had urged him down under the clutching waters of despair since he'd awakened for the first time inside the MASH unit just before being transported to the hospital in Kabul. That heaviness had grown steadily during his physical recovery until he wished it would simply crush him and end his pathetic struggle.

But now Kristen stood here with him. Holding her, he could almost bear it—the shame, the despair, the soul-wracking regret.

A sudden wail pierced the air. Anthony winced at the volume and then resisted a desperate need to clutch at his wife when he felt her begin to pull away. The cries continued and gained force. He felt like joining in. Screams seemed to reside just below his calm facade, aching to be heard. As always, he managed to restrain himself. He allowed his attention to be drawn to the small human body clinging to his wife's leg. The wailing came from a very small girl in a ruffled pink dress.

His little girl?

Like a knife through his heart came the realization that this cute-as-a-button noise machine was his child. Despite the updates he'd received through his far-too-few e-mail exchanges with Kristen, Anthony hadn't really pictured his daughter accurately. In his mind, she'd stayed a baby. But looking at her now, he saw that he'd missed her babyhood. He'd missed it completely. Amy was a little girl.

Kristen bent to shush the child and tugged the small clutching arms free. Amy stood there, silent at last and steadier on her feet than her father was on his. Then big brown eyes looked up at him. She stared for several seconds. Anthony felt as if those round eyes held him captive.

Amy turned back to her mother. "Up," she said. At this one word, his insides leaped in surprise. She could talk, too! Had he known that? Had that milestone made it into any of Kristen's updates? God, he'd missed so much.

Kristen picked Amy up but remained close to him. "Da Da," she said to his daughter as if this was something they'd practiced.

"Da Da," Amy repeated, looking at her mother's face. For the first time in many months, amusement tugged at the corners of his mouth. His heart filled with unexpected pleasure that glimmered like a faint light within the internal darkness that had grown so familiar.

Kristen caught his gaze again. "Anthony, I'd like you to meet your daughter. Amy," she said to the little girl, "this is your daddy." Then she pointed to him, inviting Amy to look in his direction again.

Amy turned her head. Innocent eyes fastened their gaze onto his.

He looked back, awed. "Hello, Amy," he said. Then he offered her a smile—an expression he barely remembered how to produce. He felt his skin tighten in strange places. Too late, he remembered his terrible scars.

Amy whipped her face away and tucked her head into the hollow of Kristen's neck, refusing to look at him again. Anthony took a step back, reeling as if he'd been struck.

"She's just tired, Anthony," Kristen assured him. "Don't take her too seriously. Really. She's just tired and hot. Probably hungry, too. She'll be your shadow before you know it. You'll see."

But Anthony knew better. He'd seen his reflection. Amy had every right to turn away from the face of a monster. Hell, he always wanted to look away from the hideous sight, too, and he had begun to avoid mirrors.

"Let's get you both home," Kristen said, and she turned to lead the way. Amy's unblinking dark eyes peeped at him over the major's epaulette on Kristen's shoulder. Staring back at her while emptiness and a distant ache took up residence in his heart again, he couldn't move.

"A wheelchair, sir?" inquired someone behind him. The medic had followed him but hadn't intruded on his reunion.

He barely heard the question and didn't answer. Instead, he watched in fascination as Amy lifted one chubby hand and stretched out her fingers toward him as if reaching for a toy. Or beckoning to him. Anthony blinked. But his daughter's small hand remained outstretched to him, her gaze stayed locked on his, beseeching.

So he followed, finding it far easier to make his legs cooperate now. In that moment, he knew he would walk to the ends of the earth for her, if she asked it of him.

CHAPTER TWO

THERE SEEMED TO BE A LOT of stairs in the house where his wife had been living since her transfer to Germany a year ago. A comfortable house in a row of others, it had seemed welcoming from the outside. But looks were deceiving. First, there had been the three steps up to the stoop to get through the side door into the kitchen. Then there were all those additional steps to get to the bathroom. Along the way, toys were scattered everywhere. Amy seemed perfectly able to navigate through everything, even though she'd only been walking a few months. But for him, with the torn muscles along his abdomen and hip just beginning to heal, the place had all the treachery of a minefield.

"Sorry," Kristen said as she stooped to pick up the toys that stretched in an endless sea through the living room. "I know the place is a mess. We were in a rush to get out the door. I didn't want to miss your arrival. I just had to leave everything. Actually, I have to admit it's usually like this. It just seems so silly to keep picking everything up when I know for a fact that she'll have them all spread out again before…"

"It's okay, Kris," he said, wishing she wouldn't make excuses. "She's my kid, too. I'll just have to get used to it."

Kristen stopped picking up toys and stood in the center of the remaining chaos staring at Amy, who was gleefully pulling more toys out of a box. "I babble when I'm nervous," she whispered, as if they weren't familiar with each other's quirks.

Her admission startled him. "Why are you nervous?"

"I want you to like the house, to feel comfortable here," she said, and Anthony had the feeling there were other hopes she'd left unsaid. "But it's a mess and...you'll think I'm a bad mother."

"That's not possible. And who am I to judge? I haven't been here to try my hand at parenting, so what do I know? Seems to me you've done a good job so far."

She glanced at him with a shy smile lighting her eyes. "Thanks. I'm trying. But the housecleaning usually doesn't get done."

He glanced around. "Maybe I can help."

She huffed a small laugh, but when she saw he'd meant it, she sobered. "Sorry. It's just that I don't remember you doing any of the cleaning before. And besides, you need to focus on recuperating, not on running a vacuum."

He wanted to tell her he wasn't an invalid, but he shrugged instead. It didn't matter. And anyway, she was right. He couldn't remember the last time he'd done a lick of housework. It seemed as if they'd had a housekeeper or cleaning service or something at their last duty station before he'd deployed. Well, she apparently didn't have one now.

The furniture was the same stuff they'd had in their last apartment in the States. But all around the household trappings he recognized, there were unfamiliar signs of childhood. Maybe he could help put things in some sort of order for Kristen while he stayed. He certainly wasn't good for much else right now. And he had nothing else to do, given that he wouldn't be cleared for duty for quite some time. If ever. He closed his eyes against the horror of that thought. What would he do from day to day if the Army didn't let him return to duty?

"It's a nice little place," Kristen commented. "Do you want me to show you around?"

"I don't think I need a tour," he said sharply. He hadn't intended to sound so harsh, but everything tended to come out that way these days. He couldn't speak without growling, it seemed. Kristen looked so dejected at his tone that he wished he could take it back. God, there were so many things he wished he could take back, do over, try again. But people rarely got second chances. And he couldn't muster the energy to try to make conversation with Kristen right.

Amy apparently had nearly every toy she owned scattered across the carpet now. She held one up for his inspection and said, "Beebee."

It was a well-chewed baby doll. His facial muscles creaked into another unexpected smile at his clever daughter who was able to say her doll's name. But when she held up another item—this one something that could have been a stuffed animal sometime in the distant past—and said "beebee" again, he began to lose confidence. Yet his smile widened while the heaviness inside lifted slightly.

Kristen chuckled. "Everything is 'baby' to her right now. Just tell her what it really is and eventually she'll start using the right names."

Anthony cocked his head as he gazed at the toy, trying to come up with a name for the thing. "First you'll have to tell me what it is," he admitted.

"Snuffleupagus," she said, as if this would have meaning for him. "It's a Muppet," she added.

He looked down again at his daughter and her toy.

"Snup-o-gus," Amy said, and then she waved the thing at him with a huge, openmouthed smile that lit her whole face. Anthony laughed out loud. He knew he shouldn't, understood that such pleasure should be beyond him, but he couldn't help it. And before he had the chance to remind himself that laughter was a complete betrayal of his men and their fate, he carefully lowered himself to the floor next to his daughter.

"Snuff-o-lup-o-saur," he tried. Amy stared at him a moment as if stricken, and Anthony worried she would run away in fright. He was still a big man with an awful face, even if he wore a smile and sat on the floor.

She didn't run away. Instead, she tossed the stuffed animal to him. "Snup-o-gus," she repeated with a giggle.

A muffled sound came from Kristen's direction and when he looked up at her, he noted her failing attempt to hold back a giggle of her own. When she met his gaze, she tried for a serious expression. "Snuffle-up-a-gus," she advised.

"You're kidding, right? How can anyone expect a little kid to say a name like that?"

With a wide grin, Kristen held her hands out at her sides in a gesture of helplessness. "That's its name," she insisted. "You'll have to just watch *Sesame Street* with her tomorrow morning and see for yourself."

As he thought about watching a morning kids' show with Amy, he felt something stirring inside. An ache, a longing, a wish.

Did he dare to try to make a relationship with this wonderful child? Should he attempt to win over his daughter and perhaps rediscover his wife—even though his men… God, he could hardly bear to think of it, even after all these weeks.

And then there was that other thing haunting him. A terrorist madman with an American accent who'd threatened to track him down and kill him. The one he'd been so sure he'd seen trying to get into his room in the hospital in Kabul just before he'd gone under sedation. By the time he'd asked about the sighting, no one remembered the man he knew as Taaoun. And the doctors chalked it up to paranoia from post-traumatic stress disorder.

Anthony couldn't be sure if he was endangering his family by possibly leading a psycho to their home or simply burdening them with his own twisted mental condition. He shook his head a little, disgusted by the thought. A psychopathic killer on the loose or merely a delusional husband and father—hard to tell which would cause his family the most suffering.

Confusion made his head swim as he struggled with the push and pull of competing emotions. He needed to escape.

"You said the bathroom is upstairs?" he asked in a hollow voice. The pain medication had worn off and although he hated to take it, the stuff had the added advantage of dulling his senses so the memories were not as sharp and jagged. He could barely force himself to raise his gaze to hers.

Kristen's smile wavered at his mood change. "Yes, just past Amy's bedroom."

He got to his feet—no small task in his condition. Finding the facilities wasn't a necessity right then, but evacuating this happy hearth-and-home insanity seemed imperative. He didn't deserve any of this, never would, had to get away from it, needed to get away…

KRISTEN WATCHED HIM climb the stairs. His doctors had claimed he could resume normal activities as long as he didn't overdo things. But he took each step one at a time, lifting the same foot first each time, slowly and methodically. And he looked like an old man.

Don't think like that, she chided herself. He just needs time.

Before he disappeared behind the wall that began halfway up the stairway, she asked, "Can I get anything for you? Are you hungry? I've got lemonade. And plums. I remembered you used to like plums." She stopped the babble when he raised a hand, palm out, to indicate he needed nothing. Then he moved out of sight.

She forced herself to wait a full twenty minutes, plying Amy with applesauce and cheese until the child could barely keep her eyes open. "Nap time," Kristen finally said. She scooped up the weary toddler and took comfort in her sweet smell and the trusting slackness of her limbs.

Quietly, she climbed the stairs, unsure of what she might find. Could he still be in the bathroom? Maybe he'd gone into their bedroom to lie down. Would he mind if she stretched out beside him, just to be near him again after so many months? How pathetic she felt as she acknowledged the depths of her longing to press her body to his again, to feel his strength, to know she wasn't alone anymore.

But she found him where she least expected him. He stood in Amy's bedroom, in the center of the open floor, apparently staring at the wallpaper. Or maybe he gaped at the shelves of toys along the wall. Or the side-by-side pictures of their sets of parents, smiling down on Amy as only grandparents can do.

Kristen didn't want to disturb him, but Amy desperately needed a nap. "Daddy's here to say night-night to you, Amy," she whispered, partly to alert Anthony to her presence and partly to explain to Amy why the tall stranger occupied her room.

Anthony stepped a little out of the way, saying nothing. The scars on his face weren't so noticeable when he wore this slack, shuttered expression. Kristen stepped to the bed and eased Amy onto it. The girl slid like a silk ribbon onto the mattress and immediately grasped her teddy bear with one hand while popping the thumb of the other into her mouth. As Kristen sat on the edge of the bed, Amy's fatigue-glazed eyes sought the photograph on her nightstand. "Ni-ni, Da Da," she said.

Kristen felt her eyes begin to sting as she remembered all the times Amy had said good-night to her absent father through his picture. "You don't have to say night-night to his picture anymore, Amy. He's right here." Kristen beckoned for Anthony to draw nearer.

Hesitantly, he approached. Kristen took his hand and pressed it to her own cheek, closing her eyes momentarily to savor the wonder of having him here. In those seconds, she realized that his hands were the same as always—strong and warm and long-fingered. So comforting in their familiarity. "This is your daddy, Amy. Say good-night to *him* now."

Amy stared into her mother's eyes, then glanced up at her father. Then her lids began to close as if they weighed too much for her to hold open anymore. Just when Kristen thought she'd drifted off to sleep, those round eyes cracked open one last time.

Amy looked straight at Anthony and said, "Ni-ni, Da Da."

When Kristen looked up, she saw that Anthony's eyes were shiny and his lips compressed. She couldn't ever remember Anthony getting even slightly choked up before. He'd always been in such excellent control of his emotions.

Kristen smiled at him. Amy had a way of doing this to people. And he'd had so much to take in all at once. He couldn't be expected to contain it. Kristen searched for the words that would reassure him.

"She tugs on everyone's heartstrings, you know," she whispered as she stood and raised the protective railing along the open side of her daughter's bed. "My dad needed to carry a handkerchief everywhere he went while he and my mother were here." She moved to the door on tiptoes.

Anthony followed her into the hallway. "I didn't even know your parents had visited."

Kristen nodded. "Amy had them wrapped around her finger in less than an hour. Especially Dad." Anyone who knew Amy's grandfather would appreciate how unlikely this was, given his gruff, drill-sergeant mentality. If Master Sergeant Clifford Clark, U.S. Army, retired, could be brought to tears by Amy Garitano, then the child must be one that no man could endure stoically.

"You're just saying all that to make me feel better about turning to mush every time she so much as glances my way." This was the longest sentence he'd spoken since she'd picked him up at the airport.

Kristen glanced back at him as he followed her into their bedroom. "Are my tactics working?"

He shrugged. In only a few hours of togetherness, she had come to hate that gesture. She bit back a complaint about noncommittal body language and focused on what truly mattered in this moment.

Her husband had been away for eighteen months and had suffered terrible wounds in the service of his country, but he'd come back—and he stood in their bedroom with her now. A smile began to grow inside her, taking the place of petty annoyances and doubt.

She'd checked and double-checked with his doctors about whether marital relations had to be put off until he was more fully recovered. She'd been assured that he wouldn't do himself any damage and could set his own pace.

"I've missed you so much," she whispered with just a hint of seduction. She took a step toward him.

"I...I..." he said, looking everywhere but at her. He surveyed the room, turning his shoulder toward her. "It's so strange. All our things are here, but arranged to fit a different room. I've moved so many times for the military, but I've never had anyone set up my stuff for me in a new place."

"I can see how that might be weird." She glanced at the clock. Amy would only stay asleep for about an hour. They were missing their window of opportunity.

Maybe he didn't understand that. "You know," she tried, "Amy will be asleep for a while. This is just about the only alone time we're likely to get until tonight."

He raised his eyebrows as if this concept startled him. "I was thinking of taking a nap myself," he confessed.

"Oh." She did her best not to let her disappointment show. The last thing she wanted to do was make him feel inadequate as a husband when she knew he was struggling to feel worthy as an officer right now. "Okay. I do that sometimes, too. Take a nap when she does, I mean. Let's just change into comfortable clothes and take a nap. You could probably use the rest after your long trip."

He nodded and started to unbutton his battle dress

uniform. "I see there's not much closet space. Where are my civilian clothes?" he asked.

"In the shrunk."

"The what?"

She pointed to the armoire. "They call it a shrunk here in Germany. But only your summer things are in there. All our winter stuff is in storage. Not much extra space in these European houses." She watched avidly as he shrugged out of his camouflage overshirt.

He'd lost a lot of weight, but he still looked good to her. Perhaps she saw him through a wife's eyes, which refused to pay close attention to imperfections. Or maybe he hadn't lost as much muscle as she'd expected. What his T-shirt revealed made her mouth water.

Then he did something very normal and very male that made her laugh inside. He sniffed his armpit.

"I need a shower," he concluded.

"Do you need help for that?" She didn't think he still had any bandages, but she wished he'd let her assist him anyway. The very idea made her weak-kneed.

He glared at her. "I think I can handle it."

"Okay. I'll bring you a towel." If she couldn't coax him to make love, she could at least find an excuse to join him in the bathroom so she could feast her eyes on him while he washed. God, it was so good just to have him home.

She would need to time the delivery of the towel just right, so she began to change out of her own uniform. But before she could finish unbuttoning her blouse, he caught her gaze and held it. His eyes were intense. His men used to say he had formidable focus when on a mission. Now he directed that focus on her.

"Kristen," he said in a tone he might use on a new Ranger joining his team. "You have no idea how bad I look now. I'm all torn up. I look more like the Scarecrow than Tony the Tiger. Fresh scars everywhere.'' More softly he added, ''I'm not the man you knew. So, do us both a favor and just tell me where the towels are so I can shower in peace.''

A thousand divergent thoughts went through her mind as the meaning of his words sank in. What blurted from her mouth was, ''But I'm your wife!''

She tried again. ''And I'm a nurse. You can't hide your wounds from me, Anthony. We're married, for God's sake.'' Then a better concept made its way to the surface. ''And I'll love you no matter what.''

He smiled mirthlessly. ''You have no idea what you're saying.'' Then he turned his back on her and sat on the bed to unlace his boots. She wanted very much to offer to do this for him, but she guessed he'd only bark at her. So she watched through peripheral vision until he finally succeeded in baring his feet. He stood again, obviously weary, and unbuckled his belt with the jerky movements of someone deeply annoyed.

Determination filled her. She could not allow him to shut her out because of some misguided notion that she'd find his body unappealing. So she continued to undress slowly while he slid out of his pants. He dropped them onto the floor with the other dirty clothes.

His undershorts and T-shirt hid any obvious signs of what had happened to him except for the fact that his waist was a good deal trimmer and his thighs not as muscled as they'd once been. Especially his left thigh, she noticed. But before she could take in any other details, he turned and stalked toward the bathroom.

By the time she'd changed into shorts and a T-shirt of her own, she could hear the water running. She gave him another minute to ensure he was actually committed to the shower, then she fetched a towel from the dresser in the hallway where she stored the linens. He had her so tense, she actually knocked lightly on the door before she walked in—something she never would have done before he'd gone to war. But she didn't wait for a welcome that would likely never come. Instead, she went in to the small, humid room where her husband would be naked and wet.

The steam roiled through the air so thickly, she could barely detect Anthony behind the glass shower door. Undeterred, she propped the towel on the edge of the sink and shucked off her clothes before she could change her mind. Then she pulled open the clouded door to the shower and stepped into the tub with him.

He froze with his hands poised in his lathered hair. His lips parted as if he wanted to protest but couldn't make himself speak. And then—oh, thank you, yes— then his gaze darted down to take in her nakedness as fingers of steam coiled around her body. Those eyes didn't lift again for several thrilling seconds. She stood there for him, letting him look and forgetting to look herself. His gaze felt like a caress and her skin tightened in anticipation. Even her nipples hardened, despite the heat.

But then she remembered her other purpose in joining him in the shower. She wanted to look at him, too. So she watched a channel of thick lather slide slowly down his neck and over his collarbone and along his chest toward his waist. The etchings of his healing wounds crisscrossed his abdomen and thigh. They were not the neat, straight stitches of an incision, but uneven and cruel from jaggedly torn flesh being pieced together the best it could be.

"Anthony," she whispered as she took in the reality

of how badly he'd been hurt. But then the nurse in her commented, "You're lucky to have the use of all your limbs." Not to mention the use of another part of him that clearly indicated his interest in her naked presence, whether he wanted to admit his desire or not.

"Yeah. Lucky," he said in a monotone.

When she stretched a hand out toward him, he turned his back to her. That's when she saw that some of the scars reached like clutching tentacles around his waist.

Dear God, she thought, how could he have survived such wounds for the hours she knew he'd lain amid the debris of the blast? She would have hoped he'd been unconscious most of the time, except she already knew he'd been aware during at least some part of it. The psychological evaluation she'd read in his medical file said he'd wanted the medics to take care of his men first. "Can't you hear them crying out?" he'd said. But the medics had been quite certain only one person remained alive by then. Clearly, Anthony had witnessed the torment of those members of his team who had not died instantly.

Feeling her throat tighten as tears began to choke her, she stepped forward and pressed her slick body to his back. Her arms encircled him from behind, just to hold him and feel him breathe. Alive. He was alive. Gratitude spilled from her eyes and mixed with the cascading water of the shower. Anthony seemed frozen in her arms, but she didn't care. She just needed to hold him. Her man had come home and this seemed astounding to her, like some kind of supernatural phenomenon.

She silently swore that she would make the most of this gift she'd been given, no matter what the odds. Reward for her vow came almost immediately when Anthony turned in her arms and clasped her to his hot, wet body.

Then his mouth sought hers.

CHAPTER THREE

HE'D WAITED SO LONG to have her in his arms again, Anthony simply couldn't deny himself for another moment. His physical need consumed him. Clearly she wanted him, too. Her kisses were as hungry as his.

That's because she didn't know the whole truth, he remembered as his hands slicked over her smooth, wet skin. If she did, she wouldn't let him lick the water from her tender throat or cup her full, round breast with a greedy palm. The truth would make her pull back so that he couldn't slip and slide his erection against her abdomen while instincts worked out how best to maneuver himself inside her.

Because the truth was...

The truth was he'd sent his men ahead of him into the caves—sent them to their deaths while he'd kept watch at the entrance.

Shame clawed at his insides, shredding his desire. He wrenched himself away from his wife. He turned away, pressed his palms to the tiles and hung his head between his arms. "I can't," he said. "I...I can't."

He should tell her why, he thought. But the details of that day were more than he could bear to think about, never mind speak of aloud. The psychologists had tried to get him to talk about it, and he'd given them enough so they'd leave him alone. If he couldn't tell strangers, whose opinions didn't matter, how could he ever tell Kristen?

"I'm sorry," he rasped as he heard the shower door open.

"I shouldn't push you so hard," she said softly. "You've been through hell. There's time enough in the days to come for us to be together. When you're feeling better."

He kept his back to her and nodded, not daring to speak. Then she said the one thing guaranteed to make his burning tears spill.

"I love you, Tiger." He heard her wrap a towel around her lovely body and quietly slip out of the steamy room.

Anthony hit the side of his fist against the tiled wall. The sting of it did nothing to ease the pain raging on the inside.

KRISTEN HAD BEEN GRANTED only a few precious days off from work to be with her husband before she had to return to the hospital and help prepare and execute an emergency readiness exercise. This was day six, the last of her special leave, and already she felt the weight of Anthony's constant gloom.

She'd tried to understand. She really had. But how could she? He refused to talk about his experiences and she wasn't a mind reader. And she could admit her compassion had been clouded by her crushing disappointment. Except for their all-too-brief embraces at the airport and in the shower, he hadn't touched her since he'd been home, though they'd been apart for so long. Worse, he refused to take an active role in his recovery.

When she'd reminded him that he could go to the gym if he wanted to, he responded that he didn't have the strength. She wanted to say that he would never be strong enough if he didn't try, but he wouldn't have listened. When she asked him when he would be talking to the doctors about plastic surgery to repair his face, he said he wouldn't be. This had something to do with his depression, but she had no idea how to coax him to a better frame of mind. He wouldn't talk about his experiences—to her or to anyone else, as far as she could tell. And the pain pills weren't helping.

She knew better than to push him with obvious questions about the plastic surgery, like "Why not?" Instead, she decided she would go back to the post psychologist and see what he recommended. She dressed quickly, pushing aside her unhappiness that Anthony hadn't even slept in their bed with her since his return. After the incident in the shower, he'd gone to the living room, settled on the couch, flicked on the TV and watched programs in German. The fact that Anthony did not even speak German only added to the worry and sad irritation churning inside her. He'd been sleeping on the couch ever since.

In jeans and a T-shirt that read Nurses Do It With Patients, Kristen went downstairs. She stopped dead in her tracks when she beheld the scene in the living room. Anthony sat there with Amy. The two were snuggled on the couch eating cereal out of the box and enjoying cartoons on the TV. While Kristen stood frozen, Anthony translated several lines of the show for Amy by reading subtitles aloud. The toddler giggled at the different voices he used to imitate the characters and Anthony's face lit up with delight at the sound. Kristen raised her hand to the base of her throat as she felt emotions building there.

"Ma-ma-ma!" Amy shouted as she caught sight of

Kristen standing with one foot still poised on the bottom stair. The little girl lifted her hands and bounced, demanding to be paid some attention, but she didn't climb down from her spot next to her daddy. Kristen smiled, darted a quick glance at Anthony to find out whether his features seemed welcoming, and headed cautiously in their direction.

He watched her as she moved forward, but he neither smiled nor frowned. He simply stared and she thought she caught an intensity behind his neutral expression. She sensed his gaze taking in her clothing, the fit of her jeans, the hug of her T-shirt. All those hours in the gym and on the track after Amy's birth were paying off if she could snare even this much interest from her aloof Army Ranger.

Moving a pillow out of the way, she sat on the other side of Amy. "What are you two up to?"

Amy babbled nonsensical syllables in response, too excited to get anything coherent out.

When she trailed off, Anthony said, "Just watching cartoons. The pickings are slim on a Thursday morning, but we're making the best of it."

Kristen's heart lifted slightly. Perhaps this would lead to more "making the best of it" in other aspects of his life. That would be an improvement. She smiled at him, capturing his gaze with her own and holding it. He seemed to hold his breath a moment, then he looked away first. She could have sworn his expression was ashamed and she was puzzled by it.

Yet she couldn't be entirely disheartened. He obviously wanted to make an effort for Amy, and that was something she could build on. At least she hoped so. "I have to get Amy over to her day-care mom. I have some appointments today."

His gaze returned, this time with that burning intensity he'd applied before, only angrier. "I can watch Amy while you go out."

He'd shown interest in Amy, but taking care of her alone would be daunting for anyone. Was he really up to it? She could barely form a response. "Um...I think...well...she's a lot of work...and..."

"I can take care of Amy," he said firmly. "She's just a little kid. How difficult can it be?"

Kristen nearly choked when she tried to hold back a snort of annoyed laughter. "You have no idea."

But then she thought about his request and assessed his ability to keep up with Amy's capacity for inventiveness. Anthony moved much more slowly now than he used to, but she sensed that if he made the effort, he could be back nearly to his old speed in almost no time. The physician he'd been forced to check in with the day after he'd arrived in Germany had said there were no limitations on his activities other than the limits his body dictated. In other words, don't overdo. Amy had a way of making people reach the limits of their endurance. But still...

"Okay," she said, and her heartbeat pounded out a panicky SOS even as she said it. "But only if you promise to call me if you can't take it anymore."

"I won't need to call you, for God's sake. I can handle a one-and-a-half-year-old."

Kristen didn't blink at his cutting tone. If he spoke at all these days, his tone was always harsh. Clearly, it was nothing personal. "Maybe. But she runs me ragged and I know all her signals for napping and eating and changing her diaper. Her day-care mother, Mary Jane, says she's more rambunctious than the other two kids her age."

An unexpected twinkle came into his eyes. "A natural-born leader."

Oh, how she rejoiced at this positive comment about his daughter's abilities! "Yeah, something like that. Look, have you ever changed a diaper before?" she asked gently, trying to make sure he knew what to do without undermining his confidence.

"No, but I can take apart and rebuild an M-16 and make a shelter in any environment without tools. So I think I can figure out how to change a diaper."

Kristen gave him a wan smile and headed to the kitchen to write out emergency phone numbers. She smeared some cream cheese on a bagel for herself, then returned to the couch and handed the list of phone numbers to Anthony.

Although she knew it was hopeless, she also pleaded with him to call his mother and sister, or at least to go to the library to e-mail them. She pointed to the stack of e-mails she'd printed for him, the entirety of the correspondence she'd had with the other two women in Anthony's life. His mom and sister had been worried sick over him ever since he'd deployed to Afghanistan.

"They need to hear directly from you," she concluded.

"I'll call. I'll call," he insisted. But she knew he wouldn't.

"Your mother promised not to bother you about your dangerous career again."

He huffed his disbelief. "She'd only agree to that if she knew Anna would take up the slack and work on me from the sister's angle."

Kristen couldn't say much to that. It was true, after all. If Mrs. Garitano didn't nag him about changing his career to something safer, then Anna would. They could play good cop, bad cop better than real police officers. And maybe it would be better if he didn't take on his family while he was supposed to be looking after Amy.

She headed for the door, pausing to take one more look at the pair of them. If things had been normal between her and Anthony, she would have been gleeful at the prospect of seeing his confidence laid low by the demands of an almost-two-year-old. But things were not normal between them. She vowed to cut short her time away so Amy didn't undermine the glimmer of interest in life Anthony was showing this morning. Still, Kristen recalled how insufferably sure of himself the old Anthony "Tiger" Garitano could be. She wondered if this new Anthony would be challenged by Amy's talent for getting into things or exhausted by her boundless energy.

Twenty minutes later, Kristen took a seat in a comfy chair opposite Lieutenant Colonel Paul Farley, the full-time post psychologist. He was the only one who had been able to make time for her on short notice when she'd found out about Anthony's injuries, and he had consistently been willing to see her on an irregular basis. He smiled, reminding her that he was a handsome man. With a pang of guilt, she acknowledged that she might have been interested in him if she hadn't lost her heart to Anthony.

"So," Paul said, "your husband has returned! Was the reunion everything you expected?"

"Not exactly," she began. She gave him the short version of Anthony's homecoming and lack of communication, and felt slightly guilty for not disclosing the very personal moments in the shower. Maybe Paul would be able to help more if she could make herself spill those details. But no matter how clinical and articulate she could be about other things, she couldn't force something so intimate into words.

He looked at her for a moment, as if he suspected she hadn't told him everything. "He's been home for what—six days or so?"

She nodded. Vague discomfort made her focus on the bookshelf behind him. She felt heat rising into her cheeks. Now he would begin to probe raw wounds with the sharp scalpel of questions.

"So how was your marital reunion?"

"Not." She knew her blush deepened. Talking with Paul about her sex life intensified her uneasiness, and she found she could not make eye contact with him. And yet she knew that he studied her closely.

"We've talked about this. It could be a long time before his interest rekindles. How do you feel about that?" he asked.

Paul was a handsome man, attractive in ways that were nearly the opposite of Anthony's qualities. Instead of manly brawn and an abundance of confidence, Paul had a quiet sexuality and sensual intelligence that drew women to think about whether he would kiss as well as his finely carved lips implied. Kristen had felt drawn to him, too. She was human, after all. But she'd always remembered the husband she loved so deeply, struggling through the hellholes of Afghanistan. She'd never given in to temptation, and Paul had never crossed any lines. But this particular question from this particular man made her want to squirm.

She forced her gaze to meet his. "He's been through hell, Paul. His whole team was blown up. Don't you think he might need a little time to adjust?"

His expression softened. "I think he'll take a very long time to adjust, Kris. The question you may need to ask yourself someday—or perhaps him—is whether he will *ever* adjust enough to be a real husband to you."

"Certainly I'm willing to give him more than six days. I didn't come here to talk about defeat. I came to talk about how I can help him."

Paul nodded. "I'd like to help you. You know that. But I can't do a whole lot for him unless he comes to see me in person. I have no idea what's going on with him, why he doesn't turn to you in his distress, open up to you, if no one else."

Kristen bolted from her seat and began to pace. "I know! I know. But I don't think he'll talk to you. He has a serious aversion to psychotherapists. Most Rangers do. He told me once that the first thing psychoanalysts try to figure out is why anyone would be crazy enough to become a Ranger."

Paul's laugh was mirthless. "Well, that *is* a good question."

She suppressed a burst of irritation. "They become Rangers because they love the challenge and they love their country. Why is that so hard for people to understand?"

"Kris, sit down and take a breath. I'm not suggesting he's certifiable because he became a Ranger. But Rangers aren't known for being able to make their marriages work. They're usually hardened against seeking comfort. And although I encourage you to give him more time, I've seen cases like this before. He may be even less able to accept your help than he was before his injuries."

She hated this. Hated the painful truth that Paul's comments forced her to confront. But where else could she find ways to help her husband? There were a couple of enlisted counselors under Paul's supervision and a few part-time reservists, but no other available officers.

Finding an English-speaking German doctor would be a challenge and the cultural differences would get in the way. So, she was stuck with Paul and his pointed questions and unpleasant reality checks.

She met Paul's cool, steady gaze. "I guess our marriage isn't as safe for him as it is for me. And under the circumstances, maybe that needs to be okay for now. But if you have any pearls of wisdom to impart about ways to help him feel safer, ways to coax him to talk to me, I'd appreciate your guidance."

"You're an admirable woman, Kris," Paul said. Then he got up and pulled a book off his shelf. "Here's a pretty good discussion of post-traumatic stress disorder. It might at least help you understand. But I warn you, it doesn't offer much hope for a happy ending to what you're going through."

She went to him and accepted the book. "Thanks," she said, appreciating his encouragement. She wasn't ready to consider failure.

Paul gave her a thoughtful look. "And maybe it would help if—and I'm taking a guess here, because I can't actually suggest any treatment unless I talk to him—you just try to engage him in everyday things you can do together. Some with your daughter and some for just the two of you."

"That sounds like good advice."

He held the door open for her. "That's what I do—give advice. Whether it's good or not is usually dumb luck."

She'd taken three steps into the reception area before she heard him say her name almost too softly for her to hear. She turned back.

"Just...just take care of yourself. Make sure that giving him a few weeks or months to reconnect with you doesn't turn into a few years. If you need anything, anything at all, you know I'm here for you. You can call me night or day.''

She nodded, feeling weighted down by these ominous sentiments. Yet she tried to take heart that Paul would be there to steady her if things became too difficult. It was a good thing to have friends like Paul. But as she took care of the rest of her errands, Kristen wondered why she felt a twinge of distress about asking Anthony to go talk to Paul. Any picture she could conjure of the two of them sitting down for a therapy session just seemed wrong to her somehow. But what else could she do?

ANTHONY WISHED he could take pride in the fact that Amy was sound asleep on a blanket on the floor when Kristen arrived home. He'd listened to Kristen's expressions of admiration but didn't say much in return. That way, he didn't have to admit that during the entire time the child had been upright, he'd wondered how anyone could take care of the little hurricane 24/7.

Nothing seemed to keep Amy from darting into danger at just about every turn. First there had been the near miss when the oven door came crashing down almost on her head when he'd averted his eyes for a split second. She must have been swinging on the handle, he'd surmised as he'd picked up his startled and screaming daughter and dusted her off. Then she'd tottered nearly to the top of the toy-strewn stairs before he'd discovered her missing, even though he'd been sure she stood right beside him while he'd fixed a sandwich. She'd spilled an entire cup of juice, forcing him to make his way down onto his hands and knees, despite his stiffness, to clean it up. When a bowl of dry cereal landed on the living-room carpet not more than five minutes later, he'd yelled in frustration. She'd cried. Then she'd dragged her favorite blanket from the couch onto the floor and whimpered herself to sleep. Kristen had found him stretched out on the floor with Amy right beside him as if they'd had a peaceful day together.

At least he could honestly say that he hadn't had time to write or call his mother and sister, if Kristen interrogated him about those responsibilities. It wasn't that he didn't want to ease their minds by contacting them. But he just couldn't deal with the incessant questions he knew they would have about his injuries and the prognosis—how he'd managed to be the husband of a nurse, the son of a nurse, and the brother of a nurse was beyond him. And then they'd start in on him about what he thought of his daughter and if he was glad to be home with Kristen. All the while, his father would be somewhere in the background, flicking through the television stations and not speaking, never asking about him, forever remote.

When Kristen finished lauding him, she made a suggestion. "I still need to get some groceries and I wondered if you'd come with us when Amy wakes up?"

Even on a good day, probably the very last thing he would ever want to do was shop. For anything. Especially groceries. She must have seen the horror in his eyes, because she added a bunch of hasty arguments.

"I could really use the help with Amy. You seem so good with her, and I have such a hard time getting her to be still and cooperative in the commissary. Plus, I'm not sure I remember all the things you like. You could pick out your favorite coffee and cereal and stuff. And then it's hard to get everything into the car when I have to hang on to Amy and…"

"Okay! Okay! I surrender. I'll go with you." He might be a useless excuse for an officer and a pretty terrible husband, but he could at least help Kristen with their daughter when he was asked to.

She smiled one of those incredible smiles and a wave of lust hit him broadside like a swinging two-by-four. Seeing her this way, he knew he wouldn't be able to deny himself much longer. And yet he knew it wouldn't be right to make love to her. Not when he knew that his marriage wouldn't withstand even the slightest tug on its frazzled threads.

"I'll go change," he said.

"Wear something light. It's really hot outside."

And so, an hour later, he went to the commissary with his wife and daughter as if they were a real family. Though every moment felt heavy and thick and gray, he coaxed Amy to cooperate, picked out cereal, and paid attention to the kind of diapers Amy used. Not until the checkout line did he notice that there were no fruits or vegetables in the cart, and not a single meat item.

"How about I go back and pick out some steaks?" he said, wondering if his appetite had returned against all expectation or if he simply wanted to buy them so he could continue to pretend things were normal.

She grinned, and for a moment the sun seemed to be shining on him. "We're going to a market in town for some other things like that. They're fresher there."

He groaned out loud. Another store! Not even Kristen's smile could make him look forward to dragging his sorry self through another store.

"Buck up, Tiger. You'll like this market. Most of it's out in the open air."

Okay. That didn't sound so bad. An open-air market

might be easier to endure. Not so closed in. Not so much like caves. Not like the confining caves in Afghanistan.

Damn! Where had *that* series of word associations come from? Surreptitiously, he wiped the sweat from his brow and the images from his mind.

To regain control over his wayward thoughts, he shook his head like a dog coming out of the water—a trick he used on missions when his mind wandered. Amy laughed from her seat in the shopping cart. Hoping to distract himself, as well as Amy, he shook his head again, just to make her giggle. She put her hands on his head when he bent low to offer another shake. The sensation of those tiny fingers threading through his hair made him ache inside. He loved her so damn much already, this feisty daughter he didn't deserve. The depth of his love seemed almost intolerable. He lifted his head out of her grasp, denying himself once again. But he couldn't resist planting a kiss on her fat cheek. And then on each of her fingers with their tiny dimpled knuckles.

"All set. Let's go," Kristen said. And he wondered how she had ever done this without him as he stowed the bags into the trunk while she struggled to subdue Amy enough to buckle her into her car seat.

Kristen asked him if he wanted to drive this time and he accepted. He needed to know if driving fatigued him or hurt his leg more than usual. Best to make that discovery while he had someone to take over if he wasn't up to it. Kristen directed him off post and then guided him into the town of Wiesbaden. Many of the streets looked as if they'd come right out of a storybook. Quaint and narrow and very German, despite the American presence that had endured long past the Cold War.

He parked where she suggested and they all got out. Like a magician pulling a rabbit from a hat, Kristen unearthed a little umbrella-like stroller from beneath the grocery bags. He admitted to himself that as much as he'd have liked to carry Amy in his arms, he probably wouldn't be able to do so for long. Already weariness threatened. Having her in the stroller meant he didn't have to give in to the need for rest quite yet.

"We won't be long," Kristen assured him as if she'd read his mind. He followed her to one shop and then another, almost forgetting that he shouldn't enjoy the sun pouring down from the cloudless blue sky and the flowers blooming along the way and the laughter of his daughter as people cooed to her in German.

There were people everywhere—friendly, smiling faces. Open, honest faces all around him. So the prickle he suddenly felt along the back of his neck made no sense. He tried to ignore it as he watched Kristen pick out fruits. But then a jolt from his Ranger awareness—something that Billy Brinewater used to refer to as his spider sense, before an al-Qaeda bomb had removed that young man's humor from the face of the earth—got Anthony's attention and held it.

He maneuvered Amy's stroller in between two stalls and then edged sideways a little at a time so he could scan the area with his peripheral vision without drawing attention to the fact that he did so. Coming almost full circle, he began to wonder if he'd only succumbed to paranoia when he suddenly found what he hadn't known he'd been looking for.

There, less than twenty yards away and with the sun providing a halo behind him, stood his own personal stalker, Taaoun. The man watched him from a position half-hidden by the side of a vegetable stand. But almost as soon as Anthony identified him, he disappeared, slipping behind a building. Every cell in Anthony's body came alive with the urge to give chase. But then Amy looked up at him and said, "Da—da—da—da," and he knew he couldn't leave her and Kristen to fend for themselves. He could only stay alert, keep watch, protect his family.

And on that thought, self-doubt swamped him. He'd already proved his inability to protect anyone. Besides, the staff at the hospital in Kabul had assured him repeatedly that Taaoun had not been lurking near his room as he'd believed. They'd urged him to accept his vision as a manifestation of his fears caused by trauma. The same thing could be happening again.

Had he seen Taaoun in the hospital? He couldn't be sure.

Had he seen him now? His certainty flagged. The man he'd seen had had no turban, no beard. Why did he think he could identify him? Spider-sense just didn't seem like a valid source of solid evidence about the guy. Anthony needed to see the man again, confirm his sighting, verify the ID. He needed to be certain.

But all that would have to wait until he was alone. Right now, he had his family to think of. Instinctively, he moved closer to Kristen. And he plucked Amy from her stroller, needing to hold her in the protection of his arms.

CHAPTER FOUR

FROM HER PLACE in the passenger seat, Kristen eyed her husband with growing concern. Before he'd gone to Afghanistan, she'd been hard pressed to discern a single emotion from him that he didn't want her to see. His control had bothered her when they'd first met, but then she'd come to see it as a skill he'd honed as a Ranger. It had become an aspect of who he was. After a while, she'd come to appreciate that he would express the thoughts and feelings he wanted to share when he was ready to do so. Her patience always paid off, and it was nice that he never expected her to read his mind.

Today, even though she sensed he wasn't ready to talk, she could just about taste his tension. His furtive glances were hard to miss. When he'd reached for one of the shopping bags to put it into the car, his hand had been shaking slightly.

"What's wrong?" she finally found the nerve to say. "You seem tense."

"It's nothing." But his eyes darted to the rearview mirror over and over. She glanced behind them a few times on the pretext of checking on Amy in the back seat, but no one seemed to be following them. There appeared to be no reason for his hypervigilance. What had happened to the swaggering self-confidence that used to make him seem invincible? She told herself it must simply be on a slower plane from Afghanistan, because there was no way she would admit it would never show up again.

"Did you talk to your mother?" she asked, hoping that conversation about domestic things would shift his mood.

"No time. Amy turned out to be a full-time job," he admitted. Kristen knew he loved his mom, but he had a hard time dealing with her bubbly, emotional personality, even on his better days. His sister, Anna, was a slightly toned-down version of their mother. And Anthony was just like his father—taciturn. No sense urging her husband to call his dad. The elder Garitano might secretly worry like hell over his son, but he'd never admit it. And if a phone call came in from the child he hadn't seen in two years, Anthony senior would grunt a salutation and hand the receiver over to his wife. The males of the family were not particularly close.

"Well, maybe you could call her tonight," she gently suggested.

Once they passed through the guard gate at the entrance to the Army Airfield, he seemed more settled, but Kristen couldn't shake the sick feeling at the bottom of her stomach. This man who shared her home seemed like a stranger.

That stranger was kind enough to bring the groceries into the kitchen for her while she looked after Amy—a nice reprieve from the chaos that usually prevailed when Kristen tried to do everything by herself. And whenever Anthony passed by his daughter's high chair on his way to fetch another load of bags, he tweaked her baby cheeks and made her giggle. Kristen willed away the bulk of her anxiety as she watched this interaction. She had every reason to hope that Amy would help Anthony shake off his depression. Maybe she would also quell the tendency to check over his shoulder every few minutes that seemed to have taken hold of him.

"That's the last bag," he said as he set one on the table next to the others that Kristen hadn't yet unloaded. "Do you have a computer?"

She stopped in her tracks with a can of soup in one hand and a box of pasta in the other. "Computer?" she said.

"I need to look some stuff up. I wondered if you had a laptop with a modem stashed away somewhere. You wrote me e-mails while I was away."

"I wrote them from work or from the library or the Internet café on post. I haven't had a lot of time for a computer, so I don't have one here. I could get one, if you want. Maybe borrow a laptop from work or something." She'd go buy one on her lunch hour tomorrow at the PX, if he wanted it. Anything would be an improvement over watching him clicking through the limited German TV channels hour after hour.

He shook his head. "That's okay. Forget it. Maybe I'll go to the library tomorrow."

"There are also computers in the offices used by some of the units that pass through here on their way to the field. You could go there, if you want." She told herself not to make too much of this, but a ribbon of joy fluttered through her as she thought of him taking an interest in something. She had never known Anthony to spend more than a few hours sitting still. These long days of inactivity had been high on the growing list of things that worried her. And now he was going to get out of the house, go to the library, research something on the Internet. The future suddenly looked full of possibilities.

"What are you going to research?" she asked for the

sake of conversation as she continued to put away groceries.

He didn't respond. Kristen turned, wondering if perhaps he'd slipped out of the room when she'd had her head in the depths of the refrigerator stowing lettuce in the crisper. But he still stood in the kitchen doorway, one shoulder leaning against the jamb. He seemed to be deep in thought, a million miles away. And he looked so much like his former self—so relaxed and yet poised for immediate action, so strong and sexy—that Kristen felt her newfound sliver of happiness warm into something sensual.

Tonight, she thought. Perhaps tonight I'll coax him into our bedroom. Not for sex, she told herself. He might not be ready for that. Just for sleeping. It would be wonderful to spend the night next to his big, warm body.

"Hey, Tiger," she said in a low, playful voice guaranteed to get his attention. "You're miles away, but if you come back to earth, I promise to make it worth your while."

His gaze lifted to hers and his brown eyes went smoky. Pupils dilating—a good beginning, thought the clinical side of Kristen's mind. Had his pulse quickened? Did he feel warmth pooling at the center of his body? Did his skin tingle?

Kristen's insides went all quivery as she held his heated stare. She searched for something else to say, something that would fan the sparks into flames. But libido had gained dominion over cognition and nothing coherent came into her thoughts other than a recognition that her promise only to *sleep* with him was a big fat lie.

Amy suddenly heaved her melba toast across the room and slapped her hands onto the tray of her high chair, reminding the grown-ups that her rightful place was at the center of their attention.

Anthony's gaze slid to his daughter. "Promises, promises," he said to Kristen with a wry smile. "You're forgetting we have a kid to look after now."

She hated to admit it, even to herself, but for a minute she had indeed forgotten that there would be a third person to consider before she could lure her husband between the sheets. Damn!

No, wait. No cursing Amy's presence in her life. Not ever. But it would not be a sin of motherhood to think hard about what could be done to remove Amy temporarily from the equation. Just for an hour or so.

Kristen glanced at the clock. Not nap time. And Amy had slept a good deal in the car. The chances of getting her to sleep again were slim to none. Kristen's gaze darted to the list of numbers pinned to the small bulletin board near the kitchen phone as she wondered if it would be out of the question to call Mary Jane.

"You're a mess," Anthony said to his daughter as he grinned down at her. Amy was covered in a gooey coating of toast and baby spit, but when she lifted her two arms to be picked up, the man didn't hesitate. "I watched you give her a bath last night. You want me to go hose her down in the tub?" he asked Kristen.

The feverish scheming that had been going on in the privacy of Kristen's mind stilled. And then—poof!—it was gone. And all those warm sexy fantasies, too. So much for afternoon delights.

"Sure. That would be great," she said as she went back to stowing food. And it *would* be great to have someone else give Amy her bath. What had Kristen been thinking anyway, to imagine she could stash her goo-covered daughter with the neighbor while she got it on with her husband? Get real!

By the time she heard the tread of Anthony's boots in the upstairs hallway, Kristen had her lust under control and a smile playing at her lips again. She had harbored so many fears about how Anthony would take to Amy upon his return. It wasn't as if he'd had the chance to see her as the helpless infant she'd started out as. He hadn't shared any of those endearing milestones that bind a parent to a child's less likeable characteristics and that make the terrible twos more endurable. He hadn't helped to shape her personality, hadn't grown used to her ways over time. Amy had been thrust into Anthony's life just as she approached her most difficult stage to date. Since Amy had never been what one would call an easygoing baby, Kristen had reason to worry about how their bonding would go.

To her great relief and happiness, Anthony seemed in love with Amy. Surely it was only one small step from there to remembering to love Amy's mom.

SEEING SOMEONE bathe Amy and doing it himself turned out to be two entirely different experiences. He remembered to double-check the water temperature as the tub filled. He remembered that a few inches of water sufficed. He remembered that the little plastic ring with suction cups on the legs had to be stuck to the porcelain bottom. But he could not recall how Kristen had coaxed Amy to sit inside the ring.

For Amy, stomping her feet in the water for maximum splash became a delightful game as he struggled to get her inside the ring. No matter how he tried to stuff her chubby little legs beneath the circle so she could sit on her bottom inside of it, she managed to thwart him.

When he chanced to capture both her ankles in one hand while keeping her upright with the other, he found her legs wouldn't bend to fit under the space between the suctioned-down ring and the floor of the tub. He'd seen his daughter sitting in the thing the previous night, but he simply could not puzzle out how Kristen had managed to get her there.

Defeated by a baby's bathtub safety device! It would have snapped the final thread of his control if Amy hadn't danced and laughed with such wild abandon as he held her slippery body upright between his hands. With a chuckle, he gave up on the ring and simply sat her down where he could catch her if she tipped over.

This miracle who was his child made his insides ache with tenderness. She had Kristen's smile, but she had his eyes. And she was beautiful, so beautiful. Hard to believe he could have been a part of her creation. She was the solitary thing in his sorry existence that he could be proud of. For the first time since he'd awakened in the MASH unit in country, his heart felt full instead of heavy.

"Duck!" she demanded as she reached for the far edge where the bright yellow toy stood watch. He held her still with one hand clasped around her arm as he nudged the thing into the water, then sent it floating in her direction. She clapped her hands onto the surface, sloshing water in every direction and soaking him from shoulder to waist.

"Let's get you washed before I end up with all the water on me!" he said as he sudsed a tiny washcloth with sweet-smelling baby soap.

He'd managed to lather the top half and was contemplating methods to do the same to the bottom half when he heard Kristen enter the bathroom. "How am I supposed to wash the parts that are in the water?'' he asked with a laugh. He eyed her over his shoulder.

Her smile made his insides go all hot and quivery, but then she glanced toward Amy and froze as she stared into the tub with horrified eyes.

He looked, too. Amy sat there, happily floating her duck from side to side. ''What?'' he asked.

''She's not in the ring!'' came the shocked reply. ''She's not in the ring! For God's sake, Anthony! She could slip so easily, go right under the water! You have to put her inside the ring!'' Kristen knelt and nudged him out of the way before he could protest. ''She's still a baby! Anything could happen to her! You can't be too careful!'' And in the blink of an eye, the ring was slipped over Amy's head, around her fat tummy and suctioned to the bottom of the tub, securing the child in an upright position.

Anthony still hadn't seen how it was done and the certainty of his own incompetence made him throw his hands up in defeat rather than ask. ''She was fine,'' he said, but he knew Kristen had a great deal more experience with these things than he did. Obviously the ring was important. And he'd blown it big-time.

The spark of joy that Amy's playfulness had ignited inside of him suddenly blinked out. He was less than worthless. To his country. To his men. To his daughter. ''Shit!'' he muttered as he got to his feet.

''Don't swear in front of her,'' Kristen scolded. ''She'll copy you.''

He closed his eyes as his own ineptitude weighed down on him. ''Right,'' he said tonelessly. Thick, cloying fatigue dragged him out of the bathroom, down the stairs and onto the couch. He flicked the TV on and let the thing drone in German. It made no difference what he watched or heard as long as the pictures and sounds distracted him from his own dark thoughts.

Still, his mind drifted again and again to his own inadequacy. He couldn't even give his daughter a bath. How would he protect her from the likes of Taaoun?

His breath caught as the inevitable follow-on question crept to the forefront of his brain again, as it had in the market. What if he'd imagined Taaoun? Did he dare ignore what the doctors in Kabul had insisted? They'd assured him time and time again that no unauthorized people had been lurking in intensive care. His sighting was a result of emotional trauma, they'd said. Could the same be true today? Was he delusional?

He had to admit the possibility or become a fool, as well as a failure.

In the morning, after he'd researched this Taaoun character, he would have a better idea as to whether his mind was playing tricks on him. Until then, he needed to be on guard. He'd retained a few of his Ranger skills even if he'd proven himself an abysmal leader of men. The least he could do was use those skills to protect his child. And his wife—for as long as she chose to remain in that role.

He glanced down at his body, assessing his physical condition. When he lifted his hand from his thigh and held it out, it trembled slightly. Damn. Master Sergeant "Scopes" Spiro had told him once that he had the hands of a surgeon—or a sniper. "If I needed backup for my sharp-shooting duties, I'd pick you every time," he'd said. And Major Tiger Garitano had taken that as some of the highest praise he'd ever received. Scopes knew everything there was to know about long-range shooting.

Had known everything, before his untimely death in Afghanistan.

Anthony's jaw clenched so tightly his teeth hurt. That's what it took to hold back the tide of loss that threatened to swamp him. He was nothing without his men. Less than nothing.

The creak of the steps alerted him to Kristen's descent. As he passed a hand across his eyes, erasing any hint of self-pity that might be lurking there, Anthony saw that his wife carried Amy in her arms. His daughter looked smaller when she was in her pajamas. They were the kind of jammies that covered her from shoulders to toes and zipped up the front. They fitted her closely, revealing chubby legs and a rounded tummy. She looked so cute, Anthony had to force his eyes away or risk another emotional moment.

He fixed his gaze on the TV, but he couldn't turn off his peripheral vision, through which he saw Kristen set Amy on the floor near the toy box. Amy reached for two toys at once and pulled them out. Then his view was cut off by Kristen's body as his wife came to stand in front of him.

He refused to look up and continued to stare straight ahead as if she had not blocked the TV. Undaunted, she lowered herself to her knees so that her eyes were now level with his. Then she moved forward, placing herself between his knees with her hands on his thighs.

Impossible not to look at her now. Impossible not to think of sex.

In his mind's eye, everything around them melted into darkness, leaving only the two of them. He could see her sliding her hands forward, reaching for his belt buckle and then his fly. He imagined her drawing him out, then giving him a wicked smile before lowering her head and sliding her hot, slick mouth around his...

"I'm sorry, Anthony," she said.

He used some of those latent Ranger skills to return his heart rate to normal and to control his breathing. He glanced at his daughter, sitting less than ten feet away, and felt ashamed of himself. If he could only keep her presence in mind, he ought to be able to keep his fantasies in check.

"I shouldn't have said those things to you upstairs," Kristen continued. "The words just spilled out of my mouth without passing through my brain."

He wanted to tell her she had no reason to apologize, that she'd been right and he'd been inept. But he couldn't trust himself to speak.

She looked at him, unblinking. "I just panicked because seeing her without the ring reminded me of something I did when she was six months old." He saw her swallow hard.

She was about to confess some parental mistake, he felt sure. He didn't want to hear it. "Don't," he said. He didn't think he could stand to hear about someone else's guilt. He had enough of his own.

"No. I need to tell you this so you'll understand. My little tirade in the bathroom wasn't about you. It was about me and what happened before. I had her in the tub. She had been sitting up on her own for weeks and so I didn't think anything of it. I was right there next to her, but I reached for the shampoo bottle that I'd left by the sink. I don't know how it happened, but Amy slipped." Anthony could see tears shimmering in his wife's lovely eyes. They had no business being there. He struggled for words that would make them go away, but then he felt the index finger of her right hand begin to trace patterns on his thigh. A circle, a spiral, a loop. Her tension spilled out of her and seeped into him. He realized that every muscle in his body was flexed and taut.

"I heard her head hit the porcelain," she said and Anthony winced. "It was the loudest sound. Almost like a bell. I turned and somehow, in the split second that passed, Amy had slipped under the water. She got water down her throat."

A tear streaked down Kristen's cheek and, without thinking, Anthony reached forward and wiped it gently away with his knuckle.

"I'm a nurse and I knew what to do. I scooped her out of the tub and made sure the water came out of her. She coughed and choked so hard, I could hardly stand it. And there could have been a head injury, so I took her to the emergency room to make sure she would be okay. They said she'd be fine, but they lectured me for an hour about water safety. Me! I've given those same lectures myself."

"It was an accident," he whispered. "And she was okay." He glanced Amy's way, marveling at how well she played by herself at her toy box. Ultra independent and hard to kill, just like her father.

"It was Mary Jane who told me about the bath ring. She can't slip under the water as long as she's secured inside it. So when I saw Amy in the water without it today, I remembered that horrible day."

He nodded. He understood more than she could imagine how the past could twist the here and now. Guilt was a terrible and unforgiving vice, squeezing the present into contortions that had nothing to do with objective reality.

She swiped at her tears. "I'm sorry for the things I said. I realize you had a good hold on her. You wouldn't let anything happen to her."

Unexpectedly, Kristen leaned forward and rested her head over his heart. Anthony's arms moved on their own to encircle her shoulders. A comforting gesture from a loving husband. It felt good to offer this to her. It felt good to hold her.

Except he had no right to feel good. And Kristen should not be finding comfort in *his* arms. She should leave him. Leave him and find someone else to depend upon.

"I'll always do my best to protect Amy," he said. "But..." But he might have led a terrorist madman to her doorstep, putting her in far more danger than anything she might face in the bathtub. Or he was a madman himself, imagining dangers where they didn't exist.

All at once, he set Kristen away and stood. He had to extricate himself from the scene immediately. He could see the hurt and confusion in his wife's eyes as he walked away from her, away from the lure of need and comfort.

"Anthony," she whispered, but he kept on going. He went to the door, grabbed a jacket from the coat tree, and headed out into the night. He wished he were a drinking man so he could go to the Officers' Club for a while. Hell, he'd go there anyway, he decided. Maybe it wouldn't take more than a shot or two to exorcize the ghosts that haunted him.

But he'd miscalculated again. There was no peace waiting for him at the O Club. In fact, he came face to face with the exact opposite. Because, against all expectation, a group of fresh young Rangers had gathered around a table there. And the minute they saw him, they called him over.

He wasn't wearing the tan beret that marked him as a Ranger, but they all seemed to know him anyway. He hadn't put on his uniform since his arrival at his Wiesbaden home. But he wore his green woodland camouflage pants and his black boots and a green-brown T-shirt, just because they were comfortable. So he didn't look very different from these men. Anthony knew a few of them by sight. The others he knew as Rangers by the berets they had each folded and tucked neatly into the pockets of their brown desert camouflage pants.

"Where are you heading?" he asked. Perhaps, if he got them talking about their reason for passing through Wiesbaden, he would not allow himself to think that the man to his left looked a great deal like Billy Brinewater, whose voice had been the last he'd heard in the long hours before the medics had arrived to take him on the agonizing transport to Kabul.

The man who answered wore a name tag that read McCain. The fresh, young face of Cool McCool, the youngest man to die that day, came leaping into Anthony's mind's eye, forcing his lids to close for a moment against a tide of pain. "Heading for Iraq," McCain answered without elaboration.

Anthony could guess what the Rangers would be doing in Iraq. Whatever their mission, it would be dirty and difficult. But they would succeed or die trying.

In the hour that followed, these untested Rangers toasted Anthony's team about a hundred times, reverently giving the Army's "Hoo-ah" at ever-increasing decibels. Dead Rangers were never forgotten by their living brethren. The burning need to carry on with such memorials was fueled partly by the fact that Rangers served in silence and died without much recognition. Ordinary people were never to know what Rangers were up to in their quest to defend freedom throughout the world.

Anthony participated in the drinking without joining in the eulogies. Through his thoughts danced the repetitive conviction that he shouldn't be here to listen to these people make appropriate remarks about his dead team. He ought to be dead, too. Instead, he had a daughter and a wife and an endless span of days ahead of him to slog through. The unfairness of it all nearly choked him. And the never-ending self-pity that had him in its grip shamed him to his toes.

"Have you spoken with Sergeant Grim's widow, Major?" someone asked. "How is she holding up?"

Anthony blinked. Weasel had a wife? Yes, he remembered that now. Anthony had come home to his own wife—a woman who still seemed to want him in her bed, if this afternoon had been any indication—while Weasel had left a young widow whom he'd married only a few months prior to deployment. Weasel had been a very private man, but Anthony had approved the Sergeant's occasional departure to the base camp's Internet café to correspond with his spouse. And if he hadn't been nearly killed himself, he would have been the one to write the condolences to Mrs. Grim on official Army letterhead. Someone else higher up in the chain of command must have done it. But Anthony knew he should have written himself by now, to give the women a personal account of Weasel's heroism. He should write to all the other families, as well. It was the least he could do. Duty demanded it of him, no matter what the cost to his state of mind.

Without responding to the question, Anthony stood. A few of the men laughed when he had to steady himself with his hands on the table. Too much to drink. The alcohol hadn't done a thing to dull the morbid memories, but it sure had made him tipsy. Kristen certainly wouldn't make the mistake of coming on to him now!

"You're not driving, are you, sir?" asked a man Anthony remembered from a training op a few years ago. Batsin was on his name tag. His somewhat muddled mind recalled he was a serious man, Captain Dave Batsin.

Anthony shook his head. He'd walked. And he'd walk home now and plan what he would say to Mrs. Grim, who was far too young to be a widow. And perhaps he should talk to his own wife, explain that the pending failure of their marriage was not in any way her fault, that he'd been killed in Afghanistan in many ways except the one that really counted. And there was no way an almost-dead man could carry on a relationship with a woman. Especially one as loving and warm as Major Kristen Clark.

CHAPTER FIVE

KRISTEN ROSE EARLY on Friday, showered and dressed in her class B uniform—light green short-sleeved blouse with open collar, dark green slacks with the darker officers' stripes along the outer seam. Then she packed her BDUs—battle dress uniform—into a gym bag along with her combat boots. She was likely to be better off wearing the BDUs once the exercise began. Amy watched her mother the entire time. Neither of them had seen or heard Anthony since his departure the night before. Kristen could only hope he was downstairs sleeping on the couch.

When she was ready, she picked up Amy and made her way downstairs, eager to get on with her work at the hospital and yet reluctant to leave Anthony to his own devices—assuming he'd come home. Would he really go to the library or would he waste another day pretending to learn German by osmosis from the TV? Her doubts tripled as soon as she saw him sprawled on the couch with one arm hanging off the edge and the other crooked over his eyes. The morning light streamed through the window, advertising a beautiful day, but he'd blocked it out. She wondered what time he'd come home and where he'd been. Did he realize he'd made her cry when he'd stormed out the door?

Amy had been upset, too, and the two of them had enjoyed a cathartic weep, the way moms and daughters occasionally should. But Amy had too many other things to do besides sit around and feel sad, so the festival of tears had ended within a matter of minutes. Still, Kristen had felt better because of it—and because of the cookies she'd made with Amy watching from her high chair.

The cookie plate still sat on the coffee table near her comatose husband. There were only two left of the dozen that had remained after she'd shared a pile with Amy the night before. Maybe he'd had cookies for dinner. She stood Amy on her own feet and reached for the plate to put it away. As she bent nearer to Anthony, an over-whelming whiff of stale alcohol hit her nose.

She reeled from the stench and stood looking down at the source with shock. In all the time she'd known Anthony—and, admittedly, they hadn't spent many months together—she had never known him to drink. He was a Ranger and his body was a temple, after all. The fact that he'd been out drinking last night proved he was not the man she'd married. Disgust crept over her and she backed up a few steps, then turned and fled to the kitchen.

She put the plate down next to the sink and then leaned against the counter with her hands gripping the edge, trying not to hyperventilate. She'd read about how war changed people, but the current reality lying on her living-room couch boggled her mind. Understanding that his depression had likely driven him to whatever bar he'd gone to did not in any way quell her distaste at finding him in this condition.

She glanced at her watch. No more time to wallow in self-pity over the shambles her marriage seemed to be in. Anthony would have to deal with his hangover alone. The hospital needed her. Thank God. She had an excuse to escape.

Returning to the living room, she saw that Anthony was squinting against the morning glare. Amy stood very close to him. Her constant chatter, at a distance of five inches from his ear, must sound like drums inside his throbbing head, but he didn't ask his daughter to be quiet. In fact, a weak smile seemed to be hovering around the edges of his mouth. Seeing that lightened Kristen's mood a little.

"I'm off to work," she said, a little more loudly than she needed to. She felt almost sorry for him when he squeezed his eyes closed against the sound of her voice. Almost.

To his credit, he sat up, wincing, and held up a hand. "What do you mean? Is your leave over?" If she didn't know better, she'd swear he sounded panicky at the idea of being home alone.

"Don't worry, Amy's going to day care."

"I wasn't worried about Amy. I can take care of her. I just thought…"

She waited for him to finish the sentence, but he didn't. She considered prodding him to do so, but she wasn't sure she wanted to hear what he wanted to say. Instead, she said, "If you'd wanted your wife to work regular hours, you shouldn't have married a nurse. I've been off for six days and now I have to go back. In fact, I was lucky to get six days in a row with the stepped-up tempo we've been dealing with this past year."

He ran his fingers through his already sleep-mussed hair and it stood on end at odd angles. He looked boyish, almost cute. But his appealing appearance couldn't overcome the memory of his stench. "Yeah, okay," he said. "We'll be fine." He looked at Amy, who waved her baby doll in the air with wild abandon.

"She's going to day care," Kristen said again as she swept her daughter up and settled her onto a hip.

"Why? I can look after her. She'll be safe with me," he insisted, putting up more of a fuss than Kristen would have expected.

She bit her tongue, trying hard not to say hurtful things. Staring at him as the pressure of her forced silence built up inside her, she wanted to scream, "Look at yourself! You're hungover and smelly! How could you think yourself capable of taking care of this child?" But somehow, she managed to keep the words from spilling out.

He stood and approached, limping slightly on his injured side. The instant her gaze drifted to where he'd been hurt, he straightened. "I'll look after Amy while you're at work," he asserted as he reached for their daughter.

Kristen's body moved automatically, without waiting for instructions from her brain. She turned herself aside enough to put the hip on which Amy sat as far from Anthony as possible. The shock and hurt on his ravaged face made her want to cry. But she couldn't regret the decision. "Amy's going to day care, just as she always does."

He let his hands fall to his sides and his jaw muscles flexed. Was he angry? He had no right to be. If he wanted to take care of Amy, he needed to clean himself up and act like a responsible adult. But his stare bored into her until she found herself speaking what she'd tried so hard to contain. "You've been drinking, Anthony. You're hungover."

His stare turned icy, but he didn't attempt to deny her accusation. "I'm capable of taking care of my own daughter, Kristen. She couldn't possibly be safer than when she's with me."

Yes, that was true. He was a Ranger, after all. But Amy didn't need special protection. She needed a patient father who loved her and played with her and looked after her needs. He wasn't ready for that yet. "You said you wanted to spend some time in the library," she tried. "I figured you'd want to clean up and head over there to do that research."

He blinked and his gaze sliced away. He nodded his head as if just remembering. "Yeah, maybe you're right. But I can pick her up later on. Where does her sitter live? I'll bring her home after I'm done."

Well, at least by then he should be showered and clean-shaven. He'd have hours to recover from his over-indulgence of the night before. "Okay," she said, and she gave him directions.

"Have a good day," she said as she edged out the door. She thought about kissing him goodbye, the way she used to each morning. But the reek of alcohol made her hesitate.

Anthony simply nodded at her words. He didn't step forward or even lean closer. If he didn't want to be kissed goodbye, then she wouldn't bother trying to get herself past the smell of him. But it hurt, nonetheless. With a sigh, Kristen hiked Amy more securely on her hip and went to the car.

Anthony stood in the doorway and watched them drive away. The sight of him there on the stoop looking alone and a little lost made her eyes sting. She would call him later, she decided. But then she turned the corner and had to focus on getting her daughter to day care and herself to work on time.

ANTHONY KNEW HIS WIFE had been right not to leave
Amy with him. But the pain that stabbed at him as he
watched his family drive away took him by surprise.
There had been a moment before they'd gone to the car
when he'd thought Kristen would kiss him goodbye.
And he'd wanted her to. Yet he hadn't been able to
move toward her. He just couldn't feel right about kissing his wife on the heels of being reminded the night
before of Weasel's widow. Still, he knew he needed to
shake off the self-pity he'd been mired in. Wallowing
didn't do his dead teammates any good.

But how? Grief for each of those men sat right under
his ribs, just beneath the surface, screaming to get out,
barely under control. It was hard to move forward when
he was under constant siege. And his mind wasn't very
sharp when the morbid, relentless chant ringing inside
his head became too loud to ignore: *They're dead, all
dead.*

He swallowed hard and ran his fingers through his
hair. The movement brought his own body odor to his
attention. He needed a shower. Badly. And even half an
hour with a toothbrush probably wouldn't begin to elim-
inate the fuzziness in his mouth. But he ought to make
the effort to erase the evidence of last night's lack of
judgment before trying to accomplish his goals for the
day. And although he would have liked to spend time
with Amy, he had things to do that might be easier without his daughter at his side.

It was time to find out everything he could about an
al-Qaeda sympathizer who called himself "Taaoun." He
hoped to God he hadn't delayed too long. And there
were letters to write to the families of his teammates,
who had waited too long to hear from him.

After spending a while under the hot water of the

shower, he dressed in his BDUs because that was the uniform he felt most comfortable in. As he did so, he recalled for the first time since his return to civilization that he had abandoned his usual ritual of running in the morning and lifting weights in the evening. In the first weeks after his rescue, he could barely lift his head without help, so running had been out of the question. But his doctors had told him he could go back to his usual pursuits, as long as he took it slow. Perhaps tomorrow morning he would see what he was capable of. The biggest challenge would be to accept how much strength and stamina he'd lost.

Today, he'd be glad to get through the day without drifting back into listlessness. His first stop was the Division Commander for Support of the 1st Armored Division, which was headquartered in Wiesbaden. It was past time for him to check in and renew his participation in the investigation into what had happened in Afghanistan. He'd been interviewed several times already, but he needed to make himself available for whatever would come next. Besides, he needed to know whether he was to be officially blamed for the disaster. Not that it mattered what the authorities said. He knew the truth. He just hoped he could protect his wife and daughter from suffering the taint.

His energy seemed to drain right out of him with that thought. He sat down on the edge of the bed, suddenly exhausted, and rested his head in his hands. His gaze fell on a photograph of Kristen hugging Amy that stood on the nightstand. If it weren't for them, he would not have any reason to go on, he realized. But he needed to make sure they were safe, that no terrorist stalkers were near them.

A few deep breaths revived him and he forced himself

back to his feet. Grabbing his beret, he trudged down the stairs and headed out. Walking should have been nothing, but all the scars across his abdomen and down his leg began to sting. After a block or so, he was glad he'd been told what to expect, because otherwise he might have thought he'd torn open his scars. Soon, the repaired muscles beneath his flesh began to burn and pull. But he went on. Tomorrow he hoped to go running, and the discomfort of that would be many times worse. Still, he had to pace himself, and by the time he arrived at headquarters there was a sheen of sweat on his brow. He wiped it away and fought off embarrassment as he entered the aging building.

General Jetyko happened to be standing in the reception area talking to a subordinate. He looked up and recognition lit his face, though he didn't smile. Holding out his hand to shake, he said, "Major Garitano. Glad to see you. Come on back to my office."

When the men were settled on opposite sides of the big desk, Jetyko got right to the point. "Two investigators arrived here yesterday. They plan to call you tomorrow."

"Yes, sir. I'm ready to do whatever I can."

Jetyko gazed at him for a few seconds and Anthony had to resist the unfamiliar urge to squirm. Had he ever been so hard-pressed to maintain eye contact?

"How are you, Major?" asked the General with sympathy in his voice.

Anthony didn't answer right away. He couldn't. His throat seemed to have closed around a hard lump and his eyes stung as if he were in a sandstorm. But he lifted his gaze to the General's and finally managed to choke out the words, "I'm fine, sir."

Jetyko leaned back in his chair. "Clearly your definition of 'fine' is different from mine. You're *not* fine. And you deserve some time to be 'not fine.'"

Dull amusement rose inside Anthony, despite the sudden clawing of grief in his heart. "Yes, sir," he agreed, somehow holding eye contact.

After another long moment of scrutiny, Jetyko spoke softly. "It wasn't your fault, Major. From what the investigators know so far, your point man was trying to defuse the explosive when it went off. They were doing what they were supposed to do, following protocol, doing their job."

Anthony went cold and stiff. "Then why are they dead? Standard operating procedures are supposed to keep everyone alive." His voice sounded just as cold.

"It's a dangerous job," offered the General. "And war is hell."

That sounded so criminally impersonal to Anthony, he wanted to shout and throw things. Only his training kept him from doing just that. He said nothing, unable to speak past the rise of rage and sorrow within him.

The General pierced him with one of those all-knowing looks that must be taught in General Officers' school. "You know the explosion was a terrible accident. All the evidence indicates it was no one's fault, least of all yours."

Anthony didn't move. To disagree with this General, whom he didn't know well, would be foolhardy. He chose his words carefully. "I should have been inside with my men," he admitted.

Jetyko eyed him. "From the babbling the medics said you did on the way to Kabul, you were keeping a lookout for the terrorist who had sworn to come after you. And you were alone out there, drawing fire to protect your men as they went inside. Had things gone as expected, you would have been the more likely to die that day.''

Anthony couldn't deny this. He'd had to argue strenuously with his Sergeants—and finally had had to pull rank—in order to be the one who stood outside the opening to the caves.

He didn't say this aloud or otherwise comment to the General. As if accepting this wisdom from the man, Anthony silently bided his time as he planned to change the subject.

When the time seemed right, he said, ''I know formal letters probably went out to the families, sir. But I'd like to send letters of my own. May I have access to the files to get addresses and to see what was already said in previous correspondence?''

The General eyed him skeptically, as if he knew Anthony had escaped the original topic. ''Yes, of course,'' he said. ''Writing those letters might help you through this. And I'm going to order you to see the post psychologist. You have to be evaluated anyway, but I'm hoping you'll spend some time with Lieutenant Colonel Farley and work on how this is affecting you.''

''Yes, sir,'' Anthony said dutifully. He was adept at dealing with shrinks. He could handle one more. And maybe if he got a clean bill of mental health, Kristen would be able to let him leave their marriage without clinging to him out of a sense of guilt.

Kristen would want to go to marriage counseling, too. He'd do it. To make her happy. To make her feel as if she'd tried everything possible before giving up on him. He didn't want her to feel shame or guilt. God, how he wished he could be sure she would have some good memories of him when it was all over.

KRISTEN SKIDDED INTO the staff meeting a minute late
and caught the Colonel in midremark. ''…and you'll just
have to explain to your families that you'll be needed
here for the duration.'' The people around her groaned.
What had Colonel Ripsimio told them before she got
here? His next words answered her.

''When the exercise begins tomorrow, you won't be
going home at all. That's seven days, six nights. This
time, we're giving you warning. Next time, it could be
the real thing and you won't get the chance to let anyone
know for hours what's going on.''

Now Kristen groaned. She realized she'd missed the
announcement for the start of the emergency readiness
exercise she'd known was coming. As a senior nurse,
she'd be expected to put in some long hours and would
only get home if luck prevailed. Any other time, she
would have simply activated the emergency child-care
plan the Army required her to put into writing. It called
for Mary Jane to take care of Amy until Kristen could
resume her maternal duties or until Kristen's mother
could either come for an extended visit or take Amy
back to the United States, depending on how long the
emergency or deployment was likely to last.

But that plan had been based on the fact that Anthony
couldn't be counted on to stay home. Never in Kristen's
darkest nightmares about being torn from her daughter's
side by her duty to her country had she ever considered
the possibility that Anthony might be available to take
up the parenting baton. If the military deployed or if
there was an emergency to be dealt with, he would have
to go.

It still seemed inconceivable that he could look after
Amy. But now her doubts about his ability to cope with
Amy were due to his health and mental condition rather

than his duties. She shuddered at the thought of leaving Amy in his care full-time. And yet, how could she express her concerns about his readiness to look after Amy day in and day out? Even if she managed to say what weighed on her heart without hurting or enraging her husband, Kristen doubted Anthony would ever agree to put Amy into the care of anyone else 24/7 while he was available. She might persuade him to keep their daughter in day care with Mary Jane, for the routine and familiarity of it. But she would never convince him to leave her there overnight until the exercise ended. Anthony would consider himself to be completely capable, as he always did.

A month ago, she would have agreed that he would rise to the occasion and figure stuff out as he went along. She would have worried a little—that was natural for any mother. But she wouldn't have been afraid. Now, she quaked at the idea of Anthony trying to cope with Amy while he struggled with the emotional strain arising from the loss of his men and the failure of his mission, not to mention his physical limitations.

The meeting ended while she remained lost in thought. Kristen walked out of the room with the others, hoping she hadn't missed any important details in the last fifteen minutes.

"Major Clark," called a man from behind her. Turning, she saw Colonel Ripsimio heading her way. She stifled a groan as she braced herself for the man's complaints regarding her lack of attention in the meeting.

"Yes, sir," she said with a smile. Bluffing often worked better when accompanied by a confident expression.

He stopped in front of her and his face was stern. "Major, I just want you to know that if I could give you more time at home, I would."

This was so *not* what she'd expected to hear that Kristen didn't know what she should say in response. She nodded to acknowledge she'd heard him and, after a bit, he went on speaking.

"I know your husband just got back and that he suffered serious injuries. I know you'd rather be with him, easing him into fatherhood and all." Kristen stared at the man who looked just like Colonel Ripsimio and wondered where her *real* commanding officer had gone. This copy appeared to have a heart that the original lacked completely.

She groped for words. "Yes, sir. He hadn't met Amy until he got off the plane. But she already seems to adore him, so things could be worse." Saying this out loud made her realize the truth of it. Anthony and Amy got along very well, all things considered. Maybe her fears about them alone together were overblown.

"You didn't know it, but I put off this exercise for two weeks because I knew he would be coming home. I didn't want you to be in the middle of a drill when he arrived." The man looked down at his feet as if this admission embarrassed him. Kristen knew he wasn't the type who usually spent much time dwelling on the personal needs of his staff. For this Colonel, it was all about the patients and the hospital. Everyone else had to take care of themselves.

"That was very considerate of you, sir. I appreciate it."

"Well, fun's over." He gave her an awkward smile. "Time to get on with things. The folks posing as victims will be here from Heidelberg tomorrow. I'll need you here early tomorrow and you won't be going home again until it's over."

She nodded. "I understand. I'll be here."

"I knew you would be, Major." Without further comment, he turned to go. But over his shoulder he said, "And don't let me catch you daydreaming in a staff meeting again."

She knew he didn't expect a response, so she got on with her day. Throughout most of it, she alternated between certainty that she couldn't possibly leave her daughter in Anthony's care and the conviction that it would be outrageous for her not to trust him with his own child. And then Paul Farley showed up, catching her by luck on a quick break to get some food after hours on her feet.

"Hi," he said, and he slid into a seat across from her at the lunchroom table. He put a book on the Formica surface, turned it so the title faced her, and pushed it over. The cover said *Survivor's Guilt—Working Through It* by Carmella Bellamo, Ph.D. "I thought you might find it useful," he added.

Kristen eyed the book. She knew about survivor's guilt, of course. But she'd never thought Anthony would succumb. He'd always seemed invulnerable to human frailties. If he was now in the grip of a survivor's guilt, could he ever get beyond it? "Thanks."

Paul tipped his head down so he intercepted her lowered gaze. Concern darkened his eyes. The thought crossed Kristen's mind that he ought to be more reserved in his practice of psychology. If he worried this much about all his patients, he'd burn out in no time. "Are you okay?" he asked.

"Yes," she said. A half truth. Paul's sincerity drew more out of her. "How can I judge if Anthony would be okay taking care of Amy while I'm working?"

The doctor's eyebrows shot up for a second as if he hadn't expected this question, then he hid his surprise behind a smoother expression. "Well, if he seems patient with her and capable of performing basic care... Is there some reason you ask?"

She nodded. "I have to stay here round the clock for a week to work on this readiness exercise we're doing. Normally, I would invoke my child-care plan and leave Amy with her day-care provider. But Anthony will want to look after her and he seems so..."

"So what, Kris?"

She glanced away. "I don't know. He just isn't himself. He seems...nervous. He keeps looking over his shoulder. He's restless and sleepless. And he went out and got drunk last night."

She could see that it took a lot for him to keep his face neutral. But he managed it. "Did you ask him about those things? Talking is the number-one way to preserve marital harmony," he reminded her with a half grin.

She nodded. "I've asked. He won't say why he seems nervous. I figured it's a side effect of what he's been through. He went out drinking because we had an argument. At least I think that's why he went out." Reflecting on the interaction that preceded him rushing out of the house the night before, Kristen could not put her finger on exactly what had set him off. If he'd gone out before she'd had the chance to apologize and explain, she might have understood. But he'd listened to her, let her lean against him, put his arms around her, and seemed to forgive her for her outburst about Amy in the tub.

"I don't understand. Did you have an argument or not?"

"It wasn't much of an argument." Suddenly, she didn't want to talk about it anymore. Especially with Paul, whose deep blue eyes were full of concern. Her desire for those sentiments to remain focused on her seemed almost…unfaithful. It was as if there was something adulterous about accepting the attention and conversation from Paul that she actually craved from Anthony.

Waving her hand in front of her face a couple of times, she said, "Forget it. I'll read your book. Thanks." And she got up to head back to work, scooping the text into her purse.

"Kris," Paul said, making her stop to look back at him. "You know I'm here for you, no matter what you need." His voice was warm and sympathetic. She wondered if there could be more than mere friendship between them if she gave him any hint of encouragement.

The thought drifted through her mind that if she had never met Anthony, she might have fallen head over heels for Paul. She stuffed the notion aside, uncomfortable with the very idea. "I know you are, Paul. You've been a good friend," she said, hoping that would be the opposite of what he'd hoped to hear. "I appreciate everything you've done for me."

He held her gaze for a moment. God forgive her, she became aware that a longing to be held again by a man could have her running into Paul's arms in a moment of weakness.

This was not such a moment. Her mind and heart were focused on Anthony. She wanted only Anthony. So she turned and fled from Paul. Quickening her pace so as to forget the disloyal thoughts that had passed through her mind, she headed for her patients. In another three hours, she could go home and talk to her husband. She badly needed to talk to him. God, how she wished she could talk to him the way she used to. Maybe she hadn't tried hard enough. She would make a better effort tonight.

But when she was finally able to escape—knowing that she'd have to return all too soon for a week-long stay—she felt less sure of herself. So she called her parents from her cell phone while she sat in the parking lot of the hospital.

"Kris, this call will cost a fortune. When will you learn to use e-mail?" chided her practical father.

Her mother chimed in from another line in their little house in Virginia. "Cliff, you leave her alone. She can call any time she wants to. Send her some money if you're so worried about it."

"Might just do that."

"How are you, Kris?" asked her mother, ever concerned with how everyone might feel. It never failed to shock her, when she talked to both her parents at once, that the two were so completely different.

"I'm fine," she lied, not wanting to have her emotions picked apart. All she'd called to get was a little confidence, preferably from her father.

"No, you're not," said her mother, seeing through her facade even from thousands of miles away. How did she *do* that? "Things aren't going well now that Anthony is home."

"Leave her alone," argued her dad. "She'll tell us what's going on without you trying to read too much into her words. Your mother thinks she's clairvoyant, Kris."

"Sometimes I think she is," Kristen admitted with a smile. The two might bicker, but Kristen knew her parents adored one another.

"You see?" said her mom. "So how are things going?"

"Okay, I guess. It's just that he's been gone so long and we're out of the habit of talking to each other."

"Well, you need to take the direct approach," advised Clifford, the former Master Sergeant. "Just ask him straight out what you want to know. He's a soldier, so he'll respond to that."

Her mother tsked tsked into the phone. "Sweetie, there isn't a man alive who responds to the direct approach when it comes to the important stuff."

"Corrine, that's simply not true," argued her father.

"Mom, Dad," Kristen tried, knowing she had to get a grip on the conversation before the two forgot that she'd called them all the way from Germany. "I just wanted you to tell me again that Anthony and I seem made for each other, even though we married quickly."

"Oh, that's certainly true, dear. The thing I liked best about you and Anthony was how much you smiled and laughed when you were here visiting." Her mother tended to base all her opinions on the emotions of the situation. Kristen resisted rolling her eyes.

"That's true," her father agreed. "And you match each other well in terms of your practicality and core values." Kristen had to smile at that. Core values. That was *so* her father.

She talked for another minute or two with them, but when her parents began to once again speak more to each other than to her, Kristen concluded the conversation. She'd gotten what she'd called for. Her heart was filled once again with the confidence she would need to cope with Anthony.

But when she got home, her confidence faded at the sight of what her husband and daughter were doing in the living room.

Kristen didn't respond to Anthony's greeting as she eyed the long piece of metal that Amy turned over and over in her hands. It was smooth and had no sharp edges, so it wasn't dangerous by itself. But it belonged to the weapon that Anthony had taken apart on their coffee table. He was calmly polishing the pieces of what looked like a shortened M-16.

She felt the spider legs of tension creep up her spine and all the way to her scalp.

"What are you doing?" she asked as she knelt and pried the gun part out of little fingers and picked up her daughter for a hug.

"You've seen me clean my weapon before," he said.

"Not in front of Amy. Not on the coffee table. Not where a little child could pick up small pieces and put them in her mouth and swallow them and possibly choke."

He stared up at her for a moment as if he had to decipher her words. Then he looked down at the table again. She saw his jaw clench and unclench, then he began to snap pieces back together. His hands moved so quickly, they were almost a blur. In seconds, the weapon was reassembled into an M-4 machine gun. He held up the ammunition clip between his thumb and index finger, then took both gun and bullets over to the hutch in the corner. He put them on top where even an adult would have to stretch to reach them.

"I don't want that thing in the house," she said. "Guns are a main cause of accidental death among children."

He turned and his expression seemed to be a mix of anger and confusion. "For the love of God, Kristen, you're an officer in the Army! You know all about weapons. You're qualified on several of them. Give me a break!"

"I don't have them lying about in the house!"

He put his hands on his hips, looking as if exasperation had overcome his usual coolness. "You're kidding, right?"

"No," she said. "I'm not. Please get it out of here tomorrow. And when you stop sputtering, you can join me in the kitchen. I have something I have to tell you." She took Amy to the next room and put her into her high chair. Once her hands were no longer encumbered, Kristen realized they were shaking. She saw from the dishes on the countertop and in the sink that her husband and daughter had eaten. A covered plate sat in the center of the stove, presumably for her to heat up for her own dinner.

At a loss for what to do next now that this evening chore had been done for her, she gave Amy a couple of Cheerios and sat down at the table. She had her head in her hands and her fingers laced through her hair when she heard Anthony's boots cross the threshold.

"I have something to tell you, too," he said.

Here it comes, she thought. Until this moment, she hadn't known that she'd been expecting it. But now, the meaning of his inability to reconnect with her came forward in her mind and assaulted her heart. This man, whom she loved so much...

He wanted a divorce.

CHAPTER SIX

ANTHONY STOOD IN THE DOORWAY between the kitchen and the living room and wondered how he would tell her. There was no easy way to describe the facts he'd found or the suspicions they'd aroused. He would simply have to spit it out. She had a right to know.

But he could give himself a few more minutes to collect his thoughts. "You first," he said.

Her eyes were shining as she stared up at him. They looked huge and luminous under the glare of the stark overhead light. Her hesitation suddenly made him wary. Then the seconds of silence made him quake with fear.

She would tell him she couldn't go on like this anymore. She would tell him she wanted a divorce. His body went rigid and his mind froze in an overload of denial.

He'd been expecting it and had even hoped she would give in to the inevitable without a fight. But suddenly, he wished with all his heart that he didn't have to let her go. He loved her too much. He wanted, desperately, to keep her in his life.

He opened his mouth to say something, anything, that would forestall her declaration that their marriage was over. If he could only find the right words, perhaps he could put it off for a little while longer. But she beat him to it.

"I won't be able to come home tomorrow night," she said. His hands clenched and unclenched involuntarily as he tried and failed to accept that his fears had become reality.

"I'll have to be away for a week," she said, her voice thick with emotion. "We're doing an emergency readiness drill. I have to stay at the hospital throughout."

The flood of relief made his knees weak. He almost laughed out loud but managed to contain himself. "You have to be away for a drill?"

She nodded. He could tell by the torment in her eyes that his relief might have been premature. "And?"

"And we have to figure out what's best for Amy while I'm gone." Hearing her name, Amy babbled and banged a toy onto the tray in front of her, leaving crushed Cheerios behind.

"I'll take care of Amy," he said, wondering how he would do that while he attempted to track down a terrorist.

"Well, that's just it, Anthony. Is that really what's best for *her?*" Kristen looked as if the question pained her.

"What's that supposed to mean? Is this about me cleaning my weapon in front of her?" Maybe Kristen took her supermom role a little too far sometimes. He'd have to help her find a balance. To do that, he'd have to remain calm. "She looks like she survived the incident."

"No. I just thought maybe you had a lot on your mind right now. Maybe I should just have her stay the week with Mary Jane. Amy's comfortable there. It's familiar. And you might not be up to dealing with her full-time."

There it was. She thought he was inadequate. Of course. That made sense. Because he was. But the realization that his own wife thought he couldn't care for a toddler hurt like hell. He focused on breathing. In and out. In and out. It's only pain, he told himself. It will pass. But that mantra seemed to work much better with physical pain than it did with emotional pain. His gaze slid toward Amy, loudly clamoring for attention now. He moved the few paces to her high chair and plucked her out of the thing. The child quieted down. He tickled her belly and she giggled, right on cue. The sound went a long way toward easing Anthony's torment.

"She'll be fine with me, Kristen. Trust me," he said as he locked eyes with his wife. But then he saw in her gaze the torment this conversation caused her. He searched for something he could offer to ease her mind. "I'll bring her to day care, just like you always do. And I'll pick her up at night. That way, I can have some time to do what I have to do. But Amy can still come home, where she can get to know her dad."

"Dadda, dadda, dadda," Amy said. A smile leaped from somewhere in the deepest recesses of his soul right onto his face. His eyes stung with unshed tears. He would never have suspected that having a child could be so painful and so joyful at the same time.

"You can tell me all the details of her routine," he said. "Write it all down, if you want. I'll follow it to the letter," he promised.

Kristen nodded. "But none of your Rambo gear in the house, right?"

He sighed. How could he promise her that he wouldn't keep a weapon at his side when he knew that a nutcase was after them? Perhaps she would be more lenient if he explained.

"I have something to tell you, too, remember?"

She waited and he could have sworn she held her breath. Whatever she expected him to say, it couldn't be half as crazy as the story she was about to hear.

"In Afghanistan, there was a man. An enemy combatant."

"A terrorist?"

"Yes. He escaped capture when we netted all his men. And one day, he attempted to create a diversion, probably in the hope of helping his companions get away from us. He took a couple of shots at us." He watched Kristen's worried expression even as he bounced Amy on his knee. He knew that Kristen understood better than most wives that he put himself in harm's way when he worked. But talking about it must make it seem more real to her. He wished he could avoid saying more, but he had to explain.

"Just before he had to run or be captured by my guys..." he began. The memory of his agile men running after Taaoun sent grief stabbing at his insides. He forced himself to continue. "...this combatant, this terrorist nutcase, stood up and shouted that he would hunt us down and kill us. Then he said my name. He must have seen it on my BDUs through his binoculars." He looked at Kristen to see how she was taking this frightening news.

"But you're home now," she replied. "You're safe here. As safe on this military installation as anyone can be these days."

"That's just it. We're not safe. He's here. And he's after me."

Kristen stared at him with wide eyes. Anthony wished he could spare her the truth. But she needed to take precautions. He couldn't protect her when he wasn't by her side and he couldn't be with her every moment.

"Oh, Anthony, please," she whispered. "Tell me you don't really believe that some terrorist has come all the way to Wiesbaden just to kill *you*."

Okay, when she put it like that, it sounded somewhat unlikely. But everything he'd learned confirmed his fears. Or at least almost everything. One fact he'd unearthed today would be hard to explain.

Amy squirmed to be put down and he set her on her feet. She toddled off to her toy box in the next room. Kristen shifted in her seat so that her daughter remained in her line of sight. But then her gaze riveted back to his. "You need to talk to someone, Anthony," she said.

He knew she meant that "someone" should be a shrink. And there had been moments today when he'd thought so himself. But then he'd seen the man sitting in the vehicle parked along the road just outside the post's perimeter fence. The car had no business being there. And the man behind the wheel had been staring at him as he walked by. Shadow had hidden the driver's face, but there'd been something familiar about the shape of the head and the set of the shoulders. Logic told him he couldn't possibly identify the man as Taaoun. But instinct warned him that the man had been watching him, analyzing, biding his time.

"I know it doesn't sound very likely, Kristen. I'm not crazy, so I'm well aware that what I'm telling you seems unbelievable. But I swear to you that I've seen this guy. Here."

A flash of fear replaced the doubt she'd tried to hide. "You've seen him with your own eyes?"

"Yes. Today. And a few days ago." But his sense of honor wouldn't let him give her half the story. "I wanted to think that what the doctors in Kabul told me was true, but now I can't believe that."

"What did they tell you, Anthony?" Her even tone indicated the return of her skepticism.

"While I was in the hospital, I saw this guy lurking around my room."

"Lurking," she said under her breath. "In a hospital in Kabul with all those American soldiers everywhere."

Well, he hadn't expected her to believe him right away. But if he could just coax her into being careful... "He looked just like the guy from the mountains in country, only his beard was shorter. I asked the nurses about him, but they said no one was allowed on the intensive care floor who wasn't supposed to be there. The doctors told me the guy wasn't real, that the medications and my emotional trauma combined to make me believe I saw him when I didn't." Anthony looked carefully at his wife, but her expression had become inscrutable.

"I swear I caught a glimpse of him again when I was in transit to the plane that brought me here. Just when I began to believe the doctors had to be right, I saw him again. Still, I figured a terrorist wouldn't follow me out of the country all the way to Germany. And I didn't want to think about Afghanistan anymore. I didn't want to see stalkers haunting my every move. I wasn't looking for him here. But there he was."

"Where, Anthony? Where do you think you saw him here in Germany?" she asked quietly.

"At the market where we bought the fresh food. Not on post. I don't think he can get on post. At least not easily. So Amy should be safe at her day care while I look for this guy. I'll capture him and we'll be able to relax again."

Kristen slumped against the back of her chair and sighed. "Don't you think you should just take your information to the authorities?"

"Damn it, Kristen, I *am* the authorities when it comes

to this guy," he answered. "There's no one more qualified to take out a terrorist than me." She opened her mouth, clearly preparing to protest this assertion, but he rushed on before she had the chance. "Besides, I've done some research today on him. He's an American citizen who sympathizes with al-Qaeda. His real name is Theodore Bjornvik."

He had to tell her all the facts, because he knew she'd probably be on the Internet looking things up for herself if he didn't. If he tried to keep details from her just because they didn't support his story, he'd never convince her to trust him. He took a breath and told her the rest. "The only thing is, the CIA has him listed as deceased, even though my men and I saw him alive and firing a weapon at us in Afghanistan long after he was supposed to have died."

There, now it was all out in the open. The CIA report on Taaoun had given him pause when he'd read it. For a few hours this afternoon, he'd begun to believe he really could not have seen Taaoun, also known as Theodore Bjornvik. He'd started to agree that he should get himself on some sort of antihallucination drugs as soon as possible. But then he'd seen the shadow of Taaoun sitting in a car, just outside the Army Airfield, beyond his reach and gone by the time he'd made his way to the spot. Anthony had known beyond any shadow of a doubt that he had not imagined what he'd seen. And even if his certainty wavered under the bright light of the kitchen, his training urged him to trust his guts.

Still, now that he'd said everything out loud to Kristen, he could see that a great many aspects would seem implausible to her. He appreciated that she hadn't been there in Afghanistan when Bjornvik had been silhouetted by the sun, his frame clearly outlined. She hadn't seen him turn into the waning light just before he ran. His face had been illuminated. The details had been indelibly imprinted on his mind, but not Kristen's. So he couldn't blame her for her doubts. There were even some lingering doubts of his own.

"Anthony. Listen to yourself. Try to look at your story objectively."

He waved his hand in the air as if he could make the insanity go away so that only the sensible aspects remained. "I know. It sounds crazy. *I* sound crazy. But I know what I saw. And can you really say that it's beyond the realm of possibility that an American who's turned al-Qaeda sympathizer wouldn't take it into his deranged head to go after the American who thwarted him?"

"Anything's possible with terrorists," she conceded.

"There's one more thing, Kristen." He leaned forward with his elbows on his knees so he could take her two hands in his. It was the first physical contact he'd volunteered to have with her since their initial embrace at the airport. "I wanted to write letters to the families of my men today. But when I went looking for addresses and what had already been sent to them, I found out some startling facts."

"I'm glad you're writing letters," she said, tears shimmering in her eyes. "Write to your mother while you're at it."

"But that's just it, Kristen. I can't write letters to the families of my men. There's no one left to write them to."

Her eyes widened. "What do you mean?"

"Weasel's wife died in a car accident. McCool's parents caught some mysterious lung disease at nearly the same time and died within a week of each other. Billy's fiancée disappeared and no one knows where she is. JJ's ex-wife suddenly took his kids and moved out of state leaving no forwarding address. Scopes's mother is in an old folks' home after a fall down a flight of stairs. The report says she suffers from delusions.''

Kristen squeezed his hands, opened her mouth to speak, closed it again and stared at him. Her eyes darted away and back to his face several times as she seemed to struggle for the right words. After a moment, she asked very gently, ''So what do you think that all means?''

''It means this Bjornvik guy couldn't go after my men because they were all dead, so he went after their families, just like he promised he would. He said he'd kill us and our children. Well, he's doing just that.''

Kristen's gaze shifted to where Amy sat on the floor in the living room, happily stacking things and knocking them down again. ''You're scaring me,'' his wife whispered as she disengaged her fingers from his grasp and withdrew her hands.

''I'm *trying* to scare you. For God's sake, I need you to be afraid. Be afraid enough to take extra precautions. Don't go outside alone if you can help it. Don't get into your car without checking the back first, carry a weapon if you can. I want you to take this seriously and be careful!''

The volume of his speech had escalated and Amy turned to see what the shouting was all about. In a flash, she'd gone from laughing and carefree to confused and worried.

''Sorry,'' Anthony said to her. ''It's okay, honey. Everything's fine.'' He even tried to smile for her, but he knew it would look more like an evil grimace because of his scars. Still, Amy seemed somewhat mollified. She toddled to her mother but didn't start crying. Kristen picked her up and set her on her knee. She gave her daughter a forced smile. Then, apparently to hide the fact that her expression crumbled into one of anguish, she hugged Amy close.

A few moments later, Kristen seemed to have pulled herself together. Her eyes were still dark and brooding, but she'd checked her emotions. She set Amy back down and gave her a cookie. Then she opened the cupboard where the pots and pans were kept and Amy shrieked with happiness. She crawled over on hands and knees at speed and began noisily taking things out and banging them onto the linoleum.

Over the racket, he heard Kristen say, "Let's assume that it isn't more than sheer coincidence that the families of your men are all having problems right now. I mean, let's figure that it's impossible that a young woman would have a car accident or that elderly parents would get sick and die. We'll suppose the disappearing fiancée did not jump off a bridge or run away to forget about her loss. And let's figure that old women with dementia don't sometimes fall down stairs." She kept her tone even, but her words smacked of sarcasm. "Instead, we'll assume that all these things are related to one another in some sinister plot for vengeance by an American turned terrorist."

He'd known it would sound like this even before she spelled it out for him. But he couldn't let that stop him from trying to protect his family, no matter how foolish he seemed in the eyes of those he cared about. Frustration forced Anthony to stand up and pace the length of the small kitchen. "You think I'm crazy. But I'm not. I saw what I saw. I was ready to give up when I read the CIA report. I was ready to agree that it was all my imagination from a blow to the head during the explosion or something. But I saw him sitting in that car.'' When he turned to walk back the other way, he saw that Kristen stood rigidly next to the counter.

Her gaze searched his face. ''Even if we assume that none of this is coincidence and that you did, indeed, see a terrorist stalking us the other day and seated in a car today, don't you think we ought to report it instead of just upsetting ourselves?''

Now he had to admit this, too. ''I already did. They said they'd look into it. But the implication was that they'll look into it when hell freezes over. I could tell— they think I'm not really recovered from the shock of my trauma.'' Unlike Kristen, he made no attempt to hide his sarcastic tone.

She looked as if she wanted to cry, but instead she moved toward him and wrapped her arms around his neck. Taken off guard by the suddenness of her action, he wrapped his arms around her. It seemed so natural to do so. She hugged him tightly, and the warmth of her seeped through his BDUs to his skin. He breathed in the scent of her shampoo and lost himself in the sweetness of this human contact, of this beautiful woman in his arms. The subject they'd been discussing evaporated in the sudden heat and unexpected desire that threatened to consume him.

He needed this. Needed it so much. This human contact that he didn't deserve. His self-denial only made him crave it all the more. Made him crave her.

''I don't think you're crazy, Anthony,'' she said.

His arms pulled her tighter against him so he could feel the length of her body all along his own. He wanted to float in the pleasure and wonder of it forever, forgetting everything else.

She drew back her head so she could look into his face. Her eyes glistened with moisture as she searched his face. "You're not crazy. But you need to talk to the psychologist. Paul can help you work through whatever has its hold on you."

He held her for another second or two before the meaning of her words overtook his desire to maintain this fleeting escape from his responsibilities. Anthony dropped his arms and took a step back. Kristen's reversal cut deep. She might not question his actual sanity, but she sure as hell didn't trust him much if she wanted him to see a shrink.

Amy chose that moment to begin crashing two pans together, hammering the red-hot spike of a headache straight through his temples. "Paul?" he asked coldly.

"Dr. Farley. Lieutenant Colonel Paul Farley. The psychologist on post. I've been seeing him, trying to prepare myself for your arrival. So he knows about you and maybe he could help you cope with the loss of your team. He knows a lot about..."

"You're on a first-name basis with a psychologist you consulted?" To his horror, he watched a faint blush creep up Kristen's cheeks. Nothing could have made his half-formed doubts turn into full-blown fears as fast. He wanted to flee, to protect his already battered heart from whatever it was that blush implied. Instead, he took a defiant step toward her. "Because I'm not sure what to make of you being so chummy with a shrink who outranks you that you call him Paul."

His insides were ablaze with anger and suspicion. When her blush intensified, jealousy filled him to the bursting point. He wanted to rip Paul from Kristen's life, from her very memory. Thoughts of pummeling the faceless stranger flitted through his mind. He had less confidence in his ability to win her away from her connection with the psychologist through charm and romance, but he suddenly felt willing to try just about anything.

"He's been helpful, nothing more," she said, but her flaming cheeks proved that there was something she wasn't saying.

"You've never been very good at keeping things from me, Kristen." He took another step closer to her, pushed by some primitive need to claim her. To her credit, she seemed unafraid. He thought he detected a strange combination of defiance and welcome in her eyes. When he grasped her by her shoulders and drew her closer, her palms flattened against his chest. But they didn't push him away.

Softly, she said, "When I realized your emotional injuries would be as bad as the physical ones, I wanted to learn how to help you, or at least how to understand. Paul was there for me and…"

"Well, *I'm* here for you now, Kristen. You don't need to turn to any other man." One more step and he had her pressed against the kitchen wall. A roaring in his ears and a quickening in his loins blocked everything else from his mind. He could hardly breathe past the desire building and building inside him. "Not ever again."

"I would never…" she began.

But her words were cut off as he took possession of her mouth with his.

CHAPTER SEVEN

KRISTEN INSTANTLY FORGOT everything that had been weighing on her as passion carried her to that place beyond intellect where she could lose herself in Anthony's long-awaited kiss.

"Does he make you feel like this?" Anthony asked, as he kissed her at the sensitive place beneath her chin that he'd come to know during the months of their marriage.

"No," she said on a sigh as she tried to let go of the secret guilt she felt over her vague attraction to Paul.

"How about like this?" he inquired, as he skimmed a finger down the side of her neck and then smoothed a palm past her collarbone until he cupped her breast. Her nipples hardened as her expectations blossomed.

"No one else can make me feel like this," she admitted. No one but Anthony had ever been able to make her feel so alive. "Only you, Anthony." Her admission seemed to encourage him and he found her mouth again. He kissed her deeply, thoroughly, passionately—the way she loved him to kiss her. He made her feel as if there were only the two of them in all the world.

And then Amy reminded them both that she was in their world, too. She crashed some pans again, making Kristen's heart skip a beat in surprise. Anthony must have been equally shocked because he leaped back, releasing her so suddenly she stumbled forward. Guilt flooded through Kristen as she realized she'd forgotten all about Amy during those moments in her husband's arms.

"Da da da da! Ma ma ma ma!" Amy shouted, demanding attention in no uncertain terms. She must have been sitting right there, not ten feet away, watching her parents kiss passionately as if she wasn't there.

"Um," Anthony said. His cheeks were flaming, from passion or guilt, Kristen couldn't tell which.

"I can put her to bed. It'll take just a couple of minutes." That was an outright lie, but if she told him it would take her an hour or more to ease Amy to sleep, she'd have no hope of picking up where they'd just left off. And she could think of no better way to ease the rift that made every problem seem insurmountable. If they could just get past whatever had kept them physically apart until now, then everything else could be solved, too.

But Anthony shook his head. "No. Don't rush. I remember from these past nights how long it takes. I'll just go…" he gestured toward the stairs then fled in that direction.

Disappointment warred with her maternal instincts. He was right. She shouldn't rush Amy. But, oh how she wanted Anthony to sleep with her tonight, to take her into his arms, to touch her, caress her, make her soar the way only he could.

By the time Kristen had pulled herself together enough to scoop her daughter up for the hugs and attention the child craved, she could hear the water from the shower overhead. She assumed the spray sluicing over Anthony's body would be ice-cold. He'd have a better grip on his libido than Kristen had on hers by the time he was done. And what would her chances of rekindling the flame be after that?

None, apparently, she realized a few minutes later as she sat on the edge of Amy's low bed. The lack of steam coming from the bathroom doorway told her that her assumptions about his shower had been correct. While she read Amy her story, she heard him opening and closing drawers. When next she saw him, he was dressed in clean BDUs.

He stopped on the threshold of Amy's room. "I have to go out. I want to check on some things." By that, Kristen assumed he wanted to secure the perimeter or some other soldierly thing that would make him feel as if he were doing something constructive against the threat he perceived. She hoped to God it didn't mean he would go to the bar again. Tired of fighting with him, sad that their moment had passed without satisfaction, she gave him a jaunty salute.

"Ni-night, Dada," Amy said from beneath drooping lids.

Anthony looked startled for a moment, then he cautiously approached. Seeing this, Amy came back to life and leaped to stand precariously on her mattress. Anthony caught her just before she toppled over and swung her around in a circle before drawing her in for a hug.

Kristen sighed. As good as it was to have Anthony taking such interest in their daughter, she couldn't help the spark of irritation that coursed through her. Amy had been just about asleep. Now Kristen would have to start all over, easing the little scamp back into that quiet state from which she would topple into dreamland.

For the first time, Kristen understood the complaints of other mothers she knew. Remarks about husbands who swept in for the giggles and play while remaining blissfully unaware of the whining and work suddenly made sense. She knew she was being unfair—Anthony had only just arrived and couldn't be expected to understand the details yet. But that fact just served to remind her of her other worry—that her husband wasn't ready to care for Amy while she worked the bioterrorism readiness exercise at the hospital.

Not to mention that there was every possibility he was delusional.

She heard him leave the house to go tilting at windmills. Or perhaps there really was a threat and he took his life into his hands to protect them from danger. She simply couldn't be sure which was right. But suddenly she wished she'd told him to be careful or reminded him that she loved him. If anything happened to him now, when so much unfinished business stood between them, she wouldn't be able to forgive herself.

Coaxing Amy back under the covers proved as difficult as she'd expected. But soon the toddler had eyelids at half-mast again. Before Kristen turned to the last page of the book, Amy's deep and even breathing indicated she was fast asleep. Kristen slipped off the bed and raised the railing that kept Amy from tumbling twelve inches to the floor. For long minutes, she watched the small chest rise and fall and rise and fall, all maternal irritation completely forgotten. Was there anything so sweet as a sleeping child?

But after a while, the weight of her troubles began to press down on her again. She could lose herself in the wonder of her daughter for only so long. Reluctantly, she trudged down to the kitchen to reheat the food Anthony had prepared for dinner and to think over what had transpired between them.

An hour later, she'd made little progress in deciding

whether Anthony's story could have any shred of truth to it. It seemed far-fetched, but she couldn't be certain that being stalked by a terrorist was beyond the realm of possibility. With a sigh, she decided to suspend her judgment for the time being. The only decision she needed to make immediately was about Amy's care during the readiness drill at the hospital.

If she activated her child-care plan with Mary Jane, Anthony would be livid. And he might not abide by it, making things awkward for Mary Jane if he tried to retrieve Amy from her home. One thing was for certain—Kristen would not take chances with Amy's safety. Under the circumstances, Anthony seemed riskier than Mary Jane. If Anthony's story turned out to be true, then their daughter would still be better off away from the house where she'd be a less likely target. If not, then Kristen would have better luck coaxing him to get help when he wasn't burdened with Amy's care.

Kristen only hoped she could convince Anthony of this when he got home. Meanwhile, she had to call Mary Jane and let her know the situation. Her depression lifted slightly as she dialed the phone. Even such a small decision felt like a major accomplishment today. "Hi, Mary Jane," she said into the phone when she heard the other woman's voice. "I hate to do this to you, but I have to activate my care plan for Amy."

"Ohmigod! Are you deploying?" Mary Jane asked in a voice charged with alarm. "Where are you going? What's happening?"

Mary Jane's husband was an officer in the 1st Armored Division and she justifiably worried about his safety when he was in Iraq instead of rotated home for a few weeks of rest. "No, no!" Kristen rushed to say. "Honestly, I'm not deploying. I'd tell you, I swear. It's just that I have a week-long readiness drill going on at the hospital, starting tomorrow. I'm lucky I got to come home tonight.''

"Oh, that's okay then," Mary Jane said. "Sure, I can keep Amy for the week. We were planning to drive to Klopp Castle on Saturday. Mind if we just take Amy with us?''

Kristen's stomach knotted and she chewed on her lip. What if the CIA report was wrong and this Theodore Bjornvik person was still alive? What if he really was out for revenge, stalking them, biding his time until he could strike?

And what if he wasn't? Should she live in fear because her husband's strained mind and emotions had conjured up a threat that, in all likelihood, did not exist? The facts Anthony had presented were far from convincing. In fact, they tended to prove a profound lack of credibility.

"If it's a problem, we can put it off another week," Mary Jane offered when Kristen hesitated.

"No, don't do that. I know you don't get much family time all together. Go to the castle. Take Amy with you.''

"Is it Anthony? Are you worried he won't like us taking her there for some reason? I mean, he doesn't know us very well." The depth of this woman's perception reminded Kristen of all the reasons she trusted Mary Jane with the care of her child.

"Yeah, it's Anthony. He's struggling right now. I don't know what to expect from him one minute to the next. The doctors all say it will take time. Unfortunately, this readiness drill has come up at the worst possible moment.''

"I'm sorry, Kris. I can't imagine what he's going

through—or you, either. Just let me know if there's anything I can do.''

"Taking care of Amy this week will be more than enough," she said.

"And your husband's okay with me keeping her the whole time?'' Mary Jane asked hesitantly. "You sure he wouldn't rather pick her up in the evenings?''

"Maybe, but I'd rather she stay with you.'' Even as she said it, an acidic worry settled into her stomach and began to claw its way up her esophagus. Anthony would be very angry about this. He'd already said he wanted to bring Amy home at night. Who could say how he'd react to being overruled? Given his fragile state of mind, Kristen had no idea what to expect. But she couldn't leave Amy in his care until she knew he was dealing more successfully with his emotional issues.

Also, there was his desire to have weapons in the house ready for a defense against attacks by terrorists. That alone was enough to make Kristen prefer Mary Jane's home for Amy, even if Anthony hadn't told her his wild tale tonight.

"I'll explain things to Anthony, so don't worry about that. She'll be more comfortable with you. Besides, he isn't likely to be home if we have a real emergency rather than just a drill. They'll need him to help, even if he isn't completely healed yet. And I really need to test my child-care plan anyway.''

"Well, we could use the extra cash. Tell him that, too, and maybe that will soothe him some.''

Kristen managed to crack a smile over that comment. "Yeah, maybe. I'll let you know how it goes with him when I see you tomorrow morning.'' She closed her conversation with Mary Jane, but sat at the table for a long time, thinking about the situation and waiting for her husband to come home.

Several more hours passed before she concluded that Anthony might not be returning for the night. She finally called his cell phone, got his voice mail, left a message to call home and slammed the phone receiver onto its cradle in frustration. Then worry set in. What if something had happened to him?

Just when she began to wonder if she should call someone to search for him, he called her back. "Go to bed, Kristen," he said. "I'm fine, but I have some things to do that can't wait."

What could she say to that? "Okay. I wanted to tell you I asked Mary Jane to take Amy the whole time I'm gone. I figured, after everything you said, you'd need to be free to take care of things." Saying this felt somewhat dishonest to Kristen. Her motivation had nothing to do with wanting to keep Anthony free to pursue his fantasies. But she needed to say something that would gain his acquiescence with minimal fuss.

A long silence beat at the ear she had pressed to the receiver. At last he said, "Maybe you're right. Let's leave her with Mary Jane."

Relief flooded through Kristen. One less thing to weigh on her mind, she thought. "Thanks, Tiger. We'll talk some more when the drill is over, okay?"

"Okay. Don't worry about me. I'll be fine. Just stay vigilant, for your own safety."

"Yes, I will." Other words crowded through her mind, demanding to be spoken. Too many of them. What was it she had wanted to say to him in case one of them were hurt or killed? He'd already said goodbye and waited for her to say it, too. But there should be more, shouldn't there? "Anthony," she said, stalling for time.

"I don't want you to think there was anything between me and Paul. There never was."

Another long silence came, bearing down on her heart. What could she say if he chose not to believe her? "Then what was that blush for when I asked you why you were on a first-name basis?"

Oh. In the heat of their discussion, she hadn't realized that this was what had made him suspicious. She hated having this kind of conversation on the phone. She couldn't see his eyes or gauge his reactions. "I've always been honest with you, Anthony, and I won't start trying to make up stories for you now. The truth is, he's attractive and..." How to express the rest?

"And you're attracted to him," Anthony filled in.

She sighed. "No, not really." Then she added, "He isn't you."

"But?" How had he known something else weighed on her mind?

"But there have been times in the past year and a half when I missed you so much. I missed being held and having someone just lend me some strength, physically and emotionally. I probably blushed because once or twice, I might have wondered... You've probably wondered, too, about women you've met," she concluded lamely.

"No. I haven't. Not many women to wonder about in the middle of those barren hills of rock. If he touches you, he's a dead man," Anthony growled into the phone.

Coming from anyone else, that might have sounded ridiculously primitive and brutal. But Kristen knew Anthony and understood the side of him that made him say such things. Reassurance seemed in order. And all at once, she remembered what she'd wanted to say to him, those incredibly important parting words. "I love you, Anthony. More than ever."

She thought she could detect sounds of lost composure on the other end of the phone and she chose not to wait for a reply. She knew he loved her, too. Someday soon, she'd hear him say it again. But not today. He'd had enough emotion for one day. "I'll call you tomorrow if I get the chance," she said, then she hung up the phone and went to bed.

WITHOUT HIS TEAM, Anthony felt as if he'd lost a vital part of his body. Everything was harder to do, compensating for what was missing put him off balance, and the pain associated with the loss sometimes exploded almost past endurance. During his search outside his house and just beyond the post's perimeter fence, he wished he had Weasel with him. He'd been an excellent tracker. And when he sat at the computer doing research, tracking the life of Theodore Bjornvik, a.k.a. Taaoun, he longed for JJ's able fingers flying over the keyboard to manipulate search engines and cut through deep classified sites with the precision of a surgeon. And damn if he didn't wish he could talk to young Lieutenant Billy Brinewater, just for a few minutes. That boy had looked up to Anthony with worshipful eyes at times, but at other times, the kid could be exceptionally clear-thinking and frank.

It would be nice to have Billy here to tell him straight out if he was full of crap or really on to something serious here. Anthony even spent some time trying to think like Billy, going over the information he'd collected and turning it around and upside down to see if it would add up to something more conclusive, one way or the other. But none of that helped. The CIA had DNA evidence

that Taaoun had been killed in Afghanistan months prior
to Anthony's team arriving in country. Hard to refute
that.

Except that Anthony had *seen* him. He was almost
certain of it. If only he could get a glimpse of the
stalker's hand, the missing finger would put an end to
this nagging doubt that clouded his mind. But that
wasn't likely. He finally sought out one of the Rangers
he'd met at the bar, the guy he'd remembered from his
days in South Carolina.

"Thanks for meeting me here, Dave," Anthony said
as he took a seat across the coffee-shop table from Captain Batsin.

"No problem. S'up?" Anthony knew that Dave knew
he'd called him to simply talk stuff over. But the pair
of them would never openly admit to getting together
over coffee to have some sort of chatfest like a couple
of girls. There had to be a reason for their meeting and
Anthony had come prepared for that requirement.

"I need your help with a private operation," he said,
taking the other man's measure with a steady gaze.

"Uh-oh. A personal agenda. Bad news. Not my thing.
Sorry, man. Not sure I can help you."

Anthony had been prepared for this, too. Dave would
never turn his back on a fellow Ranger, but he needed
to show deep resistance now in case things got messy
later. He could honestly state that he'd been drawn into
the deal reluctantly and only because he had to watch
out for a fellow Ranger. "I just need someone to back
me up while I try to find this nutcase who followed me
over here from Afghanistan."

That got Dave's attention. "Speak on."

Anthony told him what he'd told Kristen. But this
man wore the tan beret, just like Anthony, so there was

no suggestion that the story might be in any way the figment of a tormented mind. Dave nodded gravely upon hearing Taaoun's threat, seemed angry at what had happened to the families of Anthony's men, and looked ready to go huntin' for bear at the suggestion that the terrorist was here in Germany, lurking nearby.

Dave thought over the information for a few moments as he savored a slug of coffee. "The docs think you're hallucinating and your wife thinks you're crazy," he stated.

"Yeah." He held Dave's penetrating gaze.

"But you're not."

"No."

The young Captain stared at him for a few more seconds. Then he came to a decision. "It looks like what we have here is a semiprivate operation, 'cause I'm not going to sit by doing nothing while some al-Qaeda American psycho walks around where our families live."

Anthony smiled and, for the first time, didn't mind the tug of his scars on his cheek. It felt so damned good to be part of a team again, even a team of two. "Thanks," he said. "Right now, I just need you to keep your eyes open. In a day or two, I'll have a better idea of how we can go after this guy."

Dave slapped some money on the table and slid out of the booth. "Gotta get back to the drudgery of strategic planning. War sucks. But you call me when you're ready. Ask for Fang," he said with a grin as he walked away.

Anthony made a mental note to ask him how he'd come by that nickname. It seemed so far removed from his actual name, there had to be a good story.

As good as Batsin's confidence had felt to Anthony, by fifteen hundred on the second day of Kristen's emergency readiness drill, Anthony had made up his mind to go see Lieutenant Colonel Paul Farley. At best, he'd be a sounding board to help Anthony put his thoughts in order. And if the man proved useless in that regard, at least Anthony would have checked off one requirement General Jetyko had placed on him. Besides, it'd feel good to confront the man who had made his wife blush the other day.

As he'd been doing since Kristen's drill began, Anthony did some research in the morning, walking to all his destinations. He could move faster now, almost jog. The burning in his muscles had faded somewhat. Either that, or he'd become used to it and, like a good Ranger, simply blocked out the pain.

Arriving in Lieutenant Colonel Farley's office without an appointment, Anthony decided on his approach. He would tell the man everything he'd found out and also divulge the various sightings he'd had of Taaoun. This didn't seem as risky as it would have been if Anthony were going in for an ordinary psych evaluation. For one thing, he wasn't yet fit for duty regardless of his mental health, so Farley couldn't hurt him on that account. For another, Anthony knew that he ought to manifest some obvious signs of emotional anguish and mental trauma so that he could "recover" from them when the time was right. If he decided to remain in the Army, he'd have to prove he'd overcome the effects of what had happened, emotionally as well as physically. There were few ways to prove emotional fitness, but if he overcame "visions" he'd have the evidence he needed.

Besides, there were times when his sightings *did* seem like mere visions. Farley's opinion might prove enlightening, even though he probably wouldn't be entirely objective given his interest in Kristen. Or at least the interest in her that Anthony suspected the man had. Steeling himself for verbal combat, Anthony waited in the reception area for the door to open. He knew the doctor was in because the sign said I'm With A Patient, So Please Be Patient. Cute. Very cerebral. If the sign gave any indication, his figurative joust with Farley would be a short battle of wits.

He was halfway through a *Sports Illustrated* when the door swung open. A woman with red-rimmed eyes walked past, followed by a blond guy in uniform—undoubtedly the shrink himself. The man appeared to be in good shape, but with the slim physique of a runner. Anthony could deck him in less than a second, if necessary. The thought made him feel good. When the doctor turned an inquiring eye toward him, Anthony was able to smile.

The beginning of recognition lit Farley's eyes seconds before Anthony gave his full name. The scars were a dead giveaway, he knew. The Lieutenant Colonel glanced at his name tag for confirmation unnecessarily. How many Majors in tan berets were walking around Wiesbaden with faces like this? Only one.

"Come in, Major. You've caught me with a free hour. I'm more than happy to talk with you."

I'll just bet you are, Anthony thought. Anthony had timed his arrival toward the end of the work day, hoping for just such a break.

"Thanks." He followed the man into the office beyond the reception area. There were comfortable chairs and even a couch. Anthony eyed the couch suspiciously. That would be where this shrink would have seduced Kristen if she'd been a weaker woman. Or maybe not, he corrected. Better to suspend judgment until all the facts were in. Farley didn't look like the type who would color outside the lines.

"Pick a chair and have a seat," the doctor said.

Anthony had played the "pick a chair" game before. He glanced around, decided which piece of furniture the doctor preferred and eased himself into it. He kept his expression neutral, showing none of the defiance he felt inside.

Farley didn't even blink. He simply went to the chair across from Anthony as if it didn't matter. "How are you, Major?"

"Let me get right to the point," Anthony said. "My wife is off-limits to you for any purpose other than professional."

Farley's concerned expression didn't change. "There has never been anything other than a doctor-patient relationship between Major Clark and me. Would you like to talk about your own relationship with her?"

Anthony hadn't expected a compassionate reply to what had come out as a bald accusation. "My marriage is none of your business," he said.

"Okay," Farley agreed. He sat looking amiable and patient until Anthony realized the man wasn't going to say anything else. Maybe the verbal battle would be a long one after all.

"I want your agreement as an officer that you won't interfere with our marriage." Even as he said these words, Anthony wondered what the hell they really meant. He'd known his marriage was hopeless since the day he'd awakened in the hospital in Kabul and confirmed the fate of his men.

"I would never interfere. But I will help her decide for herself what she needs and wants, Major. I wouldn't be much of a psychologist if I urged her to remain unhappy.''

Anthony leaned forward, indicating with every nuance of body language that he would throttle the good doctor if he didn't watch what he said. Even as he made the subtly threatening move, Anthony acknowledged that the man had a point. He'd been saying the same thing to himself for all the weeks of his recovery—Kristen had a right to a marriage that would meet her needs. Doubt remained as to whether Anthony could hold up his end of such a marriage.

Farley added, ''But I can't talk about Kristen with you unless the two of you want to see me for couples therapy. She has independent privacy rights. You and I need to stick to talking about you. How are *you* doing?''

Okay. Fine. He'd talk about himself. General Jetyko had ordered him to do so and Kristen also expected him to. But Anthony gave himself permission to wring the guy's scrawny neck if Farley ever implied a personal interest in Kristen.

''I'm doing pretty well for a man who lost his team in an explosion and who now sees terrorist stalkers on every street corner,'' he began. Then he told the psychologist everything he had confessed to Dave Batsin— with far different results.

DAY THREE AND THERE were bodies everywhere. Kristen saw that the emergency room and surrounding corridors were filled with them. The beds and mobile stretchers had all been used, and now the moaning people were lying on the floor. With barely enough room to walk between them, Kristen nearly stepped on an outstretched hand as she rushed toward the latest crisis. The entire day had been like this. Constant action, putting out one fire after another. An hour after the exercise began, she and her team had dealt with an actual heart attack. A few hours later, a ruptured eardrum walked in and promptly collapsed on the emergency room floor, blood pooling on the linoleum. An observer would have considered it chaos, but Kristen took it all in stride.

The people from Heidelberg had been well prepared for their roles as victims of a biological attack. They retched convincingly, poured glycerine from their noses and eyes, moaned and begged for help with acting skills worthy of Oscars. Late into her third shift in a row, Kristen had to calm down a young nurse on the verge of losing it. The Lieutenant stood immobile in the center of the hallway, stunned by the apparent insanity of it all.

Kristen pulled her to a nurses' station for privacy. "Get a grip, Lieutenant. You have two minutes. Emergencies don't slow down so you can pull yourself together."

"Yes, ma'am," said the woman. The military order got her moving.

When Kristen looked up again, she saw a familiar figure in BDUs striding toward her. He had a slight limp but otherwise stood tall. The scars on Anthony's cheek made him look like a pirate and his steady gaze resting on her made her blood heat. God, she loved this man. And the progress that he'd made physically in the days since she'd last seen him was nothing short of astounding. Blinking against the stinging in her eyes, she wished she could launch herself into his arms so that he could swing her around while he kissed her.

But she knew he wouldn't appreciate such a public display. And he clearly had something important on his mind.

"Kristen, we need to talk," he said, all business.

Her elation at seeing him so vastly improved evaporated and was replaced by dread. "What's wrong? Has something happened to Amy?"

He held up his palms in a calming gesture. "Amy's fine. She's still at day care with Mary Jane. But I need to talk to you about something else. Where can we go?"

She glanced around in search of a nearby corner and realized there would be no privacy today. "We're in the middle of the exercise. It's impossible." She turned her attention back to him, puzzled. "How did you get in here anyway? Any real emergencies have to go through triage in the ER and all the people playing victims are wearing badges. This place is locked down pretty tight. You shouldn't have been able to get through."

A slight grin crinkled the corners of his eyes, transforming him from the bitter man he'd become into the man she'd married. "I'm a Ranger, Kristen. I can get inside Camp David and sit beside the President if I need to. But I'll talk to your security officer about some chinks in your hospital armor, if it'll make you feel more secure."

With weariness clogging her ability to think, she waved him off. The hospital would have to be hermetically sealed to keep a determined Ranger out. "Never mind. Come over here and tell me what you came to talk to me about." She led the way to a corner where there were only two moaning bodies lying nearby, doing a bang-up job of pretending to be in dire straits. "This is as good as it's gonna get."

He glanced around at the chaos and nodded. Then he turned his gaze back to her. "You look exhausted," he remarked. He lifted his two hands to her shoulders, as if to steady her.

Did she really look that bad? And did she really care

when her appearance made her husband's eyes darken with concern? It was her turn to offer a slight smile. "I'm an Army nurse in the middle of a biological warfare exercise. Nothing like practicing for the real thing to tire out the medical staff."

He nodded again and dropped his hands to his sides. She could have kicked herself for reminding him that she was a capable officer when what she really wanted to do was just lean on him for a bit, after so many months with no one to depend on. Too late, the moment had escaped her.

"I've talked to one of the Rangers on post," he said. "He's one of the guys waiting for the next deployment. I told him about the terrorist. The American al-Qaeda sympathizer?"

As if she could forget. She didn't know where this was leading, so she forced her features to remain neutral while she waited for him to continue.

"He's willing to help me figure out what's going on. I told him everything I told you and he thinks it's possible this guy really did follow me here."

Well, that was no surprise. Rangers stuck together and tended to believe in the infallibility of their members, especially the officers. Hardly likely that any Ranger would consider the possibility that one of their own could be suffering from post-traumatic stress disorder or that emotional strain could lead to overreactions to simple facts.

Still, with suicide bombers cropping up everywhere and with the historical fact of the September 11 attacks on New York and D.C., how could she simply dismiss the possibility that Anthony might be right?

"I concede that anything is possible, Anthony," she

said very gently. "But I refuse to live in fear, waiting for demons to attack at any moment."

"I only came here to check on your safety and to ask you to be careful. This environment leaves you vulnerable. I need you to be on your guard."

"I can do that. I *am* doing that. Our discussion the other day made me more wary."

He gazed into her eyes as if trying to assess whether she was telling him the truth or merely humoring him. He seemed satisfied by what he saw. "Good. I'll do everything I can to find this guy before he hurts anyone." He turned as if to go, but she took hold of his arm and stopped him.

"Just make sure Amy's safe," she said. Her mind whirled with competing hopes—that Anthony be proven as in touch with reality as anyone, that his fears be entirely unfounded, that all of them stay safe in a very unsafe world. Her inability to do anything about Anthony's terrorist, real or imagined, made her want to scream with frustration.

"I'll keep her safe, Kristen. I promise." He looked as if he might say something more, but then he lifted his chin and walked away in the direction he had come, moving with grace for all his height and breadth. An ache settled behind her solar plexus and seemed to put down roots.

"Major!" called one of the experienced nurses from the doorway to the ER. "I need you to come look at someone."

Kristen followed and came to a patient writhing on a floor mat. He held his head and moaned. Then he began to cough. Kristen decided from a distance that this person was no actor and, without thinking about it, she lifted her surgical mask to cover her nose and mouth.

His breathing sounded congested, even though he had nothing running from his nose or eyes.

"I don't think this man is with the others. Did you get his vitals?" Kristen asked. They had. Blood pressure low, temperature high.

"Hurts," said the man as he patted his chest. "Breathed somethin'. Made m'sick," said the man in between racking coughs.

"When?" asked Kristen as she leaned over him, trying to keep him coherent by force of will. She saw then that he wore BDUs like everyone else. "Sergeant Peterson, can you tell me when you started feeling sick?" In her urgency to acquire this information, she nearly shouted at the man and might have shaken him in frustration if he hadn't been so sick.

"Jus' now," was all he said and that made no sense at all. And those were his last intelligible words. All he could do after that was moan and cough.

Kristen's initial reaction was that he could be having an allergic reaction. She wanted to be ready in case the doctor agreed.

"My baby! Help me with my baby!" cried a woman who had just come in. Kristen looked up and decided mother and child were part of the exercise and not in immediate danger, despite the theatrical wailing. Besides, a medic had gone to her assistance. Everything was under control regarding the actors. The people in real trouble had to remain Kristen's first concern.

She barked orders to those nearby. "This man needs a bed. Let's see what his oxygen levels are. You, get epinephrine ready, just in case. You, get Doctor Alder or Ripsimio. Hurry."

People scattered to follow her instructions as Kristen listened to the man's lungs. He wasn't wheezing, though he sounded congested, and his throat did not seem to be closing. He had no other signs of allergic reaction. She stood back and looked at him, thinking. How could pneumonia grip this robust military man so quickly? He didn't have the recognized symptoms of Severe Acute Respiratory Syndrome, but nothing else fit, either.

In another moment, Ripsimio showed up at her elbow. Kristen recited what she knew. He barked out which tests he wanted done, including a chest X-ray, then turned back to her. "Why are you so sure he's not just a good actor?" the Colonel asked over the man's moans.

"Diapherisis is hard to fake," she said.

The doctor tilted his head and looked the patient over. "He's not sweating now."

"But he was. You'll have to take my word for it."

"Good enough for me. Let's see what his blood work tells us."

The Colonel's response brought Kristen up short. It felt good to have her superior officer trust her intuition without question. Guilt flooded through her even as she went about her duties regarding her patient. Sometimes, it's important to trust instincts even when the facts may not be clear. But she hadn't trusted Anthony's usually excellent intuition. Should she have?

CHAPTER EIGHT

HE WENT RUNNING in the afternoon of the fourth day after Kristen's return to work—really running, until he moved into the zone beyond the pain. Then he slowed his pace and jogged for endurance, just to see how long he could take it. Eventually, he found himself in front of Mary Jane's house, where Amy was staying. Anthony barely knew his little girl, but he missed her so much, he ached with it. He wanted to see her, to hear her laugh. Hell, he'd be happy to hear her fuss, too.

He stopped to rest on the walkway, huffing like an overweight recruit. He still couldn't believe how difficult even a two-mile jog had become. The worst of it had been his lack of awareness of some of the essential muscles. They worked, but he had difficulty feeling them. And some were so stiff they seemed to tear every time he flexed them to any significant degree. But he'd checked with his physical therapist and knew he was doing himself no harm. He suspected the doctor probably had not meant for him to run beyond pain, but Anthony didn't care. He needed to recover his strength quickly and this was the only way he knew to do that.

Earlier in the day he'd done thirty push-ups and a whopping forty sit-ups. At this rate, in about a month, he'd be as good as his wife had been on her first day in the Army. That was a horrifying thought. But he wouldn't give up. He'd just have to redouble his efforts in the gym—his first day there had been a shock to his ego, too—and keep pushing the edges of his stamina. Somehow, his talk with Farley had galvanized his determination. The man had explained, at length, about delusions and post-traumatic stress disorder. He'd delved into survivor's guilt. And, after considering Anthony's confession about seeing Taaoun here in Wiesbaden, he'd suggested having a physician write a prescription for some kind of antischizophrenia drug.

Yeah, right. As if Anthony would ever consider taking that kind of medication when his family could be in jeopardy. He hadn't seen any sign of the stalker the previous day, but on the chance that his worries were founded in reality, Anthony would keep his mind clear and his reflexes sharp.

He scanned the area around the home where his daughter had been spending her days and, in the days Kristen had been gone, her nights. Everything seemed quiet and normal. The sky was blue, the trees swayed in a soothing breeze, summer flowers scented the air. There were no vehicles of any kind sitting along the curbs, no one hovered behind trees to watch the house, he detected no hidden surveillance devices tucked in trees or on telephone poles. For now, his daughter seemed safe. But something nagged at him and he wanted to see her with the same intensity he craved water after a long hike.

Yet, he resisted. He had things to do. And if he went in to play with Amy, there could be no telling when he'd be able to extricate himself. Besides, his clothes were drenched with sweat and he could imagine how he'd smell in the confines of the house. Despite the heat, he'd worn his BDU pants with a T-shirt—the better to conceal the semiautomatic handgun he carried inside a deep pocket. The extra clothing didn't go well with the heat, but the weapon certainly made him feel better.

He walked on, surprised by the tug of an invisible string that threatened to draw him back to his daughter. He vowed to pick her up tomorrow evening and bring her home for the night. Just one night. Kristen wouldn't even have to know, assuming he could persuade Mary Jane not to squeal on him.

On second thought, perhaps he'd call Kristen and let her know his plan to bring Amy home to sleep. The worst that could happen was that Kristen would be upset. But maybe she wouldn't be. At the hospital, she'd asked him to keep Amy safe. Clearly she trusted him to do that, despite her doubts about the terrorist. And telling Kristen would be the right thing to do even if she did get upset. What was that compared to the chance he'd have to spend some time with Amy? As a bonus, he'd use the opportunity with his little girl to prove himself as a father. He couldn't show Kristen he was capable if he never got the chance to take care of Amy.

First, though, he had to see what else he could learn of Taaoun or Bjornvik or whatever he called himself. Anthony didn't believe the man was dead, no matter what the classified files claimed. He'd found some gaps in the CIA report and he had some phone calls to make to some people he knew in the intelligence community. He also needed to spend a little more time at the officers' club. Not to drink. He'd had enough of that the last time he'd been there. But he thought it likely that Dave Batsin would go there for lunch and maybe he'd find the other visiting Rangers hanging out there, too. Their families would be safely tucked away back home near their posts in one of the Carolinas or Wisconsin. They wouldn't know what else to do with themselves if not gather at the club to be with other Rangers. He'd join them. If nothing else, he could gather information. He also hoped to become better acquainted with them in case he needed help in the near future. If Taaoun turned out to be alive, if he'd done the things Anthony suspected, then a team of Rangers would be his only way to save his family.

On his way to the O Club, he would take care of another chore, he decided. After talking to the shrink, Anthony had begun to feel the need to do something that seemed mentally healthy, regardless of his actual state of mind. So he picked up his cell phone when he went to the house to change clothes. On his walk through the post, he called his mother.

"Anthony!" she shrieked. He had to pull the phone away from his ear or risk further injury to his hearing. "You don't call! You don't write! I'm worried sick!" Then she spoke to someone else in the room with her. He heard her say, "It's Anthony!" as if the person could not have surmised that from her initial outcry.

"I'm doing fine now. Sorry to worry you," he said. God, how he wished he didn't have to talk to her right now. Having his mother on the phone only reminded him of how he'd thought of her while he'd been lying in the desert, certain he was about to die. He remembered wishing he'd told her he loved her the last time they'd talked. But saying so now just didn't feel right, either.

"Anna's here for breakfast," his mother said. "She wants to talk to you about your injuries." His mom barked at his sister to just wait her turn and stop grabbing at the phone. Carrying on two conversations at once was nothing out of the ordinary for Paula Garitano. "Are you going to be able to come home for a visit soon?" she asked.

"Probably not, Mom. But you and Dad can come over here and see Europe if you want." He felt a slight twinge of guilt as he made the offer, knowing full well what the response would be. It was a risk-free invitation.

"Heavens no! Your father isn't going to fly anywhere and certainly not all the way to Europe. And especially not while there's so much violence going on in the world. You'll just have to tell us all about it when we see you."

"You could come by yourself. Or you could come with Anna."

"No, I couldn't do that. Your father would get into all sorts of trouble if I left him here alone. If you grab for this phone one more time, I swear I'm going to lock myself in the bathroom with it!" It took him a second or two to realize this last sentence had been directed at his sister.

"Why don't you let me talk to her so she'll stop bothering you?"

There came a brief scuffling sound, then his sister's voice. "Anthony!"

Without preamble, he said, "You should talk to Kristen about my injuries, Anna. I really don't know much, except that it's taking a long time to get back to normal."

"I already talked to Kristen. I know you're doing okay. It'll take a while for you to get back into your usual my-body-is-a-temple shape. That's not really why I wanted to talk to you," she said.

"Oh?" Dread crept over his skin.

"You know, I had this car accident a few weeks ago…"

"An accident?" he asked, alarmed. "What happened?

Were you hurt? Was anyone else involved?'' The fore-boding began to ratchet up in intensity.

"I'm fine. Really. But the guy who ran into me said he knew you."

Damn! His immediate thought was that his stalker had found his stateside family, too. And yet the man couldn't be in two places at once. "When did this happen? What did the guy look like? Did he give you his name? When was this exactly? How…"

"Slow down and I'll tell you! This was about a month ago. He was actually very nice. Very polite. Said he met you in Afghanistan. Told me to tell you he said hello."

"His name?" he asked again, struggling to control his impatience.

"Flea-oh, he said. I figured it was one of those nick-names you guys give each other in the Army."

"Never heard of the guy. Did he give you his insur-ance information?"

"Nope. He paid me for the damages in cash right on the spot. Insisted on it. I didn't realize you Army types made real money," she said with a laugh in her voice. "Or maybe it's because he's out of the Army now, working in a real job."

"He paid you in cash? How did you know what it would all cost? Why would you just accept money like that without getting things checked out?" His tone threatened to expose the depths of his concern. He took a breath and eased it out of his lungs, along with some of his unproductive agitation.

"It was just a small dent. I might not even bother to get it fixed. And he gave me more than enough to cover the damages I had. I've been in enough fender benders to know what bodywork will cost. The last thing I needed was to go through my insurance company again, and he was very sympathetic.''

''Well, his name doesn't ring any bells,'' he told her, even though plenty of alarm bells were going off in his mind. ''What was he like? Anything unique about him?'' Like, was he missing a finger?

''He was just a nice guy with a weird name. He even asked me to dinner. I would have accepted, but I was already late for my shift at the hospital.''

Dread scrabbled around inside his stomach like rats with long claws. ''You aren't going to go out with this stranger, are you? He didn't even give you his real name!''

''C'mon, Anthony. I would have gotten his real name before I went out with him, for heaven's sake. But he never called, even though I asked for a rain check and gave him my number. He was so sure he knew you. Are you positive that strange nickname doesn't mean anything to you?''

''Not a thing,'' he said. ''You should be more careful about giving out your phone number to strangers and going out with men you don't even know. This guy could have been a psycho.'' *Or a terrorist bent on destroying everyone I love,* he thought.

''He wasn't like that. You had to meet him. Honestly. I swear, if he'd called to ask me out again, I would have accepted.''

Jesus, Mary and Joseph! ''God, Anna, you don't know anything about the guy!''

''Well, he's a friend of yours, so he has to be okay. But, listen, Kristen said you weren't going to have the plastic surgery on your face that the doctors recommended and I think you should know…''

''Stop! I haven't decided about the surgery. I just want

some time to recover before I think about any more hospital stays. Is that asking so much?''

''But she said…''

''She misunderstood,'' he lied. He had been very clear with Kristen that his face was of as little importance to him as his life, these days. But he didn't want to argue with Anna. ''Look, this is costing a fortune, so put Mom back on. I'll e-mail you with updates, I promise.''

''Yeah, well, I can't imagine you letting that pretty face stay messed up for long. You like your good looks too much. And I'll believe you'll send an e-mail when I see it. But here's Mom now. You take care of yourself.''

Anthony managed to get through another five minutes of conversation with his mother, just enough to feel that he'd done his duty to the fullest where his family was concerned. He didn't ask to speak to his father and his mom didn't suggest it, either. She told him that the elder Tony Garitano had been worried about him and was very relieved when news came that he'd survived. But Anthony knew he wouldn't hear any of that from his father's own lips. He'd have to take his mother's word for it.

Before he could bring the call to a close, however, his father surprised him. In the background, Anthony distinctly heard his dad say, ''Tell him he has to take better care of himself from now on. He's got a daughter these days.'' His mother repeated those sentences into the phone while Anthony stood stock-still in the center of the sidewalk, stunned into immobility that his father would have bothered to say something to him that was unrelated to sports or cars.

His mind reeled with both his sister's revelations and his father's unexpected words of advice as he responded automatically to his mother's further inquiries into the health of both Amy and Kristen. By the time he finally hit the cell button to end the call, he had regained his ability to move. Even his breathing and heart rate had returned to normal.

After a few minutes of sorting through the emotional upheaval the phone call had caused, he decided that the first order of business was to try to find out whether this nice, ordinary man who called himself Flea-oh had anything to do with Taaoun.

KRISTEN'S EXHAUSTION would have brought a less experienced nurse to her knees. But she had learned over the years how to keep going on the certainty that every situation was temporary. On the heels of several long days, this day had been the longest. The Sergeant who'd come in the night before with the mysterious disease finally seemed stable, but he didn't appear to be improving.

They'd begun administering a general antibiotic for lack of anything better to do. But if his pneumonia was viral, this would have little effect. Over and over in her mind, she heard Sergeant Peterson croak the words "Breathed something," and "Made me sick," and "Just now." She felt sure these were clues to his survival that her fatigue prevented her from interpreting.

"Major Clark," Colonel Ripsimio called. She turned to look at the man striding toward her. Transferring her attention from the reports on the desk taxed her reserves unbearably, and she blinked against a wave of dizziness. "Peterson is stable and you need to go home."

She blinked some more. "But, sir," she began. He held up a hand to forestall her protest.

"Yes, I know the exercise is still ongoing. But I believe you're on your third straight shift without sleep. You're well out of the ERD anyway, thanks to Peterson's unexpected crisis.''

She scowled, finding it difficult to think. ''What if others come into the ER with similar symptoms to Peterson's? We'll need everyone who can recognize what's going on. I can sleep on the…''

''I want you to go home. Seriously, Kristen, you're dead on your feet.'' The fact that he had used her given name startled her enough to pay better attention to what he was telling her. His expression appeared grim. ''I'll be needing you, fresh and alert, in the next few days, if any more of these cases show up. Take this opportunity to get some real rest. Things could turn ugly.'' His words sounded ominous.

''Do you have any idea what's going on with him or how he got so sick so fast?''

''Not sure yet. But I'm not done thinking about it. We need to give the lab some time to complete tests. And I'm certain you're not done thinking about it, either. That's how I know you won't get any actual rest if you try sleeping on a cot here. You'll just dwell on the possibilities. So go home to your husband and daughter. They ought to keep the problems here off your mind.''

Kristen suppressed a laugh fearing it would come out sounding a bit hysterical. Dr. Ripsimio had no idea how well her home life and the troubles in her marriage would keep her mind off the hospital.

''Are you going to report this to the CDC?'' she asked, referring to the Centers for Disease Control and Prevention.

''Not yet. We have no indication that it's a reportable event. But if we see more…''

She eyed him, feeling worried and confused without

knowing exactly why. "It's just pneumonia, right? I don't want to transmit anything to my daughter."

"Just don't cough on anyone. If you start feeling achy or tight or like you need to cough, you should come right back here and let us check you out."

She nodded. That made sense. Peterson had pneumonia. The X-rays showed that. Just because they couldn't figure out how he'd come down with such a severe case of it so quickly didn't really change his diagnosis. Pneumonia was contagious, mainly through coughing, and she'd been wearing a mask almost the entire time she'd been near the patient. Her chances of catching a disease from him were slim and the risk of giving it to someone else before she had symptoms of her own was even lower. And people who worked in the hospital would never go home if they worried all the time about what they could transmit to their families.

"Okay, I'll go home. Let me just finish up this report."

Ripsimio watched her a moment as if to reassure himself she would actually do what she promised. But then his name sounded over the loudspeaker and he dashed away. "Get some rest!" he called over his shoulder.

She would. Right after she went to talk with Paul, she thought as she glanced at the clock on the wall. Only seventeen hundred forty-five hours on day four of the drill. She had plenty of time to get to Paul's office before he left for the day. Funny that she knew his habits so well. She felt uncomfortable with that. It seemed like the threshold of a mental betrayal of her husband. Especially when the thought had crossed her mind during some of her darkest, loneliest moments that she might be able to turn to Paul for more than psychotherapy. She knew she should find another person to help her. But there were no others with whom she could talk—especially without an appointment. And there was no way she'd dare face her husband at home without checking in with the psychologist first. Not after the argument she and Anthony had engaged in by phone earlier today.

He'd called from his cell phone to announce that he would be picking Amy up from day care for a night at home sleeping in her own bed. Kristen's nerves had been stretched to the breaking point and she'd found herself railing at him. If he was right about a terrorist stalker, then bringing Amy home would endanger her, she'd said. And if he was delusional, well, she didn't have to spell out why he shouldn't be caring for Amy in that circumstance.

"You told me to keep her safe. I can do that better when she's with me," he'd argued.

"She's better off with Mary Jane, anonymous in the midst of that family," she'd countered. In truth, Kristen had no idea why she'd been so upset. She'd felt helpless and frustrated and completely confused. Then he'd delivered the *bad* news.

"I don't think this is going to work, Kristen," he'd said into the phone.

"That's what I've been trying to say…" she had begun, but then she'd realized he wasn't talking about Amy anymore.

"I mean us," he'd clarified.

Her lungs had refused to fill with air for what felt like minutes on end. The silence had stretched on and on. Finally, he'd mumbled that they would talk more about it when they could sit down face-to-face. Only the life-and-death situation unfolding with Sergeant Peterson had kept her from dwelling on what he'd said and what he'd meant and how he would do with Amy or how Amy would do with him. And how she would ever manage to go on without him if he meant what he'd said.

She'd managed to live without him for eighteen months, but that was because she'd convinced herself that his love for her endured somewhere in the world and that he would come home to her. The thought of ending her marriage to the man she loved with all her heart made her throat hurt and her head spin. She could hardly go on with her work. But she had to do just that.

As the day had worn on, she'd found minutes here and there for introspection. She'd lashed out at her husband on more than one occasion since he'd come home, and she knew she should ask herself why. Her fury at Anthony about picking up Amy, for example, seemed somewhat irrational, even to her. The fact was, she could do nothing to prevent him from seeing Amy.

Perhaps she should apologize. Maybe that would fix things, at least for now. She needed more time to figure out how to save her marriage. She had to persuade Anthony not to give up on her before she'd tried everything to save what they had together. The very thought of failure made her stomach clench with panic.

He deserved an apology, anyway, because she did not actually believe Amy would be in any sort of danger in Anthony's care. If she did, then she'd be rushing home to be sure her baby was safe. Instead, she drove to Paul's office, hoping to find some insights that would help her sort out the mess her marriage had become. Along the way, an unpleasant possibility wormed its way to the forefront of her thinking.

She could admit that her arguments with Anthony were at least partly over losing control regarding her daughter—a control she had so far enjoyed without any interference from another soul. Even her own mother could only offer her many opinions via brief phone conversations and lengthy e-mails, which Kristen tended to skim through. Though she'd bemoaned the lack of help when she hadn't been sure how to cope with certain situations, Kristen had to say that in the balance, she'd preferred the independence of raising Amy as she saw fit. Perhaps Anthony's unexpected talk of terrorist stalkers served as just the excuse she needed to thwart her husband's efforts to get between mother and daughter.

Wasn't that a telling choice of words her mind had conjured up? She'd have to confess aloud to Paul her worries that Anthony would come between her and Amy. Once she had sorted out these hard-to-admit thoughts with Paul, she would be better able to face Anthony.

ANTHONY'S HEART nearly stopped and then raced violently when he saw the car parked across the street. It looked like the same blue heap he'd seen outside the fence line the other day. The sun slanted across the windows, preventing him from discerning whether a person sat inside. But his guts told him it was the same car.

His ability to investigate was hampered by Amy, strapped into her stroller and chattering incomprehensibly in her lilting baby voice as they walked from her day care to their comfortable little home. He had to get her to safety before he could do anything else. How to get her out of the line of fire? His mind worked as fast as the pounding inside his chest.

"Let's go for a bumpy ride!" he called to her as he veered onto the grass to get her behind their house as quickly as possible. Amy laughed and waved her hands as they sped across the lawn to the rear entrance. But, as luck would have it, he'd locked the house up tightly before he'd gone out that morning. And he didn't have a key to the back door on him. Should he take the time to look for a hidden key or should he leave Amy buckled into her stroller while he returned out front? He needed to decide fast, before he lost the opportunity to confront the man in the car. It might be his only chance to end the living hell his life had become.

Defying his earlier assessments of his physical weakness, Anthony deftly lifted the stroller with Amy still in it and placed it on the porch without climbing the three steps. He slapped down the wheel lock and tossed her a toy from the net hanging at the back. Could he leave her here like this unguarded? He didn't want to.

And suddenly he realized he didn't have to. A neighbor stood in her backyard, watering her flowers. "Ma'am!" he called to her. "Could you help me? I need you to watch my little girl for a second."

The woman smiled at him. "Are you Kristen's husband? I'm so sorry we haven't met. I'm Charlene Mey—" she began. But he held up his hands to indicate he had an emergency.

"Could you just watch her for a minute while I take care of something?" He was already backing away, sure that she wouldn't turn her back on a cute little kid like Amy. And to his relief, the woman began to move toward the porch where Amy sat.

"Be good, sweetie," he called to his daughter as he edged away, eager to get back to the road and the stalker who awaited him there. "Daddy will be right back." But even as he turned the corner, he heard her shriek of protest. Her angry wails seemed reassuring somehow. At least if he could hear her cries in that same furious tone, he would know she was okay. He had to harden his heart to her upset, in the hope of taking out an even greater threat to her well-being.

He didn't retrace his steps to the front of the house, but ran full tilt through neighboring yards. At the far end, he vaulted a four-foot fence, shocked and a little exhilarated that he was able to do so. Just like before.

When he was far enough away, but still within earshot of his very unhappy daughter, he began to veer toward the street. Within seconds of leaving Amy, he could see the car again. No one had emerged from it. The car huddled lifelessly along the curb, taillights staring at him like dead eyes. He kept his sights on the vehicle as he drew his weapon and trotted toward it, careful to remain in the blind spot of the rearview mirror as much as possible.

He estimated his ETA at less than thirty seconds from the time he'd rounded the corner, but every running step seemed to take an eon. In those endless seconds, he remembered all the reasons why he should not be doing what he was doing—without a team, without so much as a single backup, without a weapon other than his handgun. But he didn't let those doubts stop him. This might be his only chance and he couldn't let it slip away.

Before his training kicked in and prevented him from taking these ridiculous risks with the million-dollar war machine the Army had made of him, he moved close and ducked low along the bumper. He hunkered down and scanned beneath the chassis for indications of explosives. Finding none, he edged along the driver's side with his gun poised and the safety off. Sensing no movement from within the vehicle, he abruptly stood and aimed, stiff-armed. The slightest movement from within would goad him into squeezing the trigger.

But he pointed his weapon at nothing. Only faded

upholstery looked back at him. No one sat behind the wheel or in the passenger seat. No one hid in the rear of the sedan, either. Confused, he relaxed his stance slightly. He'd been so sure.

The rush of unspent adrenaline made him shake. Or maybe it was the overexertion. Or the shock of being so utterly wrong. Glancing up and down the street, he hoped to God that no one had seen him.

There was no one in this car. His heartbeat began to pound in his ear. Perhaps there never had been. His head began to spin. Maybe he'd imagined everything else, too. His knees felt weak. He must be seeing demons where there were none. Blackness hovered at the edges of his vision.

And in the faraway distance, Amy cried and cried.

"SO I'M THINKING THAT at least half the problem is me," Kristen concluded, sitting across from Paul in his comfortable office. "I mean, it isn't just him not wanting to reunite with me. It's also me subtly pushing him away because he's intruded on my life with Amy." She blinked back the threat of tears. "Right?"

"Anything's possible, Kris." He hadn't said much so far. She'd simply talked and talked. She'd reviewed every detail of her arguments with Anthony, elaborated on where he'd slept on the nights she was home and how distant he'd been, left out none of the realizations she'd had about her own behavior, and skimmed over the passionate moments so she could focus on the sexual frustration. And his response was "Anything's possible, Kris"?

"Ah, d'ya think you could expand on that just a bit?" The words came out more biting than she'd intended, but she forgave herself because of a complete lack of sleep.

He chuckled. "Okay, how's this? Anthony came by here the other day. We had a long talk."

Her heart began to race. "Oh? W-what about?"

"You know I can't tell you that. But I'd be glad to meet with you both so you can tell each other what you each told me."

"Did he tell you about the terrorist he thinks is stalking him?"

"Would you like to tell me what *you* feel about the things Anthony's been saying?"

She groaned. "I just finished telling you how I feel about it all."

"No, you catalogued events and made a series of confessions about being too controlling. You mentioned frustration. But otherwise, I didn't hear much about your feelings."

Now her palms were sweating and her pulse throbbed in her ears. And anger rose like bile in her throat. "You want my feelings? Okay. How about I feel like a failure in my marriage? How about I feel like crying all the time, but I can't because I'm an officer and a nurse and a mother and a wife and I don't have time to indulge in tears?" But now the tears were right behind her eyes and in her throat, burning and choking. "I feel scared and confused! Anthony doesn't love me anymore, and I don't seem to be able to do anything that's lovable! And…" A sob escaped and she covered her mouth with her hand in an attempt to hold any others from being heard. "And I haven't had sex in about as long as I can remember. But I want to! I…" The torrent couldn't be held back much longer. Already she could feel drops leaking from her eyes and streaming down her cheeks. She leaned forward and shielded her eyes with her hand.

"Kris," he whispered as he appeared before her, kneeling in front of her, handing her tissues. "You are very lovable."

His voice came to her all warm and soft and soothing. His gentle tone invited her to let go of her self-control.

"I'm not," she protested.

"Of course you are," he insisted. "The fault isn't yours, Kris. It's the war that breaks men and hearts. And sometimes they can't be put back together."

She found herself leaning closer to him. She could smell his subtle aftershave. It had been a long time since a man had showered her with his undivided attention. His kindness swept over her, through her, around her like a soft, sun-drenched sea breeze.

"Believe me, Kris. It's not you. Sometimes things happen that are beyond a patient's ability to fix."

"You think so?" she asked, not wanting to believe him, yet yearning for the relief from responsibility that his words offered her. She felt him gently pat her on the back. How long had it been since she'd been touched with such kindness by a man?

"Yes," he said from his hunkered-down position. It seemed to Kristen as if he searched her face for unspoken feelings. "You're a wonderful nurse, a terrific mother, an attractive woman, and…"

She held her breath, wanting him to finish and also afraid that he would. She longed to hear that someone, somewhere wanted her. Before he could speak or shift away or stand up, her body responded to the primal magnetism between a man and a woman. She kissed him— a sweet, gentle, tender pressure of her lips to his.

Almost as soon as her mouth touched his, her mind

screamed, "No, no, this is wrong!" But somehow, her kiss had already deepened and her unspent passion enveloped her. She felt his hands cupping her shoulders, strong and masculine. No! But somehow she could not convince her body to pull back, to resist, to push herself away.

But in the next instant, he eased her back into her chair. His expression told her he'd been surprised by her bold move. And suddenly, she felt appalled.

"Anthony," she murmured, and all her longings were contained in that name.

CHAPTER NINE

PAUL WINCED WHEN he heard her husband's name from her lips and Kristen's heart regained control over her traitorous body. She bolted from her seat and moved away from Paul, horrified at what she had allowed to happen. Allowed to happen? Honesty demanded that she admit, at least to herself, that she'd instigated the kiss. Her vulnerability and unrequited needs served as no excuse.

Paul stayed where she'd left him, half kneeling in front of the chair she'd vacated, his head now bent—in frustration, or sorrow, or shame? She didn't care. Her own shame consumed her. It filled her right up to her throat and she felt as if she were choking.

After she took a few more retreating steps, something pressed into the small of her back. The doorknob and its promise of escape prodded her. Self-loathing tasted like bile, made her want to gag. If she didn't get out of this man's office, she would vomit all over his carpet. She dared not take her eyes off the evil temptation her doctor had suddenly become. But the knob turned beneath her groping hand and she managed to get the door open. A gust of cool air chilled her skin through the damp military shirt that clung to her like guilt.

"Kris," he said as he lifted eyes filled with torment to her face. "This was simply a case of transference. You mustn't blame yourself. Please…"

But she didn't wait to hear it. "Stop!"

Nothing he could say would save her from the sickening guilt and wretched disgrace. She'd come to him for help, but she would leave with unexpected burdens she didn't know how to handle. Running away wouldn't help, but she ran anyway. She ran full tilt down the hall of his office building, skidded to make the turn into the vestibule, slammed through the doors and rushed down the outside steps. Through the wet blur clouding her vision, she saw her car and bolted for it.

A wail of a horn, the screech of brakes, a shouted curse. She barely noticed that a car passed close to her, then she ran on without looking back.

At last she put her hot palms onto the surface of her shaded car. Like a blind person, she groped her way to the driver's door. Locked. She needed keys. Where were they?

In her purse. Which she'd left back in...

"Ma'am! You forgot this!" A young soldier trotted up to her. Concern creased his brow.

She knew she must be pale and wild-eyed, with teary and red-blotched cheeks. "I'm okay," she reassured him.

He nodded and had the grace to look away. "The officer inside said I should give this to you." He held her purse out to her.

"Thanks," she managed to say as she took the black leather bag from him. She turned away, horrified that this youthful specialist had witnessed her distress. She owed him and her uniform a great deal more than this disgraceful display of public emotion. And suddenly, she recalled that she was an officer in the United States Army and made of stronger stuff. "Thanks for bringing it out to me," she said, squaring her shoulders and arranging her features into what she hoped was a more dignified expression.

"My pleasure, ma'am. You take care now." He saluted and she returned it, even though she hadn't thought to place her beret on her head. As the specialist walked back to the building, she pulled the black felt cap from where she'd tucked it under her belt and put it on.

Tugging it at an angle over her right ear made her feel a bit more confident. If she could keep her mind on her uniform, on her rank, on her respected position in the Army, she might be able to hold herself together. With hands that shook only slightly, she found her keys, unlocked her door and slid behind the wheel.

She sat there a good long while without going anywhere, thinking about what had happened. With each passing moment came added perspective. Honesty forced her to admit that she'd been attracted to Paul over the months she'd known him, even though she'd never wanted anything from him other than his counsel. But this evening she'd been at her weakest—weary and lonely. He'd said something about transference and she knew that probably meant she'd shifted her desires for her husband onto the one other man in her life who seemed to care. Was that it? There was no way for her to know and it made no difference, in any case. She would not ever allow herself to be in a room alone with Lieutenant Colonel Farley again.

Her guilt became unbearable and she began to wonder whether she unjustly blamed herself. Had the man done anything to encourage her? If so, she should probably report him so he couldn't prey on some other female. But reporting him would embroil her in a "he said, she said" scandal that would not serve her career well. Her obligation to protect others from his lack of professionalism warred with her sense of self-preservation. Women who reported sexual harassment did not go unscathed. She thought this truism permeated all of society, but it proved particularly true in the military.

But had the man ever done anything wrong? She considered their history, but in truth she could not think of a single instance when he had led her on or been anything other than professional. Certainly, he had been kind and even friendly. But he'd never touched her, never even looked at her in that way men did when they were interested in a woman. And he'd been the one to push her back when she'd crossed the line. She dropped her head into her hands as the weight of her own guilt came crashing down on her again.

And yet, she knew her actions made no sense. Whatever attraction she'd felt toward Paul couldn't hold a candle to what she felt for her husband. As much as the incident felt like a betrayal of her marriage vows, Kristen knew she'd been thinking only of Anthony through it all. Though she berated herself for her responsibility for what had transpired with Paul, she took some consolation in the certainty that the arms she'd imagined holding her were Anthony's, the lips she'd wanted on hers were her husband's, the passion she'd felt welling inside her had been for the man she'd married.

He would be at home now with their daughter. She desperately needed to be there, too.

As she pulled into the driveway, she glanced at the dashboard clock. Twenty hundred hours. Amy would be asleep. Probably Anthony would be, too—on the couch in the living room, most likely. That would be the first thing she'd change. Hell, she'd sleep on the couch with him, if she had to. But she would sleep beside her husband again this night.

The drive gave her the time to see that her fatigue had been partly responsible for her momentary lapse in Paul's office. She was ashamed that she had allowed it to happen. Yet her weakness and his lack of self-control served one positive purpose. There was no doubt in her mind that she would fight for her marriage. She loved Anthony with all her heart and she would *not* give him up.

All she had to do now was remind him that he loved her, too, and that they could make their marriage work again.

Too tired and distraught to come up with a plan to accomplish that formidable goal, Kristen let herself into the darkened house. The silence struck her immediately. No TV. Since returning home, Anthony *always* had the TV on. Could Anthony be out somewhere with Amy at this late hour?

No note rested on the kitchen table telling of their whereabouts. Then again, why would he leave one, when he thought she'd still be at the hospital? Yet if he were home, he would have heard her come in, wouldn't he? True to his Ranger training, the man usually slept with an ear cocked for trouble. As she crept through the quiet house, she became more certain with each step that Anthony wasn't there. He saw terrorist shadows at every turn and he hadn't expected her home tonight. Surely he would have charged forth with guns ready at the first creak of a floor board.

At the foot of the stairs, she paused to listen. Nothing but the normal hushed sounds of the house came to her. The situation unnerved her and her own heartbeat seemed unnaturally loud in her ears. The thought popped into her mind that Anthony could have left Amy asleep in her bed, alone in the house. She told herself over and over that no one would do something that stupid, but she took the stairs two at a time anyway.

From the hallway, she peered into Amy's dark room. The covers were drawn back and there was a small indentation in the pillow, but no child rested on the sheets. Confusion made her head spin. She could think of nothing to do other than continue quickly down the hall to her own bedroom.

And there they were.

Kristen stopped in her tracks and her hand rose to cover her heart.

Anthony had clearly been reading to Amy. The bedside lamp remained lit and the thin picture book rested limply on his chest. He was sound asleep. Amy lay curled on her side with her back right up against him. She dreamed something that put a Mona Lisa smile on her bow-shaped lips. As weary as she was herself, Kristen stood on the threshold a long time, staring at them and filling her soul with the sight of the two people she loved most in the world.

There were dark circles under her husband's eyes and she hoped he would stay asleep while she moved Amy back to her own bed. The fact that he hadn't yet awakened proved how exhausted he must be. Carefully, Kristen lifted the small body and snuggled her close. Amy stirred but didn't open her eyes. Neither did Anthony, surprisingly.

Kristen smiled as she carried the dead weight of her daughter along the corridor. When Amy's body finally gave up the fight and decided to sleep, it did so with total abandon. Even putting her down on the cool sheets of her bed didn't rouse the child much. "Mommy?" was all Amy murmured.

"I'm here, baby. Go to sleep, sweetie." And she did.

Kristen slipped out of the small room, glancing back at her baby curled up beneath the blankets.

It would be wonderful to sleep next to her husband for the first time in a year and a half. Much better to do so in their bed than on the couch, as she'd vowed to do if she had to. But Kristen doubted that Anthony would remain upstairs once he realized she'd come home. When he awoke, he would retreat to the television again. So she put off joining him on the bed, where she would face inevitable disappointment, and opted for a hot shower to wash away all the difficulties of the day.

The pulse of the water through the old-style European pipes rivaled the clash of cymbals, Kristen thought. But it helped ease her anxiety about the incident with Paul. She needed to be clean. And then she needed the loving embrace of her husband. Only then would she feel she was on her way toward recovery.

Anthony would surely be awake by now. No matter. The cascade of water seemed to cleanse Kristen of her sins, as well as her hospital worries. She would sleep as deeply as Amy tonight. Even if she had to do so on the couch in the living room in order to be next to her husband.

Yet Anthony still slept in the queen-size bed when she returned to her room. With a skimpy towel wrapped around her body and another one tousling her hair dry, she almost wished he would open his eyes and see her. Maybe his gaze would turn lustful and he would take her into his arms. If he kissed her as he had in the kitchen the other day, surely they would make love…at last. Her body throbbed with the desire she'd pent up over so many months apart from him. And she wanted the healing touch of his hands on her body to erase Paul's specter from her mind.

She stood waiting for several minutes, but nothing happened. Fatigue finally changed her thinking and she decided it would be just as well to simply sleep at his side. She put on panties and a T-shirt, turned out the light, and slipped into bed beside her man. His scent filled her nostrils and she longed to press her body to his. But she didn't dare. Her luck couldn't hold out that far. She was fortunate to have gotten this close to him. What would she do if he opened his eyes now? If he tried to leave her, she would wrap herself around him and refuse to let him go.

Why hadn't he awakened? If not for his even breathing and the peaceful warmth that emanated from him, she might have worried something was wrong with him. He never, ever slept so soundly, at least not in the approximately eleven months she'd spent sleeping with him before his deployment. Of course, the man had enjoyed no real sleep since he'd returned to her. She'd heard his fitfulness in the night, listened to the anguished moans and sudden cries before hearing him prowling around downstairs. She suspected he'd often been afraid to go back to sleep, but her suggestion several days ago that he might do better if he didn't sleep alone had been met with stony silence.

But here he was beside her at last. As she drifted into her own restless dreams, she prayed he would be there in the morning.

THE DREAM CAME UPON HIM again, but this time there were no visions of dismembered bodies or echoing shrieks of agony filling his blast-damaged ears. This time, he heard only soft moaning. For once, the sounds of his dream didn't fill him with horror. Even when he felt someone thrashing beside him, he didn't recoil in dread as he had for so many nights. Somehow, even in his dreams, he understood that he could have done nothing to prevent the deaths of his men. He'd acted in their best interest, to no avail. Now it was over and they were gone.

His dream shifted away from the desert. The shadow of a man with a damaged hand crowded into his vision. The shadow refused to solidify, no matter how hard Anthony stared. Striding forward brought Anthony no closer, yet he could clearly see the shadowy man approach a young woman seated in a chair and shoot her from behind, execution-style.

"No!" Anthony tried to say, but his voice wouldn't work.

Then the executioner walked up to an old woman and pushed her down a flight of stairs. The scream echoed so loudly that Anthony's own voice could not be heard. In helpless panic, he watched as the shadow moved on next to an elderly couple and gave them something from his hands. As soon as they took the offering, the pair dropped to the ground and lay there without moving. Then the man drove a car at high speed toward another young woman. In the moment before impact, he recognized the woman as his sister.

"No!" he cried again. This time, he heard himself even though his heart pounded fast and furious in his ears. All at once, he sat straight up, pulling himself by sheer force of will out of the dream. But even upright, he didn't feel fully awake.

Soft sounds came from someone to his left. For one horrific moment, he thought he was back in the desert, where nightmares had haunted him as he'd gone in and out of consciousness. But then he realized that the moans that sifted through the night were quiet, sensual. The body next to him writhed, but not in pain. He blinked, trying to remember. Darkness hovered all around him, but the usual ghosts seemed to have abandoned their game of tormenting him when the lights were out, at least for the moment.

He recalled that Amy had awakened and toddled into Kristen's bedroom, where she'd found him sitting on the edge of the mattress with his head in his hands. Her sweet, sleep-softened expression had moved him in ways he could never describe. So he'd picked her up and hugged her close, realizing that he and Kristen had made this precious, perfect child together. This one beautiful girl, a product of his struggling marriage, could not be denied his love.

He'd lifted her onto the large bed to read to her, settling himself against a pillow—the one he remembered sleeping on night after night before his deployment. The slight indentation in the mattress on his side of the bed had also seemed familiar. Comfortable. With Amy curled against him, he'd relaxed for the first time in many weeks.

But this wasn't Amy shifting restlessly at his side. As his eyes adjusted to the gloom, he saw an arm flung upward, framing a head with short curly hair. Kristen. She must have tucked Amy into her own bed and taken her place here beside him.

His wife's skin looked silken smooth. When she tossed again, her face turned in his direction and he could see her furrowed brow and slightly parted lips. She whispered something he couldn't understand, but her voice seemed sultry and pleading at the same time. Her legs moved beneath the sheet, her back arched.

"Please," he heard her say. What did she beg for?

His body knew the answer to that question before his

mind did. Hot blood marched double-time to the drumbeat of rising passion and between one breath and the next, he was hard and aching. The woman beside him was his wife and in her sleep, she begged for his touch. And he needed her tonight. She had always been the only person on earth who could ease his nightmares. And although the dream was already fading, tension lingered. He wanted to hold his wife, wanted to be held by her.

No reason to resist came into his mind, so he reached out one hand. He slid it along the alabaster skin from her wrist to the inside of her elbow, wanting to soothe and excite at the same time. He hoped for comfort himself, and his body already quivered with desire.

She sucked in air, then moaned again as she leaned a little toward him. Beneath her snug T-shirt, he saw the perfect roundness of her breasts and the delicate peaks of hardened nipples. Another soft groan filtered into the air, but this time the sound came from him.

She hadn't yet opened her eyes, but she twisted and her shirt shifted to expose several inches of muscled abdomen. He recalled that in her e-mails she'd expressed worry about getting her abs back after Amy was born. No question about it—she'd got 'em back. And Anthony wanted to kiss every sexy inch of that solid stomach, which had been so beautifully round with child when he'd last gazed upon it.

Should he? Doubts nudged the back of his mind. He wanted to ignore them, but as soon as he tried, they danced forward.

He didn't deserve to feel the hot blood pulsing through his veins.

He shouldn't be here in this comfortable bed.

He wasn't worthy of the woman beside him.

He ought to release her from her marital obligations.

But then Kristen's eyes fluttered opened and focused on his, her expression lit with pleasure and seduction and understanding. Her love for him couldn't give him the redemption he longed for, but it made him consider the possibility of a life filled with something other than despair. And when she reached up and stroked his scarred cheek, he found himself turning to plant a kiss in the hollow of her palm.

"Anthony," she whispered as she drew him closer.

Doubts receded as desire flourished. He leaned toward her, caught the scent of her soap and arousal. He had to kiss her, needed to caress her, couldn't help himself.

So he took possession of her mouth with his own.

She kissed him back, opening to him. As he made his first foray with his tongue, her arms snaked around his neck and he found himself suddenly pressed to her hot, supple length. Exquisite sensations beat against his awareness—the slickness of her mouth, the softness of her flesh, the passion that emanated like heat from her soul.

He tasted along her jaw while his hands explored her waist and ribs. "Kristen," he whispered, shocked that his voice cracked with emotion.

"I'm here," she answered.

And those words nearly broke him. Clenching his teeth, he forced back the tide of emotion and channeled everything he had into loving his wife.

CHAPTER TEN

AT LAST, KRISTEN HAD her husband in her arms, in bed, while the baby slept! Her greedy hands ran over the solid muscles of his shoulders and back. She tasted with lips and tongue his throat. She licked along the edges of his scarred flesh and breathed in the manly scent of him.

Then his palm grazed her breast and her hunger for him turned ravenous. The hot spike of lust he sent through her body with his touch made her gasp. Every nerve ending came alive at once and she needed him to join with her, to be part of her, to be inside her.

"Please, Anthony. I need you," she pleaded.

She heard him groan, felt his erection pressing against her pelvis and prayed he wouldn't attempt to resist their lovemaking, as he had before. He'd nearly broken her heart when he'd pulled back from her. But then relief and excitement surged though her when he began to tug at her panties.

It took her only seconds to squirm and kick her way out of them while she also drew her husband's T-shirt swiftly over his head. That left only his sweat pants and boxers. She wanted them gone, but he'd begun suckling one of her sensitive nipples. Her nerves vibrated and her blood throbbed and her skin tingled. She wanted him now, now, now!

As if in answer to her prayers, he rolled to his back, bringing her with him. If he kept sliding his erection back and forth as he'd started doing, the barrier of his clothing would not hinder her tumultuous climax. But she wanted more than mere physical gratification, because this was Anthony, home and in her arms at last after all those long, lonely months without him. And only a complete joining of bodies and souls would satisfy her.

Nearly as quickly as she'd succeeded in getting him naked, Anthony covered himself with the sheet. But she could not allow him to hide from her. And there was no need to. She hadn't expected him to come home to her unchanged. Now was the moment when she would show him that she loved every blessed inch of him, scarred or not.

Kristen dived under the sheet and kissed her way up his injured side, giving particular attention to each change upon his person. She heard his breath catch and felt his muscles tense beneath her palms. Gratitude filled her as she once again had the pleasure of making her husband gasp with desire.

But she didn't get more than a brief taste of this erotic lovemaking with lips and tongue before he pulled away, swiftly reversed their positions, and slid himself inside her. She had only to tip her hips upward to meet him. And oh, how wonderful it felt to have him truly home at last!

She whimpered as the inexorable pull toward culmination consumed her. So close, so very close…

"Kristen," he said. He nuzzled the angle between her neck and shoulder, sending shivers in all directions. Then he slid one hand down her ribs, past her waist, over her hip, and across her thigh—until he slipped his talented fingers between their bodies and right to that tiny node that provided such dazzling results.

In seconds, she hovered breathlessly at the pinnacle. And when she sensed that Anthony had reached the same point of no return, she let herself go. Pleasure reached critical mass and shattered. The cry that accompanied her exultation would have rocked the house on its foundation, but Anthony covered her mouth with his as exquisite pleasure made her writhe beneath him.

He'd waited for her, but he couldn't seem to wait any longer. She knew when his moment came and rejoiced as he leaned back and every muscle in his body tensed. A deep growl emanated from his throat as he joined her on that plateau of contentment that follows supreme satisfaction.

A soft expression filled his eyes when he looked down at her. She smiled up at him and kneaded the muscles of his back. He surprised her by lowering his head and kissing her gently, reverently. Then he sipped at her lips as if she were fine wine. He made her feel precious and loved. She wanted him to feel that way, too.

"I love you so much," she said when he nibbled her earlobe.

He froze and seemed unwilling to speak or to raise his head. She couldn't see his expression, but she felt his resistance to her words in the muscles of his back. An ache of regret suffused her. But at least he didn't shift his body away. He only let himself slide from within her while he held her in his arms. And in another moment, he began to tremble.

Then hot, wet droplets splashed to her shoulder and she knew that tears fell from the face her husband refused to lift from the pillow beside her head.

ONE OF HIS WORST FEARS had materialized. He'd lost control in the presence of another person. Worse still, he'd lost it in front of his wife, with whom he'd just experienced the most incredible moments of passion. And he had little hope of pulling himself together any time soon. Against his formidable will, the floodgates had opened and he had no idea how to close them again. So the tears fell to her shoulder. And after an unmeasurable period of time, words began to spill, too—words he never thought he'd say aloud.

"God, help me, I love you, too. But I...I shouldn't. I don't deserve you," he said before his voice splintered and went silent.

She didn't say anything at first, but just held him to her and stroked his back. After a while, she murmured, "But you're stuck with me anyway, Tiger."

Feeling that he had nothing left to lose, he raised his head and let her see that he wept like a child. Some remnant of pride forced him to swipe away the worst of the tears before he met her gaze. But it was past time to tell her the truth and he needed to be looking at her when he did.

"I can't do it, Kristen. I can't live this life when all my men are dead. Every minute I spend in this house, guilt eats at me. Every second I spend with you, I feel ashamed that I came home to you when all of the others came back in body bags."

She gave him her full attention, saying nothing, waiting for what he would add. He knew he should disengage from her embrace, but he couldn't make himself do more than shift his weight to one side. Though he still pressed himself against the warmth of her naked body, he'd grown cold on the inside as reality strangled him. Exhausted and defeated, he let his head fall to her shoulder again. "I'm tired, Kristen. I want it to end. I just want it to end,'' he whispered, relieved to be telling her what had been weighing on his heart.

Unhurried, Kristen grasped the blankets from beside her and pulled them over their bodies. Then she stroked his arm as she gazed up at the ceiling. Her profile formed a silhouette against the faint glow from the nightlight in the hallway. He stared, hoping to memorize the slope of her brow and curve of her chin for the nights he couldn't have her beside him in person anymore. How would he go on without her?

After a few moments, she murmured, ''You're alive, whether you like it or not, Anthony. Somehow you survived when no one else did. Worthy or not, this is your fate.'' Slowly, she ran her fingers up and down his arm, reminding him that he was, indeed, alive and capable of feeling.

His fate. How could all this warmth and love be his fate?

But Kristen wasn't finished explaining things to him. ''You've been given more time than your men, that's all,'' she said. ''Who can say how much time that will be? Shutting yourself off from living a good life in the time you've been given only hurts everyone, including me and Amy. We need you. We need you to be part of our lives, for as long as we're given to be together.''

Suddenly, she turned onto her side to face him. She took his face in her hands, heedless of his scars. ''It's your responsibility—your obligation—to live, Anthony. And to do the most you possibly can with the time you have left.''

Some of the ice that had built up around his heart seemed to be melting. A hint of warmth returned to his depths.

''Your men,'' she said, then she stopped as her voice

cracked and her bottom lip quivered. "Your men," she tried again, "would expect nothing less of you. You owe it to them to live your life to its fullest, to live it the way they would want to have lived their own." Then tears filled her eyes.

He couldn't see past the blur that had returned to his own vision, so he pulled her into his arms. She felt so alive. The ice inside him receded a little more, the guilt began to ease its stranglehold on his heart. Then the flicker of internal heat grew to a conflagration of grief, hot and stinging and wretched. He had no choice but to let it out, even though he'd been sure he could not possibly have more tears to shed. Holding it in hurt—more than any physical pain he'd ever known.

"Billy and Cool were very young," she said, haltingly. And he nodded and thought about Billy with his easy smile and quick wit. Cool had been so smart that Anthony had been planning to recommend him for warrant officer school. "You were a hero to them," she said. "You can't let them down now."

"No, I can't let them down now," he repeated. His voice rasped with unfamiliar emotion.

"Weasel and Scopes were really good at their jobs. The best you'd ever seen," she added as she let her own tears fall.

He half laughed and half cried as he remembered one of the last comments Scopes had made on their long walk toward death in the desert. "His father told Scopes he'd either become a church-tower sniper picking off townsfolk or the best sharpshooter the military had ever known. Drove his son to the recruiter's office on his seventeenth birthday to make sure his boy made the right choice."

She chuckled at that and wept at the same time. ''Scopes made the right choice,'' she whispered.

''Yes, he did.''

''Even though he's gone now.''

''Even though.'' The talons of loss clawed at the inside of his throat, but he had to agree. All Scopes had ever wanted to do was defend his country and he'd given the Army eleven years of distinguished service. He'd hated that he shot at human beings, but whenever Scopes had succeeded, he'd get past the nausea by reminding himself of the innumerable American lives he'd saved with each enemy hit.

''And JJ,'' she said, remembering the last one to join his team, the one she barely knew.

''JJ could make a communication device out of two wires and some spit,'' he told her. ''Computers didn't dare crash when he was on duty.'' The medics had told him in the hospital that JJ had managed to send out a final message giving their location and need for rescue, just before...

Anthony clutched at his wife and grieved for his men—his friends. They'd lived with gusto to the very last moment. Anthony understood now that in honor of each of them, he could do no less.

KRISTEN AWOKE WITH A START. The phone rang again, piercing the silence in the dark room. She grabbed the receiver, hoping the unexpected sound in the middle of the night hadn't awakened Amy. Anthony turned over on his side and seemed to go back to sleep, far too exhausted after his long emotional night even to crack an eyelid.

''Hello?'' she whispered so as not to wake her husband.

"Major Clark, there's more," said the familiar voice.

She tried to shake the cobwebs of sleep from her mind. "More, sir?"

"More with the same illness as Sergeant Peterson. I'm sorry to cut short your night at home, but I need you here. You've had the most training in this sort of thing."

"What sort of thing?" she had to ask.

"Bioterrorism," Colonel Ripsimio answered.

"Oh, God. Do you know what it is, where it came from?" She'd been chosen to receive hours of extra training in bioterrorism. Most of it had centered on learning how to deal with smallpox and similar epidemics. She'd learned about evacuations, emergency inoculations, and quarantine situations. There had even been some language training, in the hope she could better understand threats to public health when information came from non-English-speaking people. But smallpox was not what had brought Sergeant Peterson to the ER. Her still sluggish mind wouldn't let her put the clues together to come up with a name for the current threat.

"Not yet. We don't even know if it's contagious. Could just be something these people were near, maybe some sort of gas. We keep testing, but we have nothing positive." The Colonel sounded frustrated.

She slipped her feet over the side of the bed onto the floor and glanced at her husband, her heart full of love and fear for him. Somehow, she resisted the irrational urge to run into Amy's room to check on her. "Did I bring something home to my family?" she asked as calmly as she could.

"Doubtful. But we'll decide what precautions we should take once you're here."

She ran her fingers through her hair as anxiety

churned in her stomach. "Okay. I'll be in as soon as I dress," she said, before closing the grim conversation.

The minute she hung up the receiver, she crept to Amy's bedside, knowing that she was letting fear take hold of her. But her daughter slept peacefully with the side of her face pressed to her pillow, making her pink lips pucker. A lock of her curly hair rested on her smooth forehead and when Kristen slid it back with her fingers, she could tell that her daughter's temperature remained normal. Taking a deep breath, she forced her intellect to dominate her emotions. This was no time to fall apart.

Her wristwatch said it was only oh four hundred. Oh dark thirty, the soldiers called it. She hadn't had enough sleep, someone had possibly unleashed something bad, and she would have to leave her child and her husband. She had no idea when she'd be able to see them again, but she wouldn't wake them for the hugs she so desperately needed. That would only send her maternal instincts into overdrive again. And it would be that much harder to go.

With a sigh, she headed for a quick shower. When she finished and stepped out through a cloud of steam, Anthony stood in front of her. He leaned against the doorjamb and held her towel in his hands. His eyes were puffy and red from the grief he'd shared with Kristen the night before. But she thought he had to be the most handsome man on earth, scars and all.

She smiled at him, despite everything.

"I missed you," he said in a sleep-raspy voice.

Oh, how she wished she could stay and see where that gleam in his eyes might lead them.

"There's trouble at the hospital and I need to get back quickly."

He stood up straight and his expression changed to one of serious concentration. "What kind of trouble?"

"Ripsimio doesn't know. We can't seem to identify what's causing the sickness. But more cases came in like the one we worked on all day yesterday." She took the towel he offered her and stifled a sigh as she thought of what might have been going on between them right now if only the world were a safer place.

"Why were you able to come home last night?" he asked. "Not that I'm ungrateful," he added with a twinkle in his eye that made her blood sing through her veins, despite her weighty thoughts.

"I'd worked too many shifts in a row and the Colonel ordered me home for some rest. But now he's ordered me back. I have no idea when I'll be able to get home again. But I'll try to call you. Carry your cell phone. I don't know if you two will need to take some precautionary medicine." She wrapped the towel around her body and took out a brush and some hair gel from the cabinet.

"I've had the anthrax vaccine," he said.

Running her gel-laden fingers through her hair, she said, "It's not anthrax. We checked for that first thing yesterday. It's more like pneumonia, or maybe an acute respiratory syndrome, except the cough isn't dry and some other symptoms don't line up."

He nodded and didn't ask her any more questions. He must know she wouldn't be able to answer them yet. She could see him in the mirror standing behind her looking thoughtful. "What about bringing Amy to day care?" he asked.

"Um." She hadn't thought of that. "I think you two should stay home until I call you. But don't worry. Ripsimio would have told us to do more if he thought we should.''

Anthony nodded. "I have some things to do today. But I'll start with phone calls and some Internet work on the laptop I borrowed from HQ.''

"What are you working on?'' Kristen asked.

He scowled and looked at his feet. Kristen watched her husband struggle with something, and with a sinking sensation in her stomach, she realized he was weighing what he would tell her. That could only mean he might lie, a skill he'd had a great deal of training in as a Ranger. She hated the thought, especially after what they'd shared the night before.

When he looked up at her, his gaze was steady. "I'll tell you straight out because you're my wife and I don't want any lies between us.''

She almost sighed with relief as she headed back to the bedroom to dress. They would be okay as long as they remained honest with each other. But his next words chilled her.

"You're not going to like it,'' he added as he followed her. "I had a weird dream. More than ever, I think all the things that have happened to the families of my men in the States are linked. I need to make a few more phone calls to see if I can get anything to fit together.''

She resisted letting her shoulders slump in defeat. She'd been so sure he'd given up his quest regarding the guy he thought he'd seen. But such a reaction now would not encourage him to tell her what was on his mind in the future. As evenly as she could, remembering how good it had felt to have her boss take her word for the initial incident at the hospital, she asked, "You still think this terrorist is after us?''

He sat down on the edge of the bed and dropped his

head into his hands. Sifting his fingers through his thick, brown hair, he didn't look much like her confident Ranger today. "No, actually I think he's in the States and messing with the families there. My sister said that a man named Flea-oh ran into her car and said he knew me. But I don't know anyone by that name."

"You talked to your sister?" The fact that he'd called his family had to be a sign of recovery.

"I called yesterday. I figured I should get it over with."

"But you no longer believe the terrorist is after us here?"

"I'm starting to think that you and the shrink are right about me. Maybe I'm just imagining it all."

He sounded so dejected. What should she say to help him? She wanted to rejoice that he might be coming to grips with the effects of his trauma, but she hated to see him lose faith in himself. "What altered your thinking?" she asked carefully.

He stuck out his lower lip and blew upward so that the longer hair at his brow fluttered. "I saw the car again. The one I thought the terrorist was using to get around Wiesbaden. I approached the car with my hand-gun drawn."

He stood and began to pace the small confines of their room as Kristen stared at him, worried that things were about to become even more complicated than they already were.

"I was so sure the guy was in there. I *wanted* him to be in that car. And I wanted to put a bullet into him, quick and dirty, so he'd never hurt you or Amy." He huffed a humorless laugh. "But you can't put a bullet into a figment of your imagination. There was no one in the car."

She waited a few beats for him to go on, but he just kept walking. "What happened after you realized there was no one in the car?" she probed.

He stopped and looked her square in the eyes. "I lost a few minutes contemplating the cosmos of my mind, then I went back to the house and let Amy out of her stroller so we could get on with our evening together."

"You had Amy with you?"

"I brought her in her stroller to the backyard first and called over a neighbor."

A thousand questions danced around in her head all at once. But she managed to keep them from being spoken. She waited for him to tell her the rest.

"You're not going to lecture me?" he asked.

Kristen slipped into a clean blouse and began to button it. "What purpose would that serve?"

"Um, I'd have a better idea of what you're thinking. And you'd let off some steam."

"I can just tell you what I'm thinking, if you want." Her calmness surprised even her.

"Okay."

"I'm concerned you left Amy in her stroller somewhere when…"

"I made sure she was safe. I had an adult watching her. I even locked the wheels."

She glared at him, but beat down her temper. "You should have called the police."

"Probably."

"Probably? You could have been hurt."

"Okay, I should have called the police. If it makes you feel any better, I did call them after I got Amy fed. I realized the car wasn't a familiar one for the street. MPs said it wasn't registered to be on post, so they towed it away. I'm hoping they towed away the whole delusional thing, too. I hate feeling like I've gone crazy.''

"You're not crazy, Anthony. Your reactions are not even uncommon. But it takes time and therapy to work things out.''

"Yeah, well, after yesterday, I'm ready to see your friend the shrink on a regular basis.''

"No!'' she said, remembering all at once her ordeal in Paul's office the day before. "I mean, I'm not so sure he's the right person to help you.''

Anthony stared at her. Afraid she would blush, she turned away on the pretext of slipping on her shoes. She told herself she would tell him about what had happened with Paul as soon as they had time, but right now, she had to get to the hospital. "So what are you looking for on the Internet?''

"Patterns. And I have some friends I can call in the States. I need to make sure that nut I shot up in Afghanistan isn't back home hurting people.''

Kristen went to him and put her hands on his shoulders. "I hope to God you don't find what you're looking for. I have to go. You should try to get some more sleep while Amy is still out. Once she's up, she'll keep you running. I'll call as soon as I can.''

Though he held her by her hips, he took a step closer so that his body pressed to hers. "I'll miss you,'' he whispered. Then he leaned in and kissed her the way he used to, with complete concentration.

CHAPTER ELEVEN

A CALL FROM DAVE BATSIN woke Anthony from the sound sleep he'd somehow managed to return to after Kristen had gone back to work. The ringing of the phone woke Amy, too, and he had to put his finger into one ear to drown out the wailing that could be heard from her bedroom when he said, "Hello?"

"I need you to come down to the MP station, Major," Batsin said without preamble. "I found something you might be interested in."

Anthony could hardly hear—and thinking was out of the question—with Amy stretching her lungs to full capacity as she was. The decibels increased as he made his way to her room. With the cordless propped between his shoulder and chin, he reached for her as he asked, "You found something about that car?"

He picked up his daughter, but that only brought the piercing cries closer to his ear. Despite his partial deafness on that side, the sound filled his entire head, pinging off the interior walls of his skull as if a raucous game of handball were being played in there. "What was that? Sorry, I can't hear you!" he called into the mouthpiece.

"I *said*," shouted the Captain, "that there were fingerprints on the car."

Anthony resisted the pull of his former delusions and prohibited his mind from leaping to any terrorist-related conclusion. "Mine, most likely. Hush, baby girl, Daddy's here," he crooned.

"What?" Batsin sounded alarmed.

"Nothing. Hold on while I try to get my daughter settled." He put the phone on the dresser and stretched Amy on the changing table. She was soaked and made the process of stripping off her wet clothing twice as difficult by kicking and squirming in deep displeasure. When he peeled the diaper from her skin, the assault on his senses made him pick up the phone again. "This is going to take a while. I'll call you back," he said and he clicked Off without attempting to hear what Batsin might say in response. At this moment, Amy had to come first.

It took Anthony half an hour to wrestle his daughter into clean clothing and then into a better mood. Dry Cheerios in a Big Bird bowl and warm milk in an Elmo cup finally turned her back into his laughing cherub. When she seemed stable at last, he called Dave back, telling himself as he dialed that he would not let the notion of fingerprints on the car suck him back into the fantasy that Taaoun was in Germany. Better to stick to the issue of whether the terrorist had ever been in the States, instead.

But Dave wasn't answering his office phone or his cell phone. Not unusual for a Ranger who trained hard almost every day. Phones could be very distracting. Anthony left messages, hoping Dave would call back soon. He needed to know what the man had found so he could reorder his thinking once and for all about Taaoun. Waiting more than ten minutes for a callback proved too much for him, so he dialed the MP station. But no one on duty knew anything about the car or the fingerprints.

Frustrated, Anthony stuck out his lower lip and blew air upward into his hair.

Amy laughed. Despite everything he had on his mind, Anthony smiled.

Looking at Amy, he realized he felt more or less content inside his own skin for the first time since that disastrous day in Afghanistan. The guilt and shame still resided within, but they were not all-consuming. And whenever his daughter laughed, Anthony's heart tripped over heady emotions that scared him and enticed him at the same time. Had he ever felt so alive? And wasn't it only yesterday he'd wanted his sorry existence to end?

But his wife wouldn't let him wither beneath the weight of his grief and self-loathing. She'd taken him by storm and loved a sense of worth into him. And although he knew he didn't deserve her, he couldn't bring himself to feel anything but gratitude. And joy. And love. Not that he'd ever admit it. He was his father's son, after all.

Nipping at the heels of that thought came the impulse to call his mother. But as he picked up the phone, he realized it would be the middle of the night where she was. He'd have to wait until later. Just as well, he thought. Not only should he avoid calling his family when he was feeling anything less than rock solid emotionally, but Amy also decided to demand release from the prison of her high chair at that moment.

They spent the day playing on the floor, taking walks around the yard, getting to know one another. When he tried to do push-ups in their living room, Amy crawled beneath him and over him until he finally had to give up. Laughter and push-ups did not mix successfully, he found.

When he discovered a jump rope on the back porch

and tried to fit in some cardiovascular exercise while Amy amused herself in the sandbox, Amy threw her ball into the rhythm of the rope, giggling whenever she succeeded in making him stumble to a stop. He restarted over and over, just to hear Amy's little-girl chortle.

He sobered when the neighbor who had helped him the day before came out to water her garden. "Are you feeling better today, Major?" she asked. "You didn't look so good yesterday."

She was probably referring to the way he'd appeared when he'd staggered back to Amy's side after finding out that no one sat in the car he'd been so sure would contain a terrorist. The discovery that his sightings had been the work of his subconscious had been devastating, because he'd been trained to trust his senses and his instincts in life-and-death situations.

"I'm doing better," he answered. "Thanks for your help yesterday." Ruthlessly, he thrust aside the vague possibilities that Dave Batsin's call had raised. He refused to let his mind draw him back into the pit of darkness from which he'd just emerged. No matter what Dave might report, Taaoun was not in Germany, never had been. Anthony could see now how unlikely that would be, how melodramatic it had been to believe that the guy would survive the war only to single him out and follow him here.

"Oh, that's okay," she said. "I watch Amy from time to time for your wife. Amy and I go way back. Don't we, sweetie?" she said as she grinned toward the child.

Amy said a series of very coherent words that made no sense together. She concluded with "Okay?"

"Okay!" said the neighbor. She looked back up at Anthony. "I'm Charlene Meyers, by the way." She held out her hand over the fence.

Anthony gave her his whole name—otherwise, she might think of him as Anthony Clark, since Kristen had not taken his last name. He didn't usually mind that she'd kept her maiden name, except when people called him Mr. Clark.

"Glad to meet you," he said, stepping forward. He almost shook her hand. At the last minute, he remembered and pulled back. Retreating a few steps, he shook his head. "Sorry. I almost forgot. Kristen said we're supposed to stay away from people today until she calls to tell us whether we're likely to have caught something contagious. Best we keep our distance. I don't want you catching the flu or anything from us."

Her face took on a concerned expression. "Nothing serious, I hope." A dog began to bark from inside Charlene's house.

"Doggy!" Amy said.

Anthony smiled at her genius and then responded to Charlene. "Not likely, or Kristen would have taken us to the hospital with her. But they're still doing some tests to figure it out and she advised us to stay home today."

She smiled down at Amy. "We wouldn't want anything to happen to our little lamb."

Those words evoked a sudden flood of protectiveness in Anthony and he scooped his daughter into his arms. "I won't let anything happen to her," he said.

"You only just met her and yet you two seem to get along as if you've been together since day one," she commented with a soft look in her eyes.

"Yeah," he said as he realized for the second time in one day that he was a very fortunate man. His daughter had taken to him wholeheartedly, accepting his scarred face and sullen moods without reservation. And his wife…

As he bade goodbye to Charlene, who had to go walk her dog, Anthony's thoughts drifted to memories of the night before in the arms of his beautiful wife. Odd that he would recall the words she'd said even more vividly than the passionate lovemaking. With each breath he took during the day, he became more convinced that she'd spoken the truth. He owed it to his men to live his life the best he could.

Everything seemed fragile and precious to him today. And like a starving man, he wanted to devour every minute he had, cherish each second. So when he put Amy down for a nap after lunch, he couldn't bring himself to part from her. He brought the borrowed laptop into her bedroom and sat on the floor with his back against her dresser while she slept. Perhaps Taaoun hadn't followed him to Germany, but Anthony couldn't shake the effects of the dream he'd had last night. He needed to be certain the man had not gone back to the United States to seek revenge.

After Amy woke up from her nap, he'd just settled her into her high chair for a snack when the phone rang. He almost spilled her juice but finally managed to get the sippy-top secured onto the cup.

When Anthony answered on the fourth ring, Dave Batsin said, "Fang here."

He laughed. "First, you have to tell me how you got the nickname Fang."

"The usual way. Batsin-bats-vampire-fang. It could have been worse."

Yes, it could have been worse, Anthony thought. The nicknames the men used in the field could be pretty wild. And some of them made no sense without a long explanation. Like the name of the guy who'd collided with his sister. "Ever hear of someone called Flea-oh?" he asked Dave.

"Nope. Listen, I have to ask you about this car," said the persistent Captain. "I'm thinking this is important."

Anthony stood up from the kitchen chair, unable to keep his mind from racing over the many reasons he'd originally thought Taaoun was nearby. For his family's sake, and for his own, he needed to let go of delusions. He needed to let himself heal so he could be a husband and father. So he could be a man.

"Go ahead." His voice sounded surprisingly steady given the rapid pace of his heart.

"Most of the car was wiped clean. I mean, someone went over it with a polishing cloth. Except there was a single handprint on the hood of the car right in the center. The MP would have missed it except some of his powder fanned over that way and he thought there might be something there. So he tested the area for prints."

"And?" Anthony's pulse had begun to thud a little louder in his ears.

"It was a handprint without the index finger, like an obscene gesture in reverse."

He sat back down abruptly. Amy laughed and threw a banana slice at him. He caught it automatically with his left hand. "Shit!" he said.

"Shthit!" said Amy with a big grin.

He frowned. "Damn," he muttered under his breath as he realized he'd just taught Amy her first swear word. Kristen would *not* be happy.

"Dahm," said Amy as she banged her hand on the tray of her high chair like an executive in a board room.

"What does it mean?" Dave asked.

"That means he's here," Anthony whispered into the

phone as he wiped the banana from his palm with a dishrag.

"Your terrorist stalker? What's up with the hand-print?" Dave wanted to know.

"We shot his index finger off in Afghanistan. The print was to let me know he's been right up close to my house and my family." One part of his mind began making plans to catch the son of a bitch while the other half went numb with relief that he was *not* delusional after all.

"Tell me what you need me to do, sir," said Captain Batsin.

"I'll meet you at the MP station in an hour." He'd have to call Kristen and let her know the bad news. She had to be watchful. And she needed to know that he wasn't crazy after all.

As he clicked the receiver back onto its cradle, his world snapped back into place. His senses hadn't lied to him. His intuition hadn't been wrong. And he knew once again that he had the skill and the will to protect his family.

But before he could do anything, he had to talk to Kristen.

KRISTEN WALKED into the afternoon meeting a minute late, but that had no effect on the mood she'd been in all day, despite her grim duties caring for the pneumonia patients.

Captain Louise Kilpatrick looked up at her with lifted eyebrows. "We have eleven cases of unexplained sudden-onset pneumonia in the middle of an emergency exercise, but you still have a twinkle in your eye and a bounce to your step. How do you do it?" she asked.

Kristen couldn't very well tell her the truth—that her

husband had made wonderful, passionate love to her last night and that it had been a glimpse of heaven after a year and a half of deprivation. "I thrive on stress," she said, as she turned to check the chart of the third patient who'd come in with the same symptoms as Sergeant Peterson.

"It must be viral," Colonel Ripsimio said to the other doctors and specialists gathered to discuss the mysterious cases. "Maybe a mutation of SARS. We tested for the usual strain and came up with nothing."

"Could be, but it isn't following the same pattern and the cough here is wet instead of dry," said a Lieutenant Colonel.

"But what if someone purposefully exposed these people to something?" Louise offered.

They had all been thinking the same thing. "A terrorist," Kristen said. Dark foreboding swallowed her good mood. "Have we looked for the standard terrorist infections?"

"Like botulism?" Louise asked. "This isn't that."

"Yeah, but *like* that. What are the other things the CDC says terrorists might use?"

"Smallpox, AIDS, bubonic plague. Most of the other things are chemical, but this looks biological. I can't imagine…" the Colonel began.

"Wait a second!" Kristen had a eureka moment. "We need to test for plague!"

"Wouldn't we have seen the lymph nodes swelling by now?" the Colonel protested. "At least on Peterson, who's had it the longest. And the computer would have identified that from blood tests by now."

"Not necessarily. It could be pneumonic plague. Not common, but possible. And it's hard to diagnose, even with blood tests. Impossible to tell from blood tests in

Peterson's case, because we started him on an antibiotic right away. But perhaps not the *right* antibiotic. Maybe that's why he's holding his own, but not recovering. He needs streptomycin or gentamicin. I can check the CDC Web page for the dosage." She ran to the computer on one side of the conference room.

"I'll write the order to change meds," said the Colonel, trusting her judgment again. "God knows changing his antibiotic is worth a try. See what you can find out about a conclusive diagnosis." The meeting broke up and everyone went into action to explore this new possibility.

Sure enough, the symptoms for pneumonic plague matched Peterson's better than any other disease they'd considered so far. Kristen printed a picture of the bacteria to give to the lab and noted that they needed to take blood from various locations in the patient's body. Because antibiotics of any kind could interfere with the tests, they would have better luck with blood from the newer patients who hadn't been on antibiotics as long.

"You might be on to something, Major," said the Colonel as he looked at the Web page over her shoulder a while later. "This stuff can even be delivered as an aerosol spray. Didn't you tell me Peterson said he breathed something?"

"Yes, sir. And not long before he showed up in the ER. This is the only thing we know of that starts to make people sick so quickly."

"Then let's see if we can get test results that match the theory. Looks like we need bronchial smears in a Wayson stain and a fluorescent-antibody test."

"And I have to get my husband and daughter in here quickly to be sure I didn't infect them, and that they don't spread this to anyone else," she said. Her steady voice belied the palpitations in her chest as she thought of Anthony and Amy succumbing to the disease. Even though plague had a very high cure rate if the correct antibiotics were given early, it could be deadly if medications were delayed.

"Everyone who worked on Peterson needs to come in to be tested. If the tests aren't conclusive, they'll need preventive streptomycin. Captain Beatty," he called to the public health specialist. "Get a list started and have someone begin making the phone calls right away. Kristen, find out what that Web page has to say about quarantine. I think isolation of patients with the symptoms will be enough, but I want to be sure. I'm going to my office to call the CDC." He turned to leave. From the doorway he added, "And call your husband."

She didn't waste a single moment. The phone seemed to ring interminably before he answered.

"Anthony, you and Amy have to come to the hospital for some tests," she said and she was pleased to note that her voice sounded much calmer than she felt. Odd that she could be so cool in the very worst crisis, but with her family at risk, she felt hysteria edging around the dark corners of her mind, waiting to attack.

"I've been trying to reach you for over an hour. I can bring Amy to you, but I have to get to the MP station to…"

"No. You *both* have to come here and have tests before you do anything else. You could be contagious."

"I had all the shots before I went to Afghanistan, Kristen. I'll be fine and…"

"Listen to what I'm saying to you. I don't want to say more over the phone. Come to the hospital for tests now." She said it without raising her voice, but the spacing of her words and the clipped syllables made her statements imperatives.

A few seconds of silence ticked by. Then, ''We're on our way,'' from Anthony.

Kristen had less than a heartbeat to savor her relief before dashing to the ward holding the pneumonia patients to oversee the drawing of blood samples. Then she needed to get over to the lab to discuss *yelsinia pestis,* otherwise known as plague.

CHAPTER TWELVE

THE LAST PLACE HE WANTED to go was to the hospital. But Kristen wasn't one to make too much of things and she'd been insistent. Before he could leave, he had to pack a bag for Amy. Snacks, juice boxes, sippy cup, diapers, toys—how did Kristen remember everything? He felt sure he'd forgotten something important.

He wished they owned a second car. There were no cabs allowed on the secured post. The shuttle bus would be a nearly impossible option. And the trip would be a long one if he had to push Amy's stroller the entire way. Should he call someone for a ride?

Normally, he would not have had to think about who to ask. He'd have had five other men on whom he could call at anytime of day or night. But those five men were dead and a fresh wave of grief clawed at the inside of his throat as he confronted this practical application of his loss. Who could he call now? He hadn't exactly been Mr. Social since his return. The only one he knew was Fang, a.k.a. David Batsin.

But Kristen had said they might be contagious. He'd hate to expose Batsin to whatever it was. "Shit!"

"Shthit!" Amy crowed.

Her delight in the new word chased away his frustration and brought an involuntary smile to his mouth. She saw it and decided a repeat was in order. "Shthit!"

Ooh, boy, he sure was gonna be in trouble when Kristen heard that. But suggesting to Amy that she shouldn't say it would likely have the opposite effect. So he remained silent and dialed the phone, feeling that he had no choice but to call Dave. Besides, Kristen would have sent an ambulance or warned him about avoiding contact with people if he were likely to spread something deadly.

"Dave, I need a ride to the hospital," he said when Batsin answered. For some reason, he just couldn't make himself call the guy "Fang" when they weren't out on a field op where such names seemed natural.

"I thought you were on your way here to the MP station?" The man sounded as exasperated as Anthony felt.

"I was. But I couldn't reach my wife and when she finally called back, she said we might have caught something from her. The flu or something. Can't be too serious because she didn't mention quarantine or anything. But the kid and I have to go in for tests. If you bring us to the hospital, they'll probably want to test you, too."

"Yeah, they can test all they want. I never catch anything. I'll pick you up in five."

"Wait," he said before the other man hung up. A sudden realization struck him—something he might have overlooked except that Kristen had made such a big deal about it the one time he'd been in the car with Amy. "I need one more thing before you come here. Go out to the hospital and get the baby car seat from my wife," he said. "No, wait!" That would take too long. He pressed the heel of his hand to his forehead, trying to think. "Any car seat for a little kid will do. Maybe it'd be easier if you could borrow one from the lending office of the Army Relief Society." Would they be open at this hour? Anthony glanced at the clock. Nineteen hundred hours.

"Where the hell is the Army Relief Society located?"

Damned if Anthony knew. "Hold on," he said as he went to the drawer under the kitchen phone where Kristen had put all their junk, including the little post phone book.

"Can't you just buckle her into the back?" Dave asked, sounding impatient, as Anthony flipped through pages, trying to locate the listing for the relief society.

An image of Kristen's apoplexy if she caught him transporting Amy without a car seat crossed Anthony's mind. The mental scene had the makings of a nightmare. "Not an option," he said to Dave. "Here it is!" And he gave the location for the place where soldiers could borrow necessities until their household goods caught up with them after a PCS, or permanent change of station. He thought he remembered Kristen telling him that she'd temporarily borrowed baby items there when she'd come over from the States. "I'll call ahead so they have it ready for you when you get there."

"I'm on my way, but I'll call back if this doesn't work out," Batsin said.

Luck was on Anthony's side. The Relief Society had evening hours only once a week, but this happened to be the day. And they had a car seat available that Captain Batsin was welcome to sign out. The Captain showed up thirty minutes later with an old but serviceable car seat lying sideways on the back seat as if he'd just tossed it in there.

"The woman behind the counter eyed me funny when she handed the thing over. I'm not wearing a wedding ring or anything. Who knows what she thought." Anthony nearly smiled at Dave's discomfort with baby stuff but managed to keep his amusement to himself.

The men loaded the stroller into the trunk and were

about to put Amy into the back seat when Anthony realized he had no idea how to install the car seat. "Shi—" he started to say, before he noted Amy's avid attention on his mouth as her new favorite word almost slipped out of it again.

"What?" asked the Captain.

"Do you know how to buckle this thing in here securely?"

Batsin's face went blank as he attempted to puzzle out a problem that had to be completely outside the scope of a bachelor's knowledge. "Just like, sit it up and wedge it in," he said after a second or two.

Anthony sighed. "It's got to be tied down somehow, with the seat belt, I think. It's dangerous to have her ride in the car loose. She could bounce around and hurt something."

The younger man glanced inside the car, looking doubtful. "Don't worry about it. There's not much in there she could break," he said magnanimously.

"Not the car. *Her!*"

The two of them looked at Amy—perched on Anthony's left arm with her elbow digging into the top of his shoulder—as if they could assess how fragile she might be. "She looks pretty tough to me," Dave said as he chucked her under her chin and pulled a face, making her laugh.

"Look, I need to figure this out somehow. Did it come with instructions?" Anthony asked as he put Amy in the front seat where she could amuse herself with the various buttons on the dashboard.

"There's words on this label back here," Dave pointed out as he flipped the thing face down. They both read the first few lines.

"What's 'tether anchorage hardware'?" Dave asked. "I don't think my car has that."

Anthony read on. "What's a locking clip?" he wondered aloud, knowing full well that Batsin wouldn't have the slightest idea.

"I don't have the slightest idea. But, look, there's a little picture of how it's supposed to go." He pointed to a diagram. "How hard can it be?" he asked as he turned the unit right side up and reached for the seat belt.

"Let me," Anthony insisted, unwilling to trust this non-father with something as important as his daughter's safety. But, like so many things in life, he couldn't do it alone and he gave Kristen a mental salute that she'd managed so well all these months as a single parent.

Installation took all the intellect they had between them and a fair amount of brawn, too. Batsin's hand was bleeding by the time they finally got the thing lodged securely. Right about then, Amy discovered the horn and began to whale on the thing with gusto.

"This is more like a military op than some of my missions," Dave shouted over the trumpeting from the car as he wiped blood onto the pant leg of his BDUs.

But the worst was not behind them. Anthony scooped his daughter from the front seat and whisked her around the back. She didn't seem to realize at first that fun time was over, but when he plunked her into the newly ensconced car seat and attempted to pull down the restraining apparatus, she bucked and hollered.

From the driver's seat, Batsin gritted his teeth and plugged his ears with his fingers. Anthony did what he could to persuade Amy to cooperate, with no noticeable results. The little demon continued to arch her back and kick and scream, making it impossible for him to lower the bar to lock her into the seat. "Shi—" he almost said. "Damn it all to hell!" finally burst from his lips.

And Amy stopped kicking and screaming to look up at him with wide, interested eyes. His little girl really liked swear words, it seemed.

Anthony wasted no time getting the restraining piece lowered and clicked into the lock between her legs. The thrill of accomplishment suffused him and he felt nearly as proud as when he'd completed an inordinately dangerous mission. When he stood back to admire his work, he realized he'd only buckled one small child into a car seat and the thrill dissipated. Feeling a bit foolish, he climbed into the passenger seat next to Dave.

"We ready?" the man asked with a slight smirk.

"Just go!" Anthony barked. Being nearly bested by a toddler did not sit well with his pride.

THE PHONE RANG at the nurses' station where Kristen had stopped to make notes on one of the plague cases. Two of the young men were responding well to the streptomycin and most of the others were holding their own. Sergeant Peterson's condition hadn't improved at all and Kristen worried about him. His breathing had become steadily more difficult over time.

"Major Clark," she said when she picked up the receiver.

"Major, I thought you'd want to know your husband and daughter have arrived. We're taking them to the lab for blood work."

"Thanks, Louise. Tell them I'll be right down."

She forced herself to finish her notes before she rubbed the weariness from her face and headed to where she would find her family. But she hadn't gone twenty feet before she heard her name being called. A second later, the code was announced over the loudspeaker.

"Peterson's gone into shock," said the frantic nurse who beckoned her. Kristen followed her at a run to the sergeant's room, grabbing a surgical mask and gloves along the way. She already wore protective coveralls over her uniform.

Alarms rang the warning that the man's blood pressure had dropped. Peterson's breathing was labored and irregular. A young doctor, Captain Sykes, already worked on him, and Kristen did everything she could to assist his efforts to stabilize the patient's condition. She and the other nurse tried to raise Peterson's core temperature by wrapping him in warmed blankets. Sykes aspirated serosanguinous fluid from his lungs by pleural tap, but not enough. Too thick.

A second doctor arrived, another young one, but a Major and senior to the first. "Give me the bullet," he demanded as Kristen gloved him.

"Advanced shock, blood pressure sixty over thirty and dropping, atelectasis," reported the other nurse, indicating that Peterson's lungs had failed.

The Major nodded, but then all hell broke loose as machines began to scream.

"Asystole! No pulse!" called Sykes as he looked at the flat line on the cardio monitor.

He began heart compressions while Kristen sent the other nurse to look for a crash cart, most of which had been conscripted for the emergency drill. Again and again Kristen squeezed the rebreather, but Peterson's lungs were simply not functioning. The doctors continued taking turns with heart compressions anyway.

"Where the hell is the crash cart?" demanded the Major as exhaustion began to hinder his ability to effectively compress the heart of his dying patient. Kristen knew this was hopeless, given the state of Peterson's lungs. But the two young doctors refused to give up until the attending physician arrived. It happened to be Colonel Ripsimio, who looked exhausted himself.

"How long with the CPR?" the Colonel asked.

"Fifteen minutes. No response. Crash cart unavailable," Kristen reported.

The Colonel shook his head and spoke Kristen's thoughts aloud. "The crash cart isn't going to fix his lungs. Call it." The Captain and Major reluctantly ceased their efforts. Kristen flicked a couple of switches to turn off the monitors.

The Colonel looked at the clock. "Time of death, twenty thirty-two."

Then, without showing the least sign of emotion, Colonel Ripsimio walked out of the room. Captain Sykes leaned on the side of the bed, head hung low between his shoulders.

"Damn!" said the Major, who looked slightly bewildered by the sudden cessation of frantic activity.

Kristen's eyes burned, but she had no time for tears. It had become increasingly clear to them all that someone had done this to the Sergeant and the other victims. On purpose. Because people don't just come down with plague all of a sudden for no reason in the heart of Germany.

That meant this had to be a terrorist act. And the one person with whom Kristen most wanted to talk to about all this was her husband. Her weary mind had begun to wonder about connections between her terrorist and his. She hurried to decontaminate herself by carefully removing her protective clothing and scrubbing down.

Then she headed to the lab where she knew Anthony and Amy would probably still be.

ANTHONY HAD ENDURED just about all the testing he was going to take for one day. But when Kristen finally showed up in the doorway of the tiny room he'd been put into, his complaints died on his tongue. She looked dead tired and her eyes seemed shiny.

"What happened?" he said, getting to his feet and going to her, despite the protest of the nurse who'd been sticking him with innumerable needles.

"Patient died," she said succinctly. "How are things going for you?"

He knew better than to probe further. His mother and sister were both nurses and he knew that every nurse had to deal with the death of a patient in whatever way worked best. Kristen didn't like to talk about the ones who slipped away.

"Fine," he said, unwilling to complain about a few needles now that the death of her patient had put his discomfort into perspective. "It's fine," he repeated as he enclosed her in his arms in the hope of lending her some strength. "You need to take a break, Kristen."

"Yeah. I'll do that when everyone is out of danger. Soon." She hugged him to her, hard, then stepped back. "Where's Amy?"

"Your friend Louise took her to another room where there are kiddy toys and pediatric needles," he said.

Kristen drew him a little away from the nurse who had been working on him. In a whisper, she said, "Did anyone tell you what we're testing for?"

"Not yet."

"It's plague," she said. "But you should be okay. Either you didn't contract it or we'll administer the right antibiotics to take care of it. The trick is to catch it early and we're doing that. You probably won't even feel sick. Promise.'' She lowered her voice a little more. ''But I'm worried about one thing. It seems to me that someone had to have deliberately released this disease on these patients. The CDC indicates that for this illness to develop so quickly in people who had no contact with each other, they'd have to breathe in an aerosol form of it.''

Anthony's insides seemed to catch fire and his heart rate soared. He remembered what Dave had told him about the handprint on the car. Taaoun lurked somewhere in Wiesbaden, waiting to strike a vengeful blow. Could he have been giving people the plague, too?

He held his wife's gaze. ''I have physical evidence that Theodore Bjornvik is in Germany, Kristen. The CIA was wrong about his death. He's alive and he's in the country. And this guy is capable of just about anything. My theory is that he spent some time in the States, hurting the families of the people on my team. But when he couldn't find us there, he tracked us down here in Germany. He's been following us, waiting for a moment to strike. I'm not sure how plague would play into all this, but we can't rule him out as a suspect.''

She put her fingers to her temples and rubbed in small circles. ''I can't believe this is happening,'' she said. ''Logically, we have no way of knowing if we're dealing with one bad guy or two. Or it could be a whole cell. This all feels like a nightmare.''

''Welcome to my world,'' he said grimly.

''You were right all along and I didn't believe you. I should have believed you,'' she said. ''I haven't been much of a wife since you've been back.'' Her eyes seemed suspiciously shiny again.

''Can we go somewhere for coffee or something?'' he

asked, wanting to get her away from her duties, at least for half an hour or so.

"No. You have to stay put until we get the test results. It should take about an hour. And I have to get back to work. We want as few people as possible exposed to this, so we're only using the staff members already on precautionary streptomycin, like me."

He let out a sigh of frustration. "Right. I'll wait here for Amy. Tell Louise to bring her back to me as soon as possible. If we're going to be quarantined here while there's a terrorist on the loose, I want us together."

"You won't be quarantined. We just want to be sure to get you on the medicine if we need to. We know what we're looking for now."

"Promise me you won't leave the hospital without me. I'll come get you when they finally let you off. Meanwhile, I'll make some phone calls to General Jetyko and security so the right people go on alert. We ought to be able to find a guy going around spraying people from a can."

Kristen nodded and hugged him again before she left, looking as if the weight of the world were on her shoulders.

An hour ticked by before Anthony, trained as he was to wait through interminable downtime on missions, began to pace. His tests were long since over, although the results were not yet in. He couldn't imagine what was keeping Kristen's friend, Louise, who was supposed to bring Amy back to him.

A few minutes later, he found out.

"Major Garitano, I'm sorry!" she said. Her hair had partly fallen from its bun at the nape of her neck, and another woman seemed to be helping her walk.

"Excuse me?" he said. "Sorry for what?" Then he

realized that Captain Louise Kilpatrick should be with Amy. And Amy was nowhere in sight. Anthony's whole body went cold.

"She's gone. Your daughter," said the Captain who swayed on her feet as if she was about to faint.

Then the other woman spoke to Louise. "Captain, you have to let me take you back to the ER. You need to be checked by a doctor."

"My daughter?" Anthony said as the cold within him turned to ice. "Where is my daughter?" He asked it calmly even though every cell of his being urged him to grab the Captain and shout the words at her. For the first time in his entire life, panic welled inside him, threatening to freeze his mind and numb his body.

"Please," said the other woman, "she's been unconscious. Some kind of drug like ether or chloroform, I think. I need to get her to the ER."

But the Captain's eyes remained locked with Anthony's. "I think someone took her," Louise said just before she sagged into unconsciousness again.

CHAPTER THIRTEEN

SEVERAL HOURS FILLED with one medical crisis after another had passed before Kristen saw her husband again. She knew something bad had happened the instant she noticed Anthony striding toward her. His eyes seemed to glow with rage, and his body moved with dangerous determination. She would not want to be the object of his wrath.

Then she noticed he wasn't alone. A small band of Rangers followed him closely. And they were armed. Inside the hospital!

"What are you doing?" she demanded when he and his men came to a halt in front of her. Her horrified gaze ranged from one M-4 machine gun to the other. The overwhelming single-mindedness of these men, standing with feet planted apart and eyes scrutinizing the perimeter, made her numb with sudden dread. What in God's name had happened?

"I'm coming to check on you before we start gathering the information we need to find Amy." She'd never seen this dangerous expression in Anthony's eyes before, and she realized this would be how he looked when on a military operation.

Then his words registered. She knew that her eyes widened, that her muscles tensed, that her pulse raced and that her lungs gasped for air. But the outcry of denial that resounded so loudly inside her mind did not escape, and the pressure of containment made her blood pressure plummet. She closed her eyes and rubbed her temples, trying to fend off dizziness. Even though her lungs continued to do their job, she felt as if she couldn't breathe. "Find Amy?" she finally managed to ask. "What do you mean? Where's Amy?"

Anthony seized her shoulders and held her upright as panic attempted to steal her ability to stand. "Jesus! Didn't the messenger find you? I sent someone before I went to gear up and gather the men…God, Kristen, I thought you already knew!"

"One…one of the patients went into shock. We…we almost lost him. We…" Her voice trailed away as she realized none of that was important at the moment. "Amy is missing?"

Anthony held her gaze as if to make certain she could handle what he was about to say. "Your friend Louise was knocked out with something soaked into a cloth. When she woke up, Amy was gone."

"H-how do you know she…she didn't just wander off?" Kristen managed to ask, scanning the area frantically as if Amy might toddle in at any moment. But Anthony shook her gently, bringing her attention back to his face, where she saw anger and frustration and guilt taking their toll on him. Seeing that, she knew the situation was very bad. Something terrible had happened to Amy. Kristen felt the barbed wire of anxiety scraping through her stomach.

"There was a note," he said. "The terrorist I've been telling you about kidnapped her to get to me. But I'll get her back, Kristen. I promise you that."

She stared deep into his eyes, hoping for strength to flow from him to her, but she saw something there that she'd never, ever seen before. Fear.

No fair, she thought as her body began to shake all over. She needed him to be as strong now as he'd always been. No fair that he would look so vulnerable when she felt on the verge of falling apart herself. But she couldn't do that now, when he clearly couldn't bear it. She had to pull herself together, regain control, find a way to keep mind and body functioning even when it seemed as if her entire world were crumbling around her. She couldn't let him deal with this alone. He'd been doing quite enough of that since he'd come home.

She forced herself to take a deep breath, in and out, and then willed her heart to beat more slowly. Sensation returned to her fingers and she realized her nails were digging into Anthony's sleeves as if such a fierce grip could possibly bring the nightmare to an end. She loosened her hold and stood back, hugging herself in a vain attempt to keep from trembling. Hardening her heart to the motherly instincts that urged her to break down and cry, she eyed the assembled men. If any group could get Amy back, this one would.

"Where did he take her? What does the note say?" she asked, fighting to sound like the field-grade officer she was.

"We have a plan," he said, but Kristen thought she heard one of the men huff slightly as if he didn't think much of the plan. Anthony ignored him. "We came back here only to get a better description of the target from Captain Kilpatrick."

The clinical part of her mind wanted to know if he'd at least waited until he'd been cleared to leave the hospital before he'd gone out in public to collect his battle gear and fetch his men, but she didn't take the time to ask about something that she could no longer do anything about. Suddenly, there seemed to be almost nothing she could control, nothing that made sense, nothing she could count on.

Except maybe Anthony's promise to get their daughter back.

They were going to go to battle against the monster who'd taken her daughter. And Kristen resolved to be part of their fighting team. She straightened her spine and stretched her neck from side to side to alleviate some of her fatigue and tension. "I'll go with you to talk to Louise," she said, then looked at the Captain standing just behind her husband. "And I want to see the note."

The Captain to whom she'd addressed the demand began to reach inside a pocket, but Anthony intervened. "No on both counts, Kristen. You're too close to the problem. I can't let you involve yourself."

She turned on him. "And you're not too close? She's not your daughter, too? Do you honestly think you can keep me from doing everything possible to find Amy?" Couldn't he see that she would succumb to useless tears and unproductive rage if she didn't *do* something to get her child returned?

When he made as if to retort, she held up her palm to him and deliberately turned away. She called to a nurse at the nearest station. "What room is Louise Kilpatrick in?"

"Two sixteen," came the prompt reply. Kristen realized everyone within earshot had been listening avidly to the discussion so far, many with both sympathy and fear in their eyes. A terrorist act like this could happen to them, too. And so they paid close attention—like drivers slowing down to scrutinize a car accident. Now Kristen knew how horrible it was to be the person in the wreckage at whom everyone stared.

Kristen led the way to Louise's room, amazed she

could make her shaking limbs do what she asked of them. Hundreds of questions whirled through her mind and she wanted answers immediately, but she conceded that talking to Louise should be a priority. Her friend had seen Amy last.

The thought that someone else had been the last to see her beautiful baby girl brought an ache to Kristen's heart so intense, she almost tripped. Why, oh why, had she not been with Amy? If she had been in the room with Amy and Louise, she might have been able to thwart the kidnapping.

Redoubling her efforts to harden herself against her maternal pain and fear, she marched toward the room where her friend lay.

"I'm so sorry," blurted Louise the instant she saw Kristen.

"You couldn't have done anything," Kristen reassured her. "It's my fault anyway, for putting my work ahead of taking care of my own daughter." Logically, she knew she'd had to do her job. But emotionally, she condemned herself. How could she have allowed harm to come to her child, she asked herself. She should have gone to her immediately to oversee her tests. She should have been there. She should have…

"We need to ask you some questions about your attacker, Captain Kilpatrick," Anthony said. Louise nodded, apparently eager to help in any way she could.

Kristen listened but didn't interfere. She paid close attention to what Louise could remember of Amy's condition—she'd seemed fussy about the blood being drawn but not otherwise in any difficulty. There had been no sign of any struggle. When she'd heard the main thrust of what Louise could tell them—that the man looked American and had dressed like an orderly, that he had been alone, that he had clearly been prepared and had even cooed to Amy as he'd wrapped the drug-soaked cloth around Louise's mouth and nose—Kristen left Anthony to continue his debriefing and went to the doorway, where the other Rangers stood guard. She wanted to see the note the kidnapper had left and she thought Anthony might try to interfere with her right to read it.

She approached the one she'd talked to just before Anthony had tried to ban her from helping. "You're Captain Batsin, the one my husband talked to about the terrorist a few days ago. It seems you believed him when no one else would."

"He's a Ranger, ma'am," he said, as if this fact made any crazy thing that Anthony might say worth listening to.

She nodded again, knowing that loyalty was very highly prized among Rangers. "Well, thanks for believing him. Now, let me see the note the kidnapper left."

Batsin looked slightly confused by the sudden request. He hesitated.

She held out her hand, palm up, and held his gaze. He looked away first, as she'd known he would. She outranked him, after all. He put the folded piece of paper into her hand. With fingers that seemed far steadier than she might have expected, she opened the note.

Garitano,
I have your daughter. Contact the authorities and I will kill her immediately. If you want to see her alive again, have your pretty wife go to the center of town, where a yellow car will pick her up at exactly 9:00 a.m. tomorrow. Do not follow or they will die. I will send further instructions when I have them both.

The note was signed Taaoun. She read the name over several times, pronouncing it in her mind.

When she looked up, she saw Batsin staring at her. "I'm sorry, ma'am," he said.

"This word at the bottom, signed like a name. Do you know what it means?"

"No, ma'am. I just know that your husband said that's what the terrorist likes to call himself."

Anthony suddenly arrived at her side. "You didn't let her read the note!" he nearly shouted. "I told you not to do that."

"She's an officer, sir. And she outranks me. She demanded to read it."

"Kristen," Anthony began in an exasperated voice.

But she cut him off. "Do you know what this word means? This name your terrorist calls himself?"

"No. It's the Arabic name that this Theodore Bjornvik goes by. Does it mean something?"

"Yes. It means 'plague' in Arabic."

They all stood stock-still, processing the implications. Anthony spoke first. "How the hell do you know that?"

"Bioterrorism training. We had to learn how certain key words sounded in other languages. The one I remember for plague in Arabic sounded just like this is spelled."

Anthony's eyebrows lifted in surprise. "So your terrorist and mine *are* the same person."

"It would seem that way," she agreed. "And it means Amy is in even more danger than we thought. This lunatic has been going around spraying plague into people's faces. There's no telling what he might do to Amy. He could even give it to her unintentionally because he might have it all over his hands. Without the right medication, she'll be dead in a day or two." Her voice cracked with emotion and she had to force herself to ignore the fact that she was talking about her own daughter, her baby girl. "I'm assuming this Taaoun is smart enough to be on antibiotics to protect himself, but Amy doesn't have any defense at all." She covered her mouth with her fingers to keep herself contained. Even so, her vision went blurry.

"Shit!" Anthony said as he ran his fingers violently through his hair and turned around in a slow circle. When he faced her again, he seemed to have regained control of himself.

So had she. And she knew what had to happen next. "So, I have to do what this kidnapper wants and meet him in the city."

"What? No way, Kristen! How do you figure?"

"I can bring her the medicine she needs, Anthony. No one else has as good a chance of getting close to her and keeping her alive as I do, given what this note says." She would do anything to save her daughter, even put herself under the control of a madman.

Anthony stared at her with disbelief etched onto his face. Finally, he said. "We'll send someone else. A medic or someone. Not you! He just wants to get both you and Amy together so he can kill you. And maybe not quickly. This is how he wants to take out his revenge on me." As he said the last words, he turned away and slammed his fist into the wall, leaving a dent in the plaster. "God! This is my fault."

"It's no one's fault," she said, but they were the words she'd been trained to say to families of patients. She used to believe they were true, but now they seemed hollow. How could it *not* be someone's fault? Surely one of them should have been able to save a single child.

Surely *she* could have protected her own daughter if she'd been with her.

Kristen wanted to comfort Anthony, but all of her emotional resources were tied up in the effort to keep her own guilt and fear from overwhelming her. She knew that if she touched him, she could very easily fall apart. Instead of risking that, she left him to finish questioning Louise and other possible witnesses, and followed Captain Batsin to the command center the Rangers had begun to set up in a nearby conference room.

If she couldn't get Anthony to see her as a capable military officer, if he couldn't get beyond his desire to protect her, she would be forced to ignore him and make plans of her own. All that mattered was saving Amy.

"Has anyone heard yet from General Jetyko?" Batsin asked when he entered the room.

"Not yet, sir. Working it," answered one of the soldiers.

"What's the plan, Captain?" Kristen asked. "And what do you need the General for?"

"The plan is to locate the terrorist, neutralize him, and rescue your daughter."

She nodded, feeling completely out of her element. Locate, neutralize, rescue. These were not activities in which she'd had much training. But she'd learned during her years in the Army always to give the appearance that she knew what she was doing. "What do we do first to find him?" she asked, trying to sound authoritative and starting with the first challenge on the list.

"Beats me," he said.

She blinked. "What? You mean you don't know how to find this guy? No clues?"

"We can't put men on the ground asking questions until we have the general's orders to go forward with the op, ma'am. Once we start asking, we'll have a better idea of how to approach the problem. We're just waiting for a 'go' from the general.''

Her blood pressure shot upward several points. ''Finding this madman who has my daughter by asking questions all over Germany could take days! Maybe weeks!''

He shook his head. ''It won't take weeks. We have some ideas about where to ask our questions so we won't be all over Germany. The general wouldn't let us do that, anyway. Too conspicuous. And we're open to other ideas, if you've got 'em.''

Ohmigod! There was no real plan at all! ''Yeah, well, it's making more and more sense to have me go in according to the kidnapper's instructions. At least I'd have a decent chance of getting close to Amy, so I can keep her alive until you guys can find us. If you're any good, you can follow me to where he's got her without being seen by him, right?''

''Finding you wouldn't be a problem even if we didn't follow you,'' Batsin said. ''We'd put a LoJack on you.''

''A what?'' Her abject terror for her daughter came down a notch when she realized that Batsin was considering letting her go to Amy. But the queasy stomach remained. She knew the horrors she might have to endure at the hands of a terrorist. And there was no guarantee that what she would suffer would mean that Amy survived. She might not even get close to her daughter.

''LoJack,'' repeated Batsin. ''Like what they put on cars to find them when they're stolen. But for humans. We implant this little device under your skin and your location blips on our computer screen.''

''A subcutaneous transponder?''

''Um, whatever you say.''

"Wouldn't they know I have it? They'd just take it out of me."

"Not likely. The bad guys don't really think of it. Most folks figure if they take all your visible hardware—and we always give you some good stuff that they can throw away—then they're safe. And this gizmo isn't easily detected. You could walk through a metal detector and never set off an alarm."

"I want one," she said. She looked at her watch to judge how much time she had left until she was supposed to meet the yellow car in town. Taaoun had demanded that she meet him at oh nine hundred. She had fewer than eight hours left. And there were a hundred things to do to prepare between now and then.

When she looked up again, Batsin hadn't moved. "Go get me the human LoJack, please. That's an order, Captain."

He eyed her another second or two and she held his gaze. Again. She hoped to God she wouldn't have to play this power game for every little thing, but she would if she had to. Finally, Batsin nodded. "I'll help you because it's the only viable plan and because you outrank us all, ma'am. But I hate like hell to go behind a fellow Ranger's back."

"Duly noted," she replied. Then he went to the phone and put in the order for the tracking device.

BY THE TIME ANTHONY JOINED the others in the improvised hospital command center, Kristen had taken over. Everyone seemed to be jumping to do her bidding and she barked orders like a drill sergeant.

"What the hell?" he asked everyone in general.

"Hello, sir," said a young Ranger sitting at a desk in front of a laptop.

Anthony ignored him. "Kristen, what do you think you're doing?"

"I'm helping your team get our daughter back," she said. Her stubborn streak had apparently decided to assert itself.

From between clenched teeth, he ground out, "Help if you can, but you're not in charge here."

The entire room went silent and still. Every face turned toward the two of them. Every person waited to find out exactly who *was* in charge, if not this female officer from whom they'd clearly been taking orders for the last hour or so. Kristen glared at him, then went back to what she'd been doing prior to his arrival.

Anthony seethed, but he kept his mouth shut. This was not the time to have a public argument. He needed to stay focused on the mission. And maybe Kristen would be able to help somehow. He knew she'd feel better if she could stay where the action was.

"Where do things stand?" he asked Batsin, wanting to know if any progress had been made while he'd been getting every possible detail about Amy's abductor.

"General Jetyko said not to get caught performing police activities on German soil. But if you *do* get caught, he has some story lined up about how the perpetrator committed his heinous crime on American soil on post here and something about hot pursuit. And if the Germans won't buy that, you're on your own, and he'll court martial you if he has to in order to make them happy."

Anthony accepted this report without surprise. He'd half expected the General to turn the case over to the local authorities and to forbid any effort by the Rangers to retrieve Amy.

He'd have had to do it anyway, against direct orders

to stand down. And he hated the idea of getting these fellow Rangers into that kind of trouble, even though he would have had no choice. So this report on Jetyko's thinking actually seemed like good news. He hadn't even ordered them to involve the German police.

"We're going to run this covert. No uniforms. No identification. Do we have someone who can pass for German?"

"Yes, sir," said a tall Sergeant hovering over a table covered with maps of Wiesbaden.

"Good. Thanks for helping. Who do we have on the ground?"

Suddenly, Kristen stood right in front of him and her eyes were just about on fire. "Please come into the hall with me, Major." Without waiting for his response, she turned and went into the hall, apparently expecting him to follow.

He did. "I don't have much time to spare for your irritation with me, Kristen."

"Is that right?" she said, and her calmness made alarms go off inside his head. "Because I have news for you, Major. I outrank you, too. By several months. And if you ever treat me like a helpless female again, I'll have you up on charges. Do you hear me?"

He stood stock-still as the sensation of being in an alternate universe engulfed him. Had she just pulled rank on him? Had she threatened him? Damn!

"I asked if you heard me and, as distasteful as this situation is for both of us, I expect an answer. Because if I don't get one, we're not both going back in there."

With his teeth clenched so hard his jaw ached, he managed to say, "I heard you, ma'am." And it just about killed him. But he couldn't leave it at that. "With all due respect, you have no training in this kind of operation. I do. A good leader would rely on those with experience."

"I'll rely on you when I believe you can forget I'm your wife and begin treating me as an officer."

He looked into her angry, determined eyes and knew the truth. "I could never, for a single second, ever forget you're my wife. Because that would mean I'd have to forget how much I love you. Not an option."

He saw that his words had found a chink in her armor, but after a momentary softening of her expression, she rallied and glared at him some more. "Look. We have no idea where this guy took Amy. Even though we have some people asking questions on the street, we have no leads. The only way to find her is for me to go through with the demands in the note and meet his yellow car in…"

"No."

She put her hands on her hips. "It's not up to you, Major. Things have already been set into motion. I've already had a tracking device implanted in my arm. I'm in the process of collecting medicine and other supplies I can carry in my BDU pockets…"

Rage spiked and he grabbed her by the shoulders. "Do you honestly think this character is going to let you keep any of that? Do you think he's even going to let you set eyes on Amy?"

"Do you honestly think I could live with myself if I didn't at least try?" she threw back at him.

He leveled his gaze to hers, holding her attention through force of will. "The only reason he would do that is so he could hurt Amy in front of you. That's the kind of stuff someone like him is willing to do."

She swallowed hard and he hated having to be so

cruel, but she had to come to her senses about this. If she didn't, he'd have to lock her up somewhere until this was all over—for her own safety and for the success of the mission.

CHAPTER FOURTEEN

KRISTEN CONCEDED that Anthony could handle waiting much better than she could. They'd done everything possible to prepare. Now they had the interminable hours to get through. Every passing minute meant Amy's condition could be worsening. Kristen barely kept herself from screaming and throwing things in sheer frustration. But between less and less frequent communications with the people looking for Amy, Anthony managed to nap.

And Kristen hated him for it. How could he sleep for even a single moment when their child was out there somewhere with a madman? A madman who had followed *him* home from Afghanistan. A terrorist Anthony had led to Amy's doorstep.

Such thoughts tormented her all the more because she knew they were unfair. She herself deserved the blame far more than Anthony. If she had trusted her husband, believed in him, encouraged him to follow up on his gut feelings, he would have nailed the son-of-a-bitch kidnapper long before now. But she'd been so certain that his sightings were products of his post-traumatic stress disorder. She'd been so superior, so sure. God! If she'd only listened with an open mind!

And then she'd committed the gravest sin of all. She'd put her work ahead of her duty to her daughter. Instead of watching over her child, as all her instincts had urged her to do, she'd gone to help a couple of doctors with a man whose condition was hopeless—as if no one else could have done the same. When had she become so arrogant as to believe that she was the only one who could do anything right?

And yet she couldn't seem to keep herself from staring at her husband's closed eyes with fury boiling inside her. He even had his feet up on the desktop, crossed at the ankles. He'd tipped his chair back slightly so that he almost reclined. How *could* he sleep?

All of a sudden, he lowered his feet to the floor and let the legs of the chair clatter onto the linoleum. In the time it took her to blink in surprise, his eyes had opened and he looked right at her without any of the dullness that so frequently accompanies initial wakefulness. "What does the word *flea-oh* mean to you?" he asked.

"What?" She knew her cheeks were flaming from guilt, as if he'd known the evil thoughts she'd had about him sleeping.

"*Flea-oh* is the nickname the car accident guy gave Anna."

"What car accident? Was your sister in a car accident? Why didn't you tell me?" More fuel for her pyre of irrational indignation against the man she'd married.

He waved a hand as if her questions were unimportant. Then he leaned forward with his elbows on his knees. "Does the word mean anything to you?"

"Flea-oh," she said, trying hard to set aside her anger to focus on what he asked of her. Then it hit her, probably because she'd just whiled away an hour reviewing the words she'd learned in her training. "It could be the French word *fleau*. I guess it's no surprise to you that it means *plague*."

He shook his head in disgust. "So the guy was in the States, too. It's like I said before. He spent some time there, looking for me and my men. He only found some family members to mess with. Then he found out from Anna that we're here in Germany.'' Anthony ran his fingers through his hair. The wavy locks stood out at odd angles here and there. Combined with the scars on his face, he looked like a mad scientist. Yet Kristen found his appearance oddly endearing. The tug on her heartstrings seemed in direct opposition to her anger of only moments ago. She didn't understand herself. And any attempt at introspection became impossible when she saw who walked through the doorway of their make-shift command center.

"Kris," said Lieutenant Colonel Paul Farley. "I came as soon as I could."

Her pulse rate quickened and her breathing accelerated. The last thing she needed right now was the stress of being in the same room as Paul. Feeling about as uncomfortable as humanly possible, she glanced at the clock on the wall. Oh-seven-fifty. Why would Paul, of all people, have heard about their crisis so early in the morning?

"Who the hell told you anything?" Anthony demanded. "This operation is close-hold."

Paul turned and looked into Anthony's eyes just long enough to make a point about rank and respect. Then he said, "General Jetyko called me. He wanted my opinion on your mental condition in regard to your ability to lead this close-hold operation."

Kristen nearly groaned as she watched her husband's nostrils flare ever so slightly at this. Anthony could be like a bull faced with a red flag when challenged. Just about anything could come out of his mouth at times like this.

But before he could speak, Paul added, "I told him

you were more capable than most men of getting your daughter back alive. Don't make a liar out of me."

After a moment, Anthony said quietly, "Thank you."

"You need to be tested for the plague," she said, sounding calmer than she felt. "I may have been contagious when I came to see you."

Paul nodded. "I'm already taking the antibiotic. How are you holding up?"

And suddenly, she felt tears fill her eyes and overflow. They streamed down her cheeks before she had the sense to turn away. Without responding to Paul's question, she walked from the room and went to the one place where neither Anthony nor Paul were likely to follow her. The women's room was blessedly empty.

She locked herself into a stall, leaned against a tiled wall, and then let her body sag slowly to the floor. With her forehead on her arms, which were propped across her knees, Kristen let her emotions flow in great, gasping sobs. Terror for her daughter choked her, fear for herself clawed at her insides. But she knew what she had to do.

Despite Anthony's protests, she had arranged with Captain Batsin to go forward with the kidnapper's demands if there were no breakthroughs by oh-eight-thirty. Her watch ticked off the minutes toward eight. In less than an hour, she would be in Theodore Bjornvik's control.

But shortly after that, she could be holding her daughter in her arms again. She had to hold out hope that this would happen. It would sustain her through whatever challenges she'd face before the Rangers could retrieve them.

The possibility of seeing Amy soon helped her regain her composure. She yanked toilet paper from the dispenser and sopped the tears from her face. She blew her nose. After another moment, she got to her feet. From a childhood memory, her mind replayed the sound of her mother's voice saying, "Wash your face now in cold water and you'll feel better." That had been her mom's favorite solution to little-girl traumas that resulted in weeping.

Sure enough, splashing cold water on her face felt really good and steadied her for the coming ordeal. Her cheeks were flushed, but not as dramatically as before. And Anthony would assume she'd lost her composure because of the long hours of worrying. She hoped he wouldn't suspect her plans to meet the kidnapper's car in the city. If he did, he'd try to stop her and she didn't want her last interaction with him to be filled with anger.

She took a few deep breaths, checked her watch for the hundredth time, and walked out of the sanctuary of the women's room. Paul waited for her just around the corner. He'd been leaning one shoulder against the wall, but straightened when she came into view.

Kristen stopped dead in her tracks. A confrontation with the psychologist was not high on her to-do list right now. She wished he would go away.

"I would have sent someone else if the General hadn't specifically asked for me. I know you're confused about our doctor-patient relationship. We can talk about that sometime or we can find you another psychologist. But I'm hoping that, just for this crisis, you'll let me help."

"I don't think you can help me," she said as she struggled to look at him without allowing her guilt to overtake her.

"I've done a lot of research on the mentality of terrorists, Kris. I read the details on this guy. That's what I've been doing since I first heard about the situation. I might be able to guide your behavior to help you stay alive. And, for what it's worth, I can give you a crash course in torture survival techniques.''

She eyed him with a new worry racing through her mind. She hadn't mentioned her intentions. He shouldn't be aware of her plans to let herself be captured. "Why would I need those?"

He gazed steadily at her. "Because I know how you think and I know you'll do anything to save your daughter. And I saw the note the kidnapper left. You're going to do what he wants in an effort to get to Amy."

It troubled her that he could read her so well. His earnest expression, the sincerity in his eyes, made her see how she could have mistakenly believed he cared for her as more than just another patient. And she knew full well that transference was not uncommon in situations such as hers. What she needed to do now was forgive herself for succumbing to it. She was human, after all.

"I love my husband, Paul. I would never do anything to hurt him." And she realized that this was true, despite her earlier anger at him for sleeping, despite her resentment that he treated her like a wife instead of like a capable soldier. "When this is over, I'm going to make our marriage work."

"I never doubted it for a single second, Kris."

She couldn't say that she forgave herself, but she knew she would eventually. She also knew she could trust herself with Paul now and could take the knowledge about terrorists that he offered. "Tell me what I need to know," she said.

He nodded. "Let's go back to the operations center."

"No," she said, holding him back by his arm. The instant she realized she was touching him, she jerked her hand away. Her explanation about Anthony not knowing about her upcoming efforts came out as babble. Hadn't she just finished saying how much she loved her husband? And yet she was about to take unilateral action against his most adamant wishes. If she survived, would he ever forgive her?

"So you see," she finished. "We can't discuss this in front of Anthony."

Paul shook his head. "That's a mistake, Kris. You need his help. And once you're taken prisoner, you'll need the extra edge of knowing you're one hundred percent on the same side. Love can carry you through almost anything."

"If I tell him what I plan to do, he'll find a way to prevent me. He's nothing if not resourceful. So we're not going to tell him. I've persuaded Captain Batsin to help me, though. He's been gathering the gear I'll need." She checked her watch. "In fact, it's time to meet him in the room where my stuff is." Her stomach flipped upside down as she realized her hour was upon her.

"You're making a mistake, but I can't stop you. You'd never be able to live with yourself if you didn't do whatever you could for Amy. Lead on."

In the small room she led him to, there was a cot covered with gizmos, a row of lockers with her gym bag hanging half out of one, and Captain Batsin. The latter took up a great deal of the space. She introduced the two men and felt as if she were underwater as she did so. They seemed to move in slow motion as they shook hands, and their voices seemed to come from far away. Everything was foggy, muffled, unreal. She knew these were reactions to her intense tension but could not remember what, if anything, she could do about them.

"You guys need to step outside while I change my

clothes,'' she said. They left her alone and she stood in the center of the small chamber trembling. *Snap out of it,* she told herself. She needed all her wits about her today. Succumbing to panic and fear would not help her. She would do what she had to do for her daughter, no matter how dangerous she knew it would be.

Action. She needed action. If she moved from one task to another without stopping too long in between, she would get through this. And in no time at all, she would no longer need to force herself to do things—the kidnapper would make her do whatever he wanted and she would only have to think about surviving.

As she reached for her gym bag, she suddenly had the irrational yearning to call her mother. Perhaps she'd thought of it because her mother's voice had advised her about the cold water. Or maybe the danger she faced made her think of loved ones and wish for more time to say goodbye. Even though they were back in the States, her parents had been so supportive while Anthony had been deployed. Funny that she would think of her mother right now rather than her father. She and Kristen had been at odds with each other when they'd lived in the same house, but once they'd gone their separate ways, their relationship had improved.

And now Kristen wanted to talk to her, to tell her she loved her, to ask her if she was doing the right thing, to beg her to explain things to Anthony if she wasn't able to do so herself later on. But talking to her would not be practical—it would be the middle of the night on the East Coast. And telling her of Amy's danger—the same danger she was about to walk into herself—would be unkind in the extreme. Maybe she'd have time to write a note, just in case she never got the chance to say the things she needed to tell her parents.

She rummaged through her locker and found paper. A pen was discovered in the gym bag. Writing "Dear Mom and Dad" at the top of the page revealed how badly her hands were shaking. Her penmanship was never good on the best of days, and now it seemed nearly illegible. Yet she persevered. She might never get another chance to tell her parents that she loved them. She closed the letter with "I love you very much," and then noticed that a tear had fallen to the page. She swiped it away, hoping no one would notice. No time to do the note over again. And she wanted to write one to Anthony. She found another sheet of paper, tattered and frayed on one end, but good enough for this emergency.

"If you are reading this, it will be because I can't be with you anymore. I had always hoped we would grow old together, always knew you were the one I wanted to be with through the years. But sometimes our duty calls us away from the life we pictured. Please understand that I didn't leave you behind willingly and that only our daughter's peril could have torn me from your side. I love you with all my heart, Kristen."

She swallowed hard as she folded the two notes and indicated the recipients on the outside of each. The papers shook as she put them on the cot so she wouldn't forget to give them to Batsin. She looked at them and had to fight for breath as the implications of what she'd written settled into her mind. If her parents or husband read those letters, she'd be dead. A daunting reality. Yet, she knew that men and women in the military all over the world kept such letters tucked away for just such an eventuality. She would try to imitate their bravery.

First, she needed to change her clothes. Once she began to do so, the tight quivering sensation in her stomach seemed to subside a bit. Yes, action would get her through this. As soon as she had donned her BDUs, she opened the door so the men could join her. She handed the letters to the Captain and he took them without a word, clearly recognizing them for what they were. He put them into an inside pocket while she sat on the end of the cot to lace up her boots.

"What do you have for me here, Captain?" she asked Batsin, indicating the pile of stuff beside her.

"We've got ourselves this cool little gizmo that makes a great sound when you push this here button, but that doesn't actually do much," he said as he picked up a small black electronic thing.

"Then why are you giving it to her?" asked Paul.

"So the terrorist can throw it away," she and Batsin said at the same time. The coincidental speech actually made her smile, despite what her near-term future had in store for her.

Batsin noted the Lieutenant Colonel's puzzled expression and added, "We give her things that look like tracking devices so they'll have stuff to take away from her. That way, they're less likely to suspect the LoJack we put under her skin."

"Got it," Paul said as he nodded his approval while Batsin put the fake transponder into her shirt pocket.

"I want you to carry your cell." Batsin handed it to her and she put it in her front hip pocket. "This guy wants to torment Major Garitano and he might like the idea of calling him on your phone. We'd like you to talk to us until he takes the thing away from you anyway. We just like to retain coms as long as possible, in case the unexpected happens late in the game."

The knot in Kristen's stomach tightened even more at

the thought of not being able to communicate. She would be very much alone.

"Here's a micro taping device that they might miss in a pat-down," Batsin continued. "It's small, but it's mighty. We'll put that in your lower pocket. And we'll replace your U.S. pin with this one. It has a camera inside. Who knows? We may get lucky with some pictures."

"What do you need pictures for? You're going to follow her and rescue her as soon as she leads you to this guy, right?" Paul asked, worry lines creasing his brow.

"Sometimes dudes slip away before we can nab 'em. This guy isn't working alone and we want to make sure we get them all," Batsin answered. "Pictures could be very helpful."

"How do I make the camera work?" Kristen asked as she unfastened the pip from the back of the dark U.S. pin on the collar of her uniform.

"Don't worry about it. It's a wireless and runs on its own. We can download pictures as we go, so there's no need for memory chips. Not the best way to ensure great snaps, but we don't think you'll be wanting to think about photo ops while you're in custody. Here's the water and food packs you ordered, and the medicine."

She stowed the consumables in other pockets, glad that the BDU had so many storage possibilities. She'd never had need to use so many of them before, not even in training. "They'll probably take all this away from me, but you never know. I might get to bring something to Amy, or they might overlook something," she said, hoping that at least the medicine would make it.

The streptomycin was in capsule form and she dreaded trying to get it down Amy's throat without water—if she even got that far. But if they took her water, she'd have to manage somehow. The medicine had to be given at four-hour intervals without exception. The capsules would normally be in a pharmacy bottle, but for this trip, Kristen had asked for them to be sealed between strips of tape. She put one strip in her pocket beneath the bottle of water. Another she would strap to her upper thigh, where there was some hope the henchmen of this Taaoun wouldn't pat her down.

But on the chance that she would be strip-searched, she also had the pharmacy seal a number of the pills into a condom. Before she left, this pack would go inside her body, the lifesaving medicine ironically inserted into the birth canal through which she'd given Amy life in the first place. The only way it would be discovered and taken from her was if she were raped—a distinct possibility, but a risk she'd have to take. Other hiding places seemed less likely to succeed. She might not be able to retain the small packet in the other body cavity that drug dealers sometimes used to get contraband past customs. She was already scared shitless and she didn't want to take the chance of losing the medicine to further fear reactions.

"You're pale and shaking," Paul said. "Try some deep breaths."

She huffed a rueful laugh. "Yeah, right. Deep breathing ought to help."

He looked away from her and ran his fingers through his hair. It was a gesture Anthony frequently made when he was upset. All at once, Kristen longed for her husband's embrace. She wanted him to reassure her, to tell her she was brave and good and loved. Only Anthony would be able to make her stronger in this hour of despair.

But she couldn't go to him. Out of love, he would

hold her back. And she would hate him forever if he managed to prevent her from going to her daughter. She wondered if her note would be delivered to him in the next few hours.

"Tell me about the terrorist, Paul. It would help me to know everything you know," she said. "Follow me to the rest room and keep talking to me through the door while I tape this stuff to my skin." She held up the tape strips holding the drugs. "I'll be listening to everything you say. Don't assume that anyone told me anything. Give me everything you think might help. Your insights could make the difference to my survival."

Before she walked out into the corridor again, she turned to Captain Batsin. "You'll have a car waiting out front in ten?" The man nodded, his expression grim. She added, "Thank you for all your help. I couldn't have done this without you."

"Just promise me that you and your daughter will come back alive, or Tiger's gonna chew me up into little pieces," he said.

"I promise," she said and gave him a small smile. "Tell Anthony…" but she couldn't think of the right words to ask Batsin to convey. Everything she wanted to say was so personal. And she'd written most of it in her note anyway.

"You'll tell him yourself when this is all over," he said firmly.

"Yeah," she said. "I'll tell him myself." And part of her believed it.

"WHERE'S KRISTEN?" Anthony asked of no one in particular. He'd followed her when she'd first run out of the operations center until he'd seen her duck into the bathroom. She'd been overcome with emotion and he'd

let her go. She needed to let out some of her pain, he
knew. He wished he could do the same. And he didn't
want her in the same room with the shrink. Bad enough
he had to put up with the guy himself.

He'd listened to everything Farley had to say about
Taaoun. Any insight could be useful in the long run,
even if it came from the same man who had so recently
believed the terrorist was a figment of Anthony's imagination. So he'd listened and even taken some notes.
Eventually, Farley had said everything he knew or suspected about Theodore Bjornvik, looked at his watch and
taken his leave.

Now Anthony consulted his own watch. Where was
Kristen? He felt sure she would have been able to com-
pose herself by now.

"I haven't seen her, sir," answered one of the members of the team.

"Stay at the coms. Find me if we get word from the
ground." He turned to the tall guy who could pass for
German. This soldier was their last hope of finding Amy
before her trail grew colder. Anthony couldn't remember
the man's name. "Gear up and get ready to go. We have
a half hour before you follow the kidnapper's car from
the center of town. If you're caught, you're German.
You have your papers?"

"Yes, sir," said the man, dressed in civilian clothes
and as ready as he could be to do whatever necessary to
find a little girl who could be anywhere.

"Sorry, I can't remember your name," Anthony admitted.

"Understandable, sir, with all that's happened. I'm
Riker, sir. Sergeant First Class."

"Riker." He nodded his head as he repeated the soldier's name, determined not to forget it again. These

men were his responsibility for now. He needed to keep them in the forefront of his mind, just as he had with the teammates he'd lost. If he didn't, the mission would be jeopardized and so would his soul. "I'm going to find my wife. If I'm not back in time, go with the plan, Sergeant Riker."

"Will do, sir."

Anthony paused when he got to the door. "I need to know where this lunatic has my daughter. I just need to know where he took her. Bring me that information, and I'll do the rest."

"I'll find out the location, sir."

Anthony nodded and moved into the corridor, knowing full well that Sergeant First Class Riker had a snowball's chance in hell of finding his daughter. But it was their only chance.

That thought stuck with him as he walked down the corridor to the nearest women's room. He knocked on the door and got no reply, so he went inside—damn anyone's right to privacy. He checked each stall, but no one was inside. Why hadn't Kristen come back to the operations center. Where had she gone?

Then suddenly he knew and cold dread raced through him, stealing his breath. Without knowing exactly how he got there, he found himself at the threshold of the op center he'd just left. "She's gone! Where's Batsin? We have to find her!"

But no one knew where Captain Dave Batsin had gone. Not even Anthony had seen him slip away. One minute he'd been there, and then sometime before Anthony had begun to wonder about Kristen's absence, he'd disappeared. Damn!

Anthony ran through the hospital like a machine after that, accosting people he met along the way, demanding to know if they had sighted his wife or Batsin, trying to discern which door they'd left from. His watch ticked quickly toward the appointed hour when the kidnapper had demanded Kristen meet his yellow car in the town center.

"Where is my wife? Have you seen Kristen Clark? Did you notice a man with a machine gun in the last half hour?" A few people gave him directions, and he pelted down the corridor toward the doors and blew through them as if they weren't there.

He had to stop her. She could *not* be allowed to sacrifice herself. He wouldn't let her. He'd do whatever he had to do to make her see reason. But as he skidded to a halt on the sidewalk under the morning sun, he saw a mottled green Humvee drive away. Though the occupants all wore camouflage clothing, he knew that the one in the black beret had been his wife.

She was going to the center of town to meet Taaoun.

CHAPTER FIFTEEN

HE HAD TO STOP HER. At the op center, he would call them and demand that the car be turned around. But when he started back, he plowed into Lieutenant Colonel Farley. And before he knew what he was doing, he had the man by the collar and shoved up against the outer brick wall of the hospital.

"You let her go, you son of a bitch! How could you let her go?" Every single nerve ending in Anthony's body itched to beat the crap out of the man he held. His brain throbbed with blood lust. Some shred of training and a force of will he didn't know he had kept him from slugging the guy.

"Let go of me, Major," said the psychologist. "And I'll pretend you did not just accost a superior officer."

Anthony let go, but he spat out a string of further accusations. "You helped her! She's walking into certain death and you allowed her to do it! You're supposed to be her doctor, for Christ's sake! You could have stopped her!"

"No, I could not have stopped her. And neither could you. She's an officer and a mother and she would have found a way. And even if you could have stopped her, what would that have accomplished in the long run? She would never have forgiven you, and worse than that, she would never have forgiven herself."

Anthony's red-hot anger pulsed, but somehow he

heard what the shrink said. It made no difference. The bastard should have stopped her. She was in no condition to make the rational choices of an officer when her daughter's life was on the line.

"You need to stay away from my wife!" he snarled.

"Yes, I know!" said Farley. "I came here today to talk to her about what happened! It was my fault, really. I should have seen it coming. But I didn't make a mistake today, Major."

Anthony went very still as he attempted to draw meaning from the words he'd heard. Something had happened between this man and Kristen? "What the hell are you talking about, Farley?"

The man's face went ashen. "You didn't know," he said. "I'm sure she was going to tell you."

Anthony's insides turned to fire. He took a step away and roared at the overcast sky, straining every muscle against the desire to kill. Just when he'd found his love for his wife again, he was betrayed!

Then he realized the psychologist was tugging on his rigid arm. "Major! You have to listen to me. It's not what you think!"

"Not what I think?" he growled. "Not what I think! Then what the hell is it, you son of a bitch?" And suddenly he had the man by the collar and up against the building again. Only this time his despair was magnified by agonizing regret and heartache.

"She loves you!" Farley cried. "It was simple transference when she kissed me. I just didn't see it coming until too late. In her mind, I was you. She even called your name. It's you she wants, even though you've treated her like dirt!"

Anthony let the man go and watched him stumble and nearly fall. "I love her!" Anthony declared, wanting to deny that he would ever treat her badly but knowing that he had. He'd rejected her in so many ways, both subtle and overt. And now he was about to lose her forever.

"I have to get to communications," he said as he strode past Farley, heading back to the operations center. "I have to talk to her. I have to convince her to come back." But he was talking to himself as he ran through the hospital corridors.

When he arrived, Captain Batsin had a headset over his ears. So he hadn't gone with her. When Batsin saw Anthony, he backed up his wheeled chair to the far wall, putting other chairs in the way as he went. Then he held up a defensive hand as Anthony plowed past the obstacles. "I've got your wife on the line, sir," he said. And it was the only thing he could have uttered to save himself from the pummeling he deserved.

Instead of planting a right hook onto Batsin's chin, Anthony accepted the headset and put it over his ears. Adjusting the microphone, he immediately launched into commands. "Kristen, turn the car around now, do you hear me? You are not authorized to do this. I'm in charge of this mission and I'm ordering you to turn around." But he knew in his heart that his command would have no effect and his voice broke on the last word. He'd never felt so helpless in his life, not even when his blood had been spilling all over the sand in Afghanistan.

"I can't do that, Anthony. You know I can't do that. This is something I just have to do," Kristen said. Her voice came to him whisper-soft, and he could almost feel her breath caressing his cheeks, as if he held her in his arms. Something he might never get to do again.

"Please," he begged, and a part of him didn't care that his men were watching him or that his eyes had filled with hot tears. "Come back, Kristen."

"You'll just have to come get me, Tiger. They have me on their locator screens. When you figure out where they've taken me, you and your guys will have to rescue me and Amy. That's our best shot and I'm counting on it."

Anthony nodded, even though he knew she couldn't tell that he did so. His voice couldn't be trusted yet. He rubbed the bridge of his nose with his fingers and thumb as he tried to regain control. He managed to clear his throat. "I'll come get you, then," he promised. And his resolve solidified around that vow. He *would* get her out. Her and Amy. He simply would not entertain any other outcome. "I see your blip on the screen. Are you still in the Humvee?"

"Yes. We're coming up to the town center now." He could hear the tension in her voice.

He knew she had to be terrified, despite her professional manner. This was not what she'd been trained to do. "Kristen, there's still time to rethink this. You don't have to get out of the car. We'll come up with another plan."

"We don't have another plan, Anthony. And you know what will happen if we don't do what he wants. I couldn't live with that. I have to do this." Yes, he could see now that she did. Her training was in saving lives and she believed that this was her best chance to save the life most precious to her.

"Look, just stay alive. Whatever it takes, just stay alive. I'll come get you and Amy, but you need to say or do whatever it takes. Understand?"

She paused a moment before answering, and he was sorry he'd made her think of the things she might have to endure. "Yes, I understand. We've stopped the car. I have to get out of the vehicle now. I don't see the yellow

car yet. But I was told to wait on the sidewalk alone.''
She gave orders to the driver to take the Humvee back
to the airfield. ''I'll stay on the phone as long as I can,''
she said to Anthony.

His throat felt too tight, but he had to say some things.
''Kristen, I want you to know I never wanted a life without you. If I said anything to make you think that, just
remember I've been a mess inside. But I see things more
clearly now and I know that I need you. I love you so
much…'' And he choked back a wave of emotion that
threatened to erupt as a sob. He covered his eyes again,
lamely seeking privacy behind his hand. He willed himself to regain control of his emotions. He'd be no good
to her if he lost it now.

''I love you, too, Tiger. I knew all along we'd make
it. We were meant for each other. Here comes the yellow
car,'' she said more calmly than he'd expected. ''The
thing looks like a mail delivery truck. One of those mini-
trucks. It even says Deutsche Post on the side.''

''Keep talking, Kristen,'' he urged. ''How many are
in the car?''

''I think there's three. No, there's only two. One of
them is getting out.''

''Look at his hand. Is there an index finger missing?''

''Yeah,'' she said and her voice wavered. Fear, no
doubt. She'd read the write-up on this guy. ''He's coming toward me. Guess I'm being greeted by the Plague
Man himself.''

Anthony heard another voice in the distance say
something to his wife. Taaoun. The madman. The
thought made acid churn in his stomach and the urge to
crush something built inside him.

''He wants to talk to you now,'' Kristen said and she
seemed more in control of herself.

"I love you, Kristen," he said, wanting those to be the last words between them until he saw her again.

"How sweet," came the male voice he hadn't heard since it shouted threats from a rocky hill in Afghanistan. "Such a shame you cannot say them in person this time. But today Allah is with you, Garitano. I won't kill your pretty wife yet. You will even get to see her one more time. I will send you the location soon and you will come. Then we will see which of us God favors."

"You hurt her or my daughter and God won't save you from what I'll do to you."

"Already with your arrogance! As if you could know what Allah has in store for any of us. But I know what's in store for your wife and little girl! Keep your phone with you, Garitano. I wouldn't want you to miss a single detail."

Then the monster clicked Off.

In another minute, Kristen's blip began to move again along the computer-generated map of Wiesbaden.

"Who do we have out there? Is someone following her?" he demanded of his men.

"Yeah, we've got eyes on," the Communications Sergeant confirmed. But the profanity that followed did not bode well. "There are something like fifty Deutsche Post trucks out delivering mail at this hour. He planned to lose himself among them and he has."

"Then we follow her blip and figure out how to get her back when it stops," Batsin said calmly.

"Let's gear up!" Anthony called to those whom Batsin had chosen to go on the rescue mission.

"Don't suppose I could convince you that you shouldn't be in charge of this operation when you're so emotionally involved, sir?" inquired the Captain.

Anthony glared at the man, then shrugged into his

Kevlar vest and fastened his utility belt around his waist. He checked his pistol—full clip in and safety on—before he holstered it. "I want the usual arsenal at my disposal. This is likely to get loud and ugly. We're gonna do whatever we have to do and come up with answers later."

"Yes, sir. The vehicles are ready and waiting. The LoJack computer is mobile."

Anthony eyed the blinking bright light that indicated his wife's position and knew that he would function more efficiently if he could make himself think of her as just another body to rescue. He grabbed his beret and headed for the door. "Then let's go follow the blip," he said.

SICKENED WITH FEAR, Kristen climbed into the small back seat of the little truck, as she had been instructed to do. Theodore Bjornvik, who called himself Taaoun, came in behind her and sat next to her. She could feel his body heat, smell his sweat. He wore ordinary jeans and a long-sleeved shirt, odd given the summer's heat outside. Though he still had the long hair, he'd cut off the beard Anthony had told her he'd worn before, probably so he could blend in with European society better. He looked like any other citizen. The driver, a big man similarly dressed, had the air-conditioning on, but it did little to reduce the thickness of the air inside the small vehicle. Kristen fought off nausea.

Neither of the men bothered to tie her hands. The kidnapper and his driver must know that she would do nothing to spoil her chances of seeing Amy. But they hadn't gone more than a few blocks when Bjornvik instructed the driver to pull into a dank, secluded alley between two aged brick buildings. Her stomach roiled, but she waited quietly and prayed for mercy.

"Out," said the kidnapper. She climbed out, keeping her eyes cast down as humbly as she could manage. Her nature would have been to face down the object of her fear with a bold glare, but she'd been counseled by Paul not to do that. Obedience and humility in front of men who had embraced the ethos of al-Qaeda might keep her alive longer.

"Come over here," the leader barked at her. The heavyset driver of the car waited in the gloom of the alley. Kristen's mind raced over any number of things that could happen next and her heart began to pound. Yet she made herself walk to Bjornvik. Somehow she sensed that this was not their destination, but only a stopping point. Perhaps they would rough her up here so she'd be less capable of causing trouble for them later.

"Take off your shirt," Bjornvik said, and the other man grinned, revealing a chipped tooth next to a gold crown.

She held back the protest that scrambled up her throat. Silently, she unbuttoned the camouflage shirt she wore. She had a T-shirt on underneath, but she thought there was a good chance she'd have to take that off, too, depending on what these guys had in mind. The overshirt held the camera Batsin had given her, as well as some of the food. One of the pockets held the fake tracking device. She took off the shirt and held it up as if to ask what she should do with it. Bjornvik snatched it from her hands and went through the pockets. Given that he could have gone through them while the garment was still on her body, she let herself hope that perhaps she'd escape for a while longer without having to cope with groping, on top of whatever else they had planned for her.

"What have we here?" he said as he pulled out the little black box hidden in her pocket. Kristen said nothing, but tried to wear an expression that indicated the worthless thing was important to her. Bjornvik pushed a button and it chirped convincingly. He tossed the thing to the ground and crushed it under his heel. It gave a realistic crunch and various authentic looking electronic things spilled out. Kristen shut her eyes for a moment as if grieving the loss. Everything else was removed from the pockets of her shirt. She only hoped he wouldn't strip off the military pin containing the camera. He didn't.

"Search her," commanded Bjornvik as he turned his attention to her cell phone, apparently searching for something among her stored numbers. Through her peripheral vision, Kristen saw the driver grin and move toward her.

She didn't flinch, even though submitting went against every impulse. The driver took great pleasure in splaying his hands over her various body parts. He found the other things Batsin had given her and the water in her pockets. Then he found the medication in her pocket. He tossed the strip of capsules to his boss.

"What's this?" Bjornvik asked as he shook it in her face.

"Medicine," she said simply, eyes lowered. The big man continued to frisk her, discovered the additional medication taped to her thigh, and took great pleasure in unfastening her belt and fly so as to reach down and rip the thing from her skin. On the way, he let his fingers drag over her body along the outside of her panties. He grinned lasciviously until the leader shoved him away from her. The driver dropped the tape of additional medication onto the filthy, broken cement that paved the alleyway. As unobtrusively as possible, Kristen refastened her pants and belt. Bjornvik circled her slowly as she did so, watching her. Her hands shook but she was allowed to accomplish the task. She began to hope that rape was not on the agenda for the time being.

He stopped and moved closer to her, perhaps less wary now that he was certain she wasn't armed. "What is the medicine for?" he said into her ear, pitching his voice to sound threatening.

She chose her words carefully. "I've been treating sick people in the hospital. They have a bad disease. I have to take the medicine so I don't get sick, too. I don't want to spread the disease to others."

He examined the capsules. "So, you figured out what's wrong with them. I had hoped it would take you longer. Did anyone die?"

"Yes," she told him. She found it difficult to talk to him without looking at him, but she managed to keep her eyes mostly downcast. "The first victim."

She caught a glimpse of his smile. His teeth showed white from within his tanned skin. "Yessss," he hissed into her ear like a serpent. She could not suppress a shudder.

Bjornvik laughed at her reaction and shoved her shirt to her. She caught it and shrugged back into it, relieved beyond reason to shroud her body in its bulky confines once again, despite the heat. He kept the medicine and motioned for his helper to continue.

The driver produced a large wand that looked like a hand-held metal detector and ran it over her body. When it came to her lower pocket, it beeped, picking up on the tiny microphone inside. The guy shoved his hand into the pocket, clutching with his fingers to cop another feel. Bile burned halfway up her throat, but she choked it down. If this was as bad as it would get, she'd rejoice.

The tiny device was found in the very depths. The driver handed it to Bjornvik, who enjoyed giving it the same heel treatment as the fake transponder. They took her watch, too. And Bjornvik also destroyed her cell phone, after writing down some data from its memory. Watching him smash it made her feel as if her lifeline had just been severed.

"Get her back into the car. We've been here long enough. And it's time to take the mother to her daughter."

Kristen *did* look up then, right into the man's eyes. Was he really going to take her to Amy? Dared she hope that she would see her baby soon?

"Ah, so I get a reaction from you at last!" he said as he followed her to the car. "Did you think I wouldn't take you to her? I told your husband that he would see both of you alive one last time. I will keep that promise. Meanwhile, there is no reason you should not be with her." His tone seemed almost compassionate now. This only made Kristen more afraid of him.

She got into the car and the kidnapper got in beside her. The small seat forced them to sit shoulder to shoulder and thigh to thigh. Kristen tried hard not to think about how awful it was to have his body pressed to hers. But Bjornvik seemed to sense her distaste. He put his maimed hand on her knee and stroked her through her BDUs. He took special care to rub the stump of his index finger along her thigh.

"These clothes don't suit you. In a short while, we'll get you out of them and see what you have to offer. I'm curious to know what type of woman Garitano finds attractive enough to marry. Perhaps I will enjoy more than looking.''

She'd tried to prepare herself, but the threat still made her blood run cold. She hoped that if he meant to rape her that he'd at least wait until she could get the second stash of medicine for Amy first. She needed to extricate it and hide it somewhere else, perhaps with her daughter or somewhere in the room where they would be held. She spent part of the drive thinking of an excuse to be allowed a few moments in which to do that before they did whatever they wanted. The rest of the time, she lost herself in thoughts about ways to exact revenge on this guy for his crimes against her family.

In another forty-five minutes—Kristen tried to note time as precisely as she could by glancing at Bjornvik's watch—they turned onto a country road and changed cars at an out-of-the-way restaurant. The sedan they got into was no more spacious inside than the postal truck. She still sat wedged against her tormentor. The car was stiflingly hot at first. She could feel sweat dripping down her spine and between her breasts. And yet, she felt cold to her very bones.

Twenty-six minutes later, they left the country road they had been on and traveled down a dirt path for a mile or so. Trees scraped at the car and rocks banged against the chassis, but the car continued through the woods until suddenly an opening spread before them. They approached a fence that appeared to be in the middle of nowhere. She noted signs at intervals along the chain-link barrier that said *Achtung! Eingang Verboten!* and *Kein Übertreten!* The place looked like an abandoned warehouse of some sort, but someone had gone to the trouble of telling people that entrance was forbidden, assuring there would be no trespassing. Germans tended to obey such signs. She could not hope to have a passing hiker come to her rescue.

The guard at the gate bent forward to see who was in the car. The instant he saw Bjornvik, he straightened and saluted. The car moved forward into the clearing. There were buildings here. And people. She quickly counted twenty-two men going about their business. Most carried weapons. All wore grim expressions. It looked just like the pictures of rebel outposts she'd seen in newspapers.

When she got out of the car, she realized she'd been taken to a terrorist camp sitting within easy reach of several major German cities. And no one knew it was here.

CHAPTER SIXTEEN

THERE WERE MOMENTS when Anthony felt as if his lungs were being compressed by a great weight and he had to struggle for air. But he did so surreptitiously, knowing well that the men who had agreed to join him on this clandestine mission might lose heart if they saw their leader succumbing to the horrific knowledge that his wife and baby daughter were in the hands of an al-Qaeda sympathizer. He could not let his men down, could not let them see him waver—because then Kristen's and Amy's chances of survival became next to nothing. So he ignored the tightness around his chest, fought past the occasional light-headedness that threatened to steal his consciousness, and forged ahead with the rescue plan they had devised.

The drive along the roads of Germany seemed interminable. Their grim purpose contrasted sharply with the beauty of the rolling landscape, the lush green of the vegetation, the enchanting colors of the summer wildflowers.

"Where the hell are they going?" Anthony asked without expecting an answer from any of the men in the van. The ride had been predominantly silent and the tension bore down on him until he could barely stand it. "What's out here, Sergeant?" he asked.

"Don't know, sir," volunteered Sergeant Mike Kazzan. "Sometimes the Germans have factories in the strangest places, tucked away in the countryside. If this guy has people helping him, as we suspect, then he must have them stationed somewhere.''

"Maybe they're not all together," offered Dave Batsin. "He could have people scattered, which would be typical terrorist tactics. We could be heading to an out-of-the-way cottage, for all we know. We need to wait and see. That's why we came with equipment to accommodate several different possibilities.''

"There's a car ahead of us, sir. You want me to pass him?'' asked the Sergeant driving the German-registered seven-passenger van that Dave somehow had waiting at the curb when they had been ready to depart.

"Yeah," Dave said. "But as you go around, pace it for a second or two so we can get a look at who's inside. I spotted that same vehicle in front of us a few miles back. I want to be sure it's just coincidence that it's on the same road as our terrorists.''

"You think it could be more of Bjornvik's people?'' Anthony asked, eyeing the vehicle with malice. God, how he itched to just pull out a weapon and blow the thing to bits.

"My suspicions are worse than that," Dave said without elaborating. "Could you all hunker down in your seats a bit so they don't ID us? You, too, sir. We don't want to be recognized." Dave did the same, shielding himself from being seen with his eyes just barely peering over the lip of the window. Only their driver, Sergeant Riker, in the civilian clothes from his aborted mission to follow Kristen, stayed upright.

Anthony slid downward and watched. Dave had become his right-hand man, almost the way Billy Brinewater had been. Despite Anthony's original anger at Batsin for letting Kristen go into harm's way, Dave had made himself so indispensable to the operation that Anthony had been forced to overcome his rage. And in the time since they had started following Kristen's blip on the computer screen, he had come to trust the guy completely. It was clear that Dave had made some careful preparations for recovery before letting Kristen go. For that, Anthony was grateful.

"Damn!" Dave blurted as he scanned the other vehicle and then quickly slid all the way out of sight. "Just what we did *not* need!"

"What?" Anthony felt the all-too-familiar band of pressure clutch at his chest again.

"We listened to the police radio for a while earlier this morning. It seems that the local law enforcement has an interest in following these guys, too. A dead delivery guy and a stolen mail truck got their attention."

Anthony groaned. This was, indeed, the last thing they needed. If the German police were involved, they could stop Anthony and his team from doing what they needed to do to save Kristen and Amy.

"Here's what's going to happen," he said, thinking fast and coming up with a twist to the established plan, as he had done so often when unexpected eventualities presented themselves on missions in the past. "We're ahead of them now and we have no reason to think they recognized us, right?"

"If they see *me,* they'll recognize me. I'm friends with the chief's daughter," Dave admitted.

Anthony blinked. "You're what? The Chief of Police, you mean? His daughter?"

Dave didn't respond, but a deeper color came to his cheeks.

Anthony assimilated this startling fact into his newly developed scheme. "Actually, that can work to our advantage. I was going to ask Sergeant Riker to keep these guys at bay, but now I think you should help him. Tell them anything you want, but keep them away from where we establish our perimeter. Promise them that they can haul the bad guys away when we're done, but keep them from interfering with our work until it's over."

"I can do that, Tony," Dave said. "They won't interfere." But he didn't look happy about it. Clearly, he was thinking about what this would mean to his friendship with the chief's daughter.

"Riker, I need you to make sure nothing gets lost in the translation. These people cannot screw up what we're going to do," Anthony said. The Sergeant nodded his agreement.

"Looks like we're turning off the main road, sir," said the driver, just as the van began to slow. They lurched off the pavement and onto a graveled road. The sunlight became dappled as the vehicle moved into thick trees. "The computer says your wife has come to a stop about a mile up ahead."

"Then we'll find a secluded place along here and begin setting up camp," Anthony said. "Batsin, if the police drive by, leave Riker to watch for them and join us. We're likely to need you."

Anthony knew from experience that he would need this Captain at his side—just as he had always needed Lieutenant Brinewater. The reminder of the men he'd lost didn't make him as weak with grief and guilt as it might have under different circumstances. The fact that these new men had followed him here today, even knowing about his last mission, helped to ease his tormented soul. These soldiers had forced him to appreciate that their lives were their own, to spend as they saw fit, regardless of Anthony's wish to protect them. They did missions like this one because it was their nature to face danger when the need arose—in this case, for the sake of a fellow soldier and a little girl.

BJORNVIK GRIPPED Kristen's arm harder than necessary as he dragged her from the back seat of the sedan. "You want to see your daughter?" he asked.

"Yes," she said, steeling herself for the likelihood that he would deny her wishes. She kept her eyes down, but through her peripheral vision, she noted how the buildings were arranged inside the small compound and where most of the human activity hovered. Could that be an ammunition depot to the left? Were those barracks straight ahead?

"I'll take you to her personally. I want to see your reaction to what you find," he said.

Oh, God! He'd already killed Amy! She must be dead for this madman to say such a thing! He would bring Kristen to her daughter's body and he would take pleasure in observing her horror and pain. Already, she could hardly make her limbs move, despite the prodding of the AK-47 at her spine. Already, a terrible numbness had begun to curl through her, leaving her cold and without hope. Amy was dead, her beautiful child gone!

And then the numbness reached her mind, and although she remained conscious and moving, as her captors demanded, no further coherent thoughts stabbed at her. Her brain had shut down under the impossible weight of her expectations.

They shoved her through a doorway and the sudden lack of sunlight blinded her. Still, she kept walking forward until one of the men grabbed her by the arm and turned her to the left. As her eyes adjusted, she saw that they were walking along a cinder-block corridor. A single exposed lightbulb burned at the end, hanging from a wire strung over a closed door. One of the men went ahead of her and unlocked the door.

The heavy portal swung inward and the opening to another room gaped at her. It seemed even darker than the hallway. Kristen's footsteps faltered as she approached. How could she face this? How would she endure it?

But she had no choice. Bjornvik pushed her forward and she found herself inside a small, naked room. There was no furniture at all and no light except what managed to trickle through the cobwebs covering the two four-inch windows at the very top of the back wall. The only thing in the room besides herself and her kidnapper was a pile of blankets thrown into one corner.

Kristen stared at the bundle of wrinkled cloth and fought back a sob of relief and disappointment. Where was Amy? Had they lied about taking her to her daughter?

But then the blanket in the corner moved ever so slightly and a small cry did, indeed, escape Kristen. Heedless of the weapons trained on her, she ran to the corner and knelt beside the tiny body. She struggled against the urge to gather her baby into her arms. But even though she performed a quick and clinical assessment of Amy's condition, without waking her, tears burned Kristen's eyes and dripped onto the filthy blanket where Amy lay curled in fitful sleep.

Relief that her child lived and rage at the toddler's condition fought for dominance inside her mother's heart. Amy had clearly not been cared for since her abduction the night before. The child's lips were parched, yet her diaper was soaked to overflowing. The stench emanating from beneath her little-girl clothes told Kristen that she would need to clean her up as soon as possible or risk damage to her delicate skin. But then Amy coughed a deep, wet, racking series of coughs that nearly broke Kristen's ability to cope. As she had feared, Amy had contracted the plague. In the hours that the baby had gone untreated, her lungs had become congested, her body feverish.

Keeping her head low, but letting her tears flow freely so that Bjornvik would win the satisfaction of seeing her suffer, Kristen turned toward her tormentors. "Please," she whispered. "If she dies, you will have one less hostage with which to lure your enemies." Bjornvik's laughter tore at Kristen's soul. Oh, how she wanted to rush at him and tear him limb from limb for what he had done to Amy! If only his men would leave them alone for five minutes, she would kill him with her bare hands.

"I'll let you comfort your daughter," he said. "Do what you can for her. I'd like her to be alive when your husband comes for you. But I'll be back for you soon, Mrs. Garitano. I have plans for you while we await your husband's arrival." He tossed her the water bottle his driver had taken from her earlier. Then he motioned to his men to follow him out.

Kristen heard the jangle of keys in the lock. The dead bolt slid into its sleeve. She and Amy were trapped inside the bare walls of the room with nothing but the grimy blanket and the bottle of water—and the hidden medicine for Amy.

THE FENCE WAS ACTUALLY a good thing, Anthony decided, as he snipped through the wires until he'd cut a man-size hole in the mesh barrier. There would be less likelihood of any of the terrorists escaping. As he finished, he looked up at the noon sky and wished night would fall earlier than usual. He'd be more comfortable with a nighttime rescue. But he wouldn't wait. Kristen and Amy could not be left in the hands of Bjornvik any longer than necessary.

"Sir," came First Sergeant Wasserman's voice over Anthony's headset. "We have visual."

Anthony retreated to where some of the equipment had been set up. Most of it remained at their original camp a half mile farther back, but the sensors and listening devices had to be close to the site they wanted to infiltrate.

Keeping conversation to a minimum, Wasserman pointed to a laptop screen where a bright green blob represented Kristen. A smaller one, which appeared to be reclining on the floor, had to be Amy. Seeing this, Anthony grinned. It felt so damn good to see those green indicators of their living, breathing, heat-generating bodies inside the building where Kristen's transponder signal had come to a relative standstill. This was the first sign he'd had that Amy still lived. The fact that Kristen's form moved around the confines of the room they were in also made him happy. She was mobile. That meant she might be able to do something for Amy if she was as sick as Kristen had feared. And they were alone—another relief. No one was torturing them. Yet.

"We have pictures of the interior, too," said Wasserman. He tapped the keyboard until half the screen showed low-density photographs of the interior that changed every half minute or so, revealing Kristen's surroundings to them, showing them what she saw. When pictures of Amy flashed by, Anthony wanted to roar with frustration. His little girl appeared sick and listless.

"How are you getting these? I can't believe they let a camera get by them," he said.

"Camera is part of her U.S. lapel pin. They didn't notice it, but they destroyed the sound device. We have pictures but no audio."

"I'd rather have pictures, if I can't have both." The two of them studied the images, gauging the size of the room, guessing at the depth of the cinder-block walls, noting the placement of the windows. "Those windows are too small and high to be much use," Anthony said. "We'd be better off going through the front door."

"I agree, sir," said Wasserman. "The only other way would be to blast through the wall over here," he pointed to the far end on one photo. "Well away from your daughter and Major Clark."

"Well, let's get the packs ready for all those possibilities." After so much inactivity and bad news, Anthony felt a boiling combination of rage and hope and determination. At least things were moving now. He'd have Amy and Kristen back in the safety of his arms in no time at all.

But his happiness was short-lived. Over his headset he heard Dave's voice. "Major, we have a problem. I need you at the camp, ASAP."

He swallowed frustration—he desperately wanted to continue to set up the perimeter with their various weapons and explosives. He did not want to run all the way back to the camp to resolve Batsin's problem. "You handle it," he ordered.

"Can't, sir. Your attention to this matter is required." In the background, he heard unfamiliar voices, but couldn't make out the words.

"On my way," he said. Batsin had all the authority he needed to take care of anything that might come up, so if he needed Anthony's presence at camp, the problem had to be big. As he jogged by, he motioned for the men to continue deploying the arsenal they'd brought. They hoped to be stealthy and then to swiftly round up the terrorists without much firepower, but if necessary, they were prepared to hold their own small version of shock and awe that would light up the local German sky. He'd do whatever it took to get his family to safety. He'd deal with the consequences later.

Except the consequences caught up with him ahead of time. In the clearing, where their vehicle had been parked and a base of operations had been established, stood the German police officers they had seen on the road before. They didn't look happy.

In a thick German accent, the leader said in English, "You have no jurisdiction here." He made a slashing gesture with one hand. "You must withdraw." He pointed toward the road. "This is a police matter." He thumped himself on the chest.

"Charlie Foxtrot," whispered Anthony, invoking a euphemism for a much worse military epithet.

"Yes, sir," came Dave's equally subdued voice over the headset.

That comment from Dave only provoked Anthony further. "You were supposed to handle this, Captain," he barked over the intercom as he glared at Batsin, who guarded the movements of the rest of the police by training his M-4 on them with calm efficiency. Anthony groaned. U.S. Army weapons pointed at German police probably violated several international laws.

"Yes, sir. The police vehicle drove on by, just as we'd hoped. I headed back toward your location as you ordered. But we're apparently not the only ones with spy equipment. They realized quickly that the bad guys had turned off. Riker tried to stop them. But short of shooting them, there wasn't much he could do.''

He should have shot them, Anthony thought as he glared back at the leader of the four-man crew of German police officers. ''Riker, get over here to translate,'' he said into the microphone.

In a matter of seconds, Sergeant Riker stood beside him. They turned off their transmitters so the parlay wouldn't tie up the radio waves as his men continued their preparations. Riker told him the name of the lead officer, then repeated all of Anthony's words in German.

''Detective Burg, I'm Major Garitano, United States Army, Special Forces. This is a military matter. A U.S. officer has been taken hostage and we're here to get her out.''

''This is German soil, Major,'' cried an outraged Detective Burg. Riker dutifully put this into simultaneous English, whispering into Anthony's ear. ''This is not one of your military bases here. You have no authority. You—''

''You need to lower your voice, Detective.'' Anthony made a soothing gesture with his hands. ''As soon as we get our officer back, we'll hand over all the criminals to you. It'll be win-win, all around.'' He waited for Riker to say this in German.

''This is unacceptable and—'' began the detective in a quieter voice, but then he was interrupted by one of his men, who motioned him over to one of the police cars. Dave eyed them as if he'd enjoy letting off a few rounds in their general direction. An electronic squawk sounded from inside one of the cars.

Riker spoke into Anthony's ear again, alerting him to what the Germans were discussing. ''They've had a communication from other police on the radio. The officer here is explaining that there's been a delay.''

"God damn!" cursed Anthony, and he noted that Riker did not translate this into German. "They're talking about us on their radios?" Anthony strode to the nearest police vehicle and grabbed the microphone out of the startled cop's hand. Then he yanked the thing loose and flung the useless remains to the ground. Reaching inside the car, he perpetrated violence upon the receiver, as well. Over his coms microphone, he said to his men, "I want all these radios out of commission ASAP! We can't do much about the cops on the other end, but we sure as hell don't need our terrorists listening to two-way chatter regarding this operation! If they haven't already figured out we're here, we'll be the luckiest sonsabitches alive.''

WHILE KRISTEN DID HER BEST to clean Amy, using part of the blanket and as little water as possible from the bottle they had let her keep, she searched for camera lenses. There appeared to be only two, hidden in small, chipped-out crevices of the cinder blocks. When she finished with her daughter's hygiene, Kristen paced the room and calculated the likely arc that each camera would capture. There were two places in the confines where she believed she would not be seen. She chose one and made quick work of retrieving the medicine she'd hidden within her body. The condom had done its work and kept the capsules clean. She could only hope that her natural body temperature hadn't overheated them.

She stowed the streptomycin in a pocket and hurriedly reassembled her clothing. The last thing she wanted was to draw the attention of her captors. Staying in their blind zone too long would surely do that. Amy lay still on the floor, but her breathing seemed reasonably even. A good sign. Now, to get some of the lifesaving medication into her.

She uncapped the water bottle again and set it nearby. Taking care to keep her back to the cameras, Kristen took out one capsule from within her pocket, hiding it in her palm. Easing Amy toward her, she opened her daughter's mouth and managed to break the medicine open so that the powder poured onto her tongue. Amy's face scrunched up with distaste. Before she could spit any of it out, Kristen lifted her up a little and put the water bottle to her lips. Some of the liquid dribbled to the floor, but most of it went in and Amy swallowed. Then she began to cough.

It was a wet, phlegmy cough and her entire small body shook. Kristen's heart felt as if it were being torn apart as she listened to it. Sitting on the dirty floor, she held her daughter, trying to lessen the violence of the coughs with the cushion of her own body. She sat there with her a long time, trying to count away the minutes into hours, hoping she would guess correctly when she should give Amy more medicine. Her baby coughed intermittently and when she did, Kristen wanted to give her another dose whether it was time for it or not. But she forced herself to wait, forced herself to follow medical protocol as best she could without her wristwatch. And while she waited and held her child, she willed Amy to recover.

And wondered when Anthony would be able to rescue them from this hellhole.

At last the angle of the weak sunlight streaming through the small windows shifted enough to convince Kristen that it was time for more medicine. Again, she put her back to the cameras. Again, she surreptitiously spilled the powder from a capsule into Amy's mouth. Again, she poured water into her mouth and urged her to swallow.

And the coughing began once more.

Kristen rocked her back and forth, taking little notice of the pins and needles in her right foot and shifting only when numbness threatened. She sang lullabies. She crooned encouragement. But Amy didn't seem to notice. At least not until the coughs subsided once more. For a few moments, the girl rested easy in the cradle of Kristen's arms. Then her huge round eyes—so like her father's—fluttered open.

Recognition was slow to come, but when it did, a slight smile trembled on her little-girl lips. "Mommy?"

"I'm here, sweetheart," Kristen whispered as she looked down into that trusting face. Love suffused her, so powerfully she ached with it. "Everything's going to be all right now. Sleep a little more, baby." Gently she rocked her again, hoping the medicine and rest would heal her. Hoping sleep would shield her from memories of her ordeal. Hoping that if the bad men came for Kristen, her daughter would not witness their abuse. Praying that Amy would be spared.

Time drifted on. When a rattle at the door announced someone's arrival—not the good guys yet, given the muffled conversation with the guards—Amy barely stirred when Kristen shifted her to the floor. By the time the door swung open on squeaking hinges, she'd tucked the ragged blanket around her daughter, pulling a corner partly over her face in an attempt to muffle sounds and inhibit vision. Kristen knew what could happen next. And she didn't want Amy to have to watch.

CHAPTER SEVENTEEN

THE HOURS STOLEN from the operation while Anthony subdued and mollified the German police officers were the longest in his life. Internally, he raged at the loss of every second. But he could not move forward with their plan until he'd reached some sort of accord—not without jeopardizing the careers of every man who had followed him to this terrorist compound.

A pack of American twenty-dollar bills had helped, along with a whole lot of diplomacy—something Anthony could force himself to engage in, but hated. The explanation of what the terrorists were likely to do if they suspected American soldiers were sitting on their doorstep put the fear of God into the Germans. Still, the cops didn't give up control easily. The sun had begun to set before Anthony had gained acquiescence of the police. Kristen and Amy remained alone and alive, according to the reports he'd listened to through his headset even as he coaxed and prodded the police into letting the soldiers do what they did best. Everyone would benefit in the end.

Darkness surrounded them by the time Anthony was able to turn his full attention back to getting his wife and daughter to safety. Not a problem—the Rangers usually did their best work at night. He would slip into the camp and get his family. Once they were safely away, the rest of them would round up the terrorists and turn them over to the cops. For the first time, Anthony began to imagine that success was within his reach.

"He's going to go nuts when we tell him this, Fang," he heard Sergeant Kazzan say to Dave over the coms. The Sergeant sounded grim and Anthony felt his hopes fly away into the night.

"Tell him anyway, Kaz," Dave said. "He'll want to know."

"Yes, sir. Is he still with the Germans?"

Anthony clicked on his microphone. "I'm listening. What's up?"

"Problem, sir. Someone's gone into the place where your wife is being held. She seems to be doing a very slow rotation around the perimeter of the room, staying out of reach of whoever is in there with her. Your daughter is stationary. Photographs aren't clear because Major Clark keeps moving."

Anthony came to a standstill and closed his eyes. This was what he'd hoped to spare Kristen. This was why his time with the Germans had been so difficult to endure. He'd taken too long and now someone—probably Bjornvik himself—was going to hurt Kristen. His lungs seemed to contract and he found himself drawing air in quick, difficult gasps.

He forced himself to breathe. Then he forced himself to think. Finally, as he strode to the second camp's computer area, where another laptop would show him Kristen's pictures, he spoke into the communicator to everyone on the frequency. "We need a diversion that won't give away our position. Anything that would require the bastard's attention. I'll take any ideas—"

Abruptly, his cell phone vibrated in his pocket. It was a military issue satellite phone, nearly impossible to geolocate, so he'd left it on, recalling that Bjornvik said he'd be in touch again.

"Yes?" he said into it.

"Major Garitano, I have your lovely wife here with me. She seems reluctant to let me get too close to her, but she won't have any choice soon. I thought you'd want to listen in on everything, maybe even give your wife a few words of encouragement."

Anthony bent forward against the acid pain that seemed to fill his stomach. Somehow, he managed to keep his cry of outrage bottled up inside him. If he said anything, he was certain he would lose his weak grip on himself. Yet he had to force himself to speak. "Where is she? Where is my daughter? You said you wanted me to see them again, so tell me where they are." The subterfuge was necessary so the terrorist wouldn't know how close he already was to the encampment or that he could see his movements on a computer screen.

"Yes, perhaps it's time to tell you how to find them and what to do. First, you must come alone and unarmed. Tricks will only get them killed before you reach them. Second, you must come here between ten and eleven o'clock."

"What happens after eleven?"

He laughed. "I have things planned and your wife and daughter will be in the way. So if you arrive after eleven, you won't see them again and my fun will be spoiled. Do you want the directions for finding them?"

"Yes." He said this even as he watched the green lights that represented Bjornvik and Kristen and Amy. He listened intently as the man gave him directions. He was expected to follow the same route they had already taken hours ago. Bjornvik told him which building and assured him that his path to the door would not be obstructed. He explained that when he arrived, the door would be unlocked. That only meant that the bastard would have to incapacitate Kristen.

"I want to talk to my wife so I know she's still alive. And I'll be calling again before I get near you, to make sure she's alive then, too."

"As you wish. Here she is."

"Anthony," said Kristen, sounding strong and in control.

"I'm here, Kristen." And he hoped she understood that he really was nearby, preparing to rescue her. "How's Amy?"

"She's sick. She needs a hospital."

"Keep her alive, Kristen. I'll come for you soon."

"I know you wi—" and she was cut off as Bjornvik took back his phone.

"I'm disappointed. No love talk, no last words. I expected more. But perhaps I'll get a reaction if I let you listen in on what happens next. Should I hurt your daughter, Garitano?"

"If you touch her, I swear I'll take you apart one piece at a time." And Anthony saw that Kristen's green light moved so that she stood between Bjornvik and Amy.

"Really? Well, you'll have to find me first. But on second thought, since your child is already nearly unconscious, she won't be much fun. So, let's see what you think of what I'm about to do to your wife..."

Anthony heard a scraping noise and then the voices seemed farther away. He realized that Bjornvik had put the phone down while leaving the line open. He wanted Anthony to hear whatever would be done to his wife.

With stomach tightened and lungs compressed, he listened. Not able to make out the faraway words, he waited for screaming to begin as he turned around and around in small, frustrated circles. Then he caught Dave Batsin's eye. Dave held up five fingers indicating that whatever diversion he'd rigged would engage in five seconds. A lot could happen to Kristen in the time it could take the kidnappers to register that there was a problem, but Anthony took heart. Whatever Dave had in mind would have to be good enough. He only hoped it would distract Bjornvik from his immediate plans for Kristen.

From the phone, he heard Bjornvik. "Take off your clothes, Mrs. Garitano. Or I'll take out my frustrations on your daughter."

KRISTEN'S EVERY INSTINCT demanded that she resist, but she knew she would not be able to protect her child for long if she did. And the bastard had a man standing just outside the closed door with an AK-47. Bjornvik had been smart enough not to come inside the room with a gun of his own. Kristen would have found a way to get it away from him and she would have shot him dead without a moment's hesitation. But she could not see even a knife on him, or anything else she could use as a weapon.

So, resigning herself to whatever she had to do to keep Amy safe, Kristen began to unbutton her camouflage shirt.

"Hurry up, or I'll do it for you," barked an impatient Bjornvik as he unbuckled his belt and began to undo his fly.

She managed to get her outer shirt off but couldn't force herself to remove her T-shirt, despite his demands. So Bjornvik rushed her and shoved her against the damp cinder blocks so hard, her head collided with the wall and stars appeared throughout her vision. Then he began to taunt her.

"Do you see this?" he said as he held up his hand with the missing index finger. "See what your husband did to me?" He pressed the stump beneath her nose and Kristen could tell the area had not been treated properly. It hadn't healed well and the stench at such close range was overpowering. Despite her training, or perhaps because of her throbbing head, her stomach turned over.

Some part of her mind remained clinical, even as her body revolted against the assault. Bile threatened to rise up her throat. And when he finally used one meaty hand to hold her head still so he could rub the hideous fingerless knuckle along her lips, she began to retch. He pulled back just in time to avoid having her vomit right into his face. Instead, she coughed up the contents of her stomach down the front of his clothing. Most of it landed in the general region of his open fly.

Kristen felt a blade of hysteria lance through her and she almost laughed. That would have been fatal, for her or for Amy. She managed to hold back, but barely. The vomit dripped from him as he stood still, looking down at himself in disbelief and growing horror.

In the next instant, before she could brace herself, his fist came whizzing toward the side of her head and she went airborne. First she was weightless and then she hit the cement floor, shoulder first. The pain didn't register for what seemed like a long time. He shouted at her, but she couldn't tell what he said through the echoes within her skull. Then the side of her face seemed to go up in flames where his blow had landed. Next, her skin on her shoulder began to scream from being scraped along the rough floor. The muscle and bone beneath the raw flesh were the last to be heard from, but what finally registered felt sharp and intense. Blackness hovered around the perimeter of her vision. But she refused to allow herself the relief of unconsciousness. Her daughter needed her.

Kristen struggled to her hands and knees. She retched again, but nothing remained in her stomach to come up. Ignoring the protests of her body, she somehow got to her feet, preparing herself mentally for his next attack. This time she would do better at submitting to him, now that she had real pain to focus on. Recalling what Anthony had said to her earlier, she steeled herself to do whatever it took to keep them both alive.

But Bjornvik didn't come after her again. A second or two passed before she realized he stood on the opposite side of the room, conferring with some men in the doorway. Bjornvik gave a roar of frustration. He turned and came toward her, anger pouring from every cell. She cowered, prepared for more violence. But he stooped halfway to pick up his phone. Snapping it shut, he glared at her.

"I'll be back. Soon. You can look forward to it." Then he turned and quit the room.

"Sir, the target appears to be leaving the room," said Sergeant Kazzan. "I guess our distraction worked."

Anthony looked over the heads of the team members monitoring the computers and listening devices and made a motion across his throat for Sergeant Riker to stop what he'd been doing. Riker, who'd been waiting for just such a signal, released the button on the side of the police radio microphone into which he'd been impersonating a German cop.

"It worked?" Dave asked as he eyed Anthony for some sign of success.

Anthony nodded. "Don't sound so surprised. There's

no way they could ignore radio communications from German police indicating the cops were closing in on their hiding place." Anthony's tension had only just begun to ebb. He took a deep breath and let it out.

He'd watched the screen intently, had wanted to do violence when he'd seen the light that represented Kristen go flying to one side from an apparent blow, had felt his eyes sting with a painful mixture of pride and relief and fury when he'd seen her figure get back on her feet. Now, he stared at the screen that once again showed Kristen and Amy alone in their cell.

"I wasn't sure they'd be smart enough to be monitoring the police communications," Dave said. "I'm glad it worked. Now we need to get Major Clark and your daughter the hell out of there."

"I'll take Kazzan with me," Anthony said.

"Yes, sir," said Kazzan at the same time that Dave said, "No way, sir."

Anthony glared at his second in command. Dave returned the look. "This is a military operation, Major. You are not the one best suited to retrieve the captives."

"The hell I'm not! And last I checked, I'm in charge here. Kazzan, get your pack." And Anthony stalked toward his gear, resting against a tree.

"With all due respect, sir," said Dave, dogging his heels and murmuring with his microphone off. "You must know that you can't go in there. You'll take too many chances with your own life to save your wife and child and that will put the whole mission at risk."

Anthony ignored him, reached for his backpack and hoisted it onto his shoulders.

"Tony!"

Anthony scowled. "You're not married, are you, Batsin?"

Dave admitted he was not.

"No children?"

"No, sir."

"Then shut the hell up." He looked over to Sergeant Riker who was making nice with the Germans. "Make sure you're ready to get Amy and Kristen quickly to the medevac helicopter the police have on its way. Kazzan!" And with that, Anthony and the Sergeant left the small camp and headed into the woods toward the hole Anthony had cut into the fence line hours before.

KRISTEN HAD ONLY ENOUGH time to put her clothes back in order and stroke Amy's hot brow a little before her tormentor came back, crashing through the door so violently that Amy began to cry. She had only a moment in which to notice that her baby's coughing seemed slightly easier than it had been. If Amy could be rescued soon, then she might survive. And hadn't Anthony implied that he was nearby and coming to get them?

Bjornvik grabbed Kristen by the arm. When Amy clung to her, the man shoved the child aside and pulled Kristen upright. Amy's outrage became loud enough to nearly split eardrums and Kristen cooed, even as she was dragged to the center of the room. There was no telling what these people might do to Amy if they thought her an inconvenience.

And Amy seemed to understand the desperation of the situation, because she scooted back into the corner with her dirty, tattered blanket and whimpered while her huge round eyes watched what the bad men were doing. Kristen hadn't realized that her captors had brought in a wooden chair until they plunked her into it. They'd dragged other things into the room, as well.

Bjornvik put his face close to hers. "I don't have

much time. We'll have to advance our schedule a bit. Sorry to disappoint you, my dear, but I won't be able to enjoy you after all.''

She tried once to get up from the chair as she saw the others taking out rope and something attached to electrical wires. But Bjornvik pressed her down onto the wooden seat with a heavy hand to her shoulder. Fear coiled inside Kristen as she watched the men sort through the things they'd brought in. She suddenly felt very cold. Her fingers were freezing. And yet her heart beat so hard, she thought everyone in the room must be able to hear it.

''I'll do whatever you want,'' she said. ''Just don't hurt my little girl.'' She knew she was begging and that it was hopeless to do so, but she couldn't keep herself from trying.

Bjornvik hunkered down on his haunches and looked up into her face while one of his men tied Kristen's hands behind the back of the chair and began to wrap the rope around her body and legs. ''I've decided that you are very brave and perhaps a good mother,'' he said to her in a soothing voice, making Kristen shiver with revulsion. His expression would have been compassionate on any other face. ''So I won't make this any harder than necessary for you or for your daughter. The crimes are not yours, and yet you will pay a high price for the vile man you married. That is the way the world works.'' And he ran the back of his injured hand gently down her cheek, which she realized then was wet with tears.

''It will be quick,'' he said. ''I promise you that. And your last sight will be that of your husband and daughter. You will be together. That is all I can offer you.''

Before she could spit in his face—the only act of defiance she had left to her now that she was immobilized—he stood up and spoke to his people in what sounded like Arabic. The man who had tied her up departed and another came close and took up her field of vision. He had dark, intelligent eyes, but they were devoid of emotion. He set to work with the wires and what appeared to be a timing device.

That's when she knew. The bulkier parts that lay at her feet were explosive packs. The wires and timing device would be attached to it, to be exploded whenever Bjornvik wished. But the reality turned out to be still worse than the picture she'd pieced together. For when they were finished, the timing device was set for thirty seconds and the trip wire was threaded to the door.

When Anthony came in to rescue her, he would set off the bomb that had been wrapped around her torso. Everyone within a hundred feet of her would die, too. They would have thirty seconds to make eye contact and perhaps say a few words. But then the end would be quick, just as Bjornvik had promised.

Unless she could warn Anthony in time. She wished to God that her tiny microphone hadn't been found and destroyed when they'd searched her. Still, she could at least keep shouting warnings in the hope that her voice wouldn't run out before Anthony heard her.

Then Bjornvik stood in front of her again. He had a length of cloth and a small rubber ball in his hand. He tossed the ball back and forth from hand to hand. Kristen closed her eyes against despair. But when the vile man pushed the ball into her mouth she didn't dare resist, for fear that she'd set off the explosives prematurely. He wrapped the cloth around her mouth and tied it behind her head. There was no way she could warn Anthony now. And she'd be denied the ability to tell him she loved him in those thirty seconds they'd have before the end.

THERE WERE PLENTY of trees inside the fence, as well as outside. They were old and bulky and provided excellent cover. Although it took a considerable amount of time, there was a half moon and Anthony and Kazzan had no trouble making their way unseen in the semi-darkness to the side of the building where Amy and Kristen were being kept. They communicated mostly in hand signals, not daring to speak into the communicators except when necessary. Slowly, they crept to a position where they could see the door and the area in front of the target building.

The two men stretched out on the ground side by side on a rise and scanned the area through their night-vision goggles. Resisting the impulse to go down Rambo-style to save his family in a blaze of gunfire, Anthony activated his microphone. "Status?" he asked of his men back at the camp, who were watching Amy and Kristen on their equipment.

"They had visitors while you were in transit. Major Clark is now in the center of the room, sir. Appears unable to move. Maybe tied to something. From the position of her limbs, they might have tied her to a chair. Your daughter is able to move and she tried to get closer to your wife, but then she stopped and went back to her corner. The photographs are static shots of a wall."

Anthony thought hard about what this could mean. The two were alone in the room, so why weren't they huddled together? For the first time, he wished he could trade in the photographs her equipment sent them and get sound instead. If Kristen had retained the transmitter, she'd be giving them details of her situation now.

"Is she moving at all, attempting to communicate?" Anthony asked.

"Hold on," said the voice into his ear. The silent seconds that followed seemed like an eternity to Anthony. Finally, "We think maybe she's moving her hands in a set rhythm. We're attempting to get heat signals from a different angle to confirm."

"We don't have much time," Anthony grumbled. Then he did what he'd been trained to do and waited. While he did so, he thought about the situation. What would Bjornvik have intended by putting Kristen in a chair in the center of the room? A terrible thought ran through his mind.

Bjornvik had wanted Anthony to see his family one more time, but Anthony certainly couldn't have expected to live through the experience if he'd done things Bjornvik's way. Having set traps of his own during his career as a Ranger, Anthony realized that he'd taken too long in coming for Kristen and Amy. If he went through the front door as he'd planned, something terrible would happen.

Just then, his headset squawked at him again. "She might be attempting to do Morse code," said the voice.

"Let me help you out," said Anthony. "She's trying to warn me away."

A moment's hesitation, then Dave's grim voice agreed. "Yes, sir, she's spelling the word *bomb*. My guess is that when you open the door, everything goes cablooey."

Anthony let his forehead drop to his arm. He'd hoped to neutralize any guards and ease through the only door. That wouldn't be possible now. "Get ready to make some noise. Blow something up near the gate when I give the word."

"Yes, sir," Dave said and Anthony thought the man sounded more than ready to start setting off explosives.

"Just a small distraction. Not the whole show. At least not until I have them safely away."

"Got it."

Kazzan's gaze lifted from his own set of goggles and swiveled to Anthony's. "There's no one near the building, sir. That means they're expecting some big fireworks that they don't want to be caught in."

"But they're watching the show from somewhere. My guess is cameras, which we need to neutralize before we enter the target area."

"There's some activity from that water tower over there." Kazzan pointed.

There were people there, but Anthony couldn't discern whether any of them was actually Bjornvik. "Make sure you point out that particular spot to Captain Batsin when the cavalry arrives to scoop up these bad guys. No one escapes."

"Yes, sir."

"Do we have a bomb defusion expert with us?" he asked Dave through his microphone.

"No, but I'll patch one through the coms if you give me some time to get one on the phone."

"Do that. But we don't have much time." Then Anthony motioned for Kazzan to follow and the two made their way across and then down the hill toward the back of the building. They found and cut the wires to the cameras first, but doing this made Anthony's blood run cold. Bjornvik might be able to blow Kristen up remotely and he could decide to do so once he realized his cameras had gone dead. Time was running out.

He and Kazzan worked silently and efficiently. When they were done, there was a small explosive device set against the back cinder blocks. It wasn't enough to knock a hole through—that would risk injuring the people on the other side and setting off the explosives within—but just enough to loosen things up so he and Kazzan could make an opening through which the hostages could be extricated.

Anthony was good at setting up explosions. He knew exactly how much to use for just the right effect. Making something blow up wasn't hard. Making something *not* blow up was much harder. He hadn't had much to do with defusing bombs. There were other experts for that. Defusing bombs had been one of Weasel's specialties. What Anthony wouldn't give to have Weasel at his side right now.

"You don't know anything about defusing bombs, do you, Kazzan?" he asked as the two made their way back up the hill with a detonation line unrolling behind them.

"I took a class once," said the Sergeant.

"Forget it," Anthony said as he took cover behind a sturdy tree trunk. When he was certain Kazzan had done the same, he said into the headset, "Five seconds, Fang."

"On your mark, sir."

"Mark," said Anthony and he tripped the device that would send a current through his wire to the little bomb he'd made outside the prison wall. Five seconds later, his explosives went off. But the sound was obliterated by the much larger explosion that lit up the horizon near the gate. Dave had provided the necessary distraction in spades.

"Let's go," he barked to Kazzan. And the two raced toward the smouldering side of the building.

KRISTEN HAD BEEN struggling to continue her feeble attempt at sending a message to her rescuers with the only part of her body she could still move. She didn't dare do more for fear of setting off the explosives wrapped around her body, but she could lift her tied hands and let them fall in a certain rhythm. She could only hope she remembered enough Morse code to make sense to the men who might be able to see her.

At first, she'd been worried that Amy would toddle too close and accidentally set off the bomb. But Amy had heeded her mother's frantic grunts and muffled shouts and had returned to the corner with her blanket, still too sick to make more of an effort to get close.

Now, Kristen feared losing consciousness and falling over. She'd been awake for well over forty hours, unable to take those quick cat naps that Anthony had been trained to grab whenever he could. And she'd sustained an injury to her head when Bjornvik had shoved her against the wall. Now, her inability to move, combined with all the other factors, made it difficult to keep her eyes from drifting closed, despite the gravity of the situation.

If she lost her battle to stay conscious, she might not wake up again. But she'd already hummed through her gag all the lullabies she could remember, both to remain awake and to soothe her daughter. She'd mentally reviewed the alphabet in Morse code and had begun sending her message, such as it was, keeping time with her muffled humming. But her hands had gone numb from the tight rope holding them and her eyelids wouldn't cooperate. When they slid closed, she dreamed in slow motion that her daughter looked at her with a trusting gaze even as the chair began to topple. Slowly, slowly the wire went tight as the chair tilted. The timing device tripped and thirty seconds ticked by, then there was a sudden explosion.

Her eyes snapped open just as she heard the terrible sound and for a moment, she couldn't understand why she was still alive and able to see. Then she realized that she hadn't set off her own bomb. Instead, there had been a huge detonation outside the building. She could still hear debris falling to the ground. Through the window, she heard people shouting far away.

A closer sound came to her ears then—a noise like the rasping of huge claws along the outer wall behind her. Amy whimpered, but stayed where she was. Kristen realized her daughter would need more of her medicine soon, but there was nothing she could do about that now.

The clawing noise came again. Then fresh air touched her nostrils from a breeze that seemed to come through the cinder blocks. She couldn't turn her head far enough to see what was happening. But she heard the rasp and scrape of bricks being moved.

"Kristen, I'm coming," came a voice she'd thought she might never hear again. A welcome voice, a cherished voice. "We know there's a bomb attached to you. Just hold still and hold on."

As if she would or could move. He was here, just as he'd promised! And he knew about the danger and hadn't come through the booby-trapped door. Everything would be okay, now. They would get Amy to a hospital in time. They would survive!

And then he stood in front of her, and there was fire in his eyes. "I'm going to get you out of here, Kristen," he promised as he very carefully unfastened her gag and took the ball from her mouth.

Her jaw muscles spasmed, but she forced herself to speak. "Get Amy out first, Anthony," she said. "You'll need to take your time untangling me from this mess, so leave me and take her out first.''

"I've got another man on guard outside. I'll just hand Amy to him and come right back. I won't leave you," he said as he rushed to the dirty mound that was his daughter in the corner. Anger flashed in his eyes as he scooped her up.

"Make sure he gets her to a hospital. He shouldn't wait for us. She needs help right away," Kristen said.

"Dada?" Amy whispered as she nestled into the protective comfort of his arms.

"I'm here, sweetie," he said and Kristen could tell there were tears in his heart, too. But as he made his way toward the opening in the back wall, they both heard the pop, pop, of a gun, followed by shots close by. It had to be the man Anthony had sent to guard, returning fire.

"Five minutes to clear up what's going on out there and to get Kazzan on his way," Anthony said. "I'll be back for you."

She gave a slight nod and he moved out of her peripheral vision. Before he slipped through the opening, she heard him shout to his man outside and then position his own weapon for firing. "I love you, Kristen," he called back to her.

Then he and Amy were gone and Kristen sat alone, without anyone for whom she had to be brave or fierce, but with the explosives embracing her body and abject fear clawing at her heart.

CHAPTER EIGHTEEN

ANTHONY MADE SURE the way was clear, and then carried Amy to where Kazzan hunkered down behind some rusted barrels. "Take her back to camp. Get her on the medevac. Don't wait for us," he ordered.

"Sir?" said the Sergeant as if he couldn't believe his ears. "I can't leave you here alone. Let's call for someone to come get her and—"

"There's no time for that," Anthony said over the arrhythmic staccato of gunfire. "She's not doing well. So this is an order, Sergeant—take my daughter to safety. I'll cover you. Get her onto that helicopter and out of here."

Kazzan looked as if he wanted to protest further, but he took Amy when Anthony thrust the child into his arms.

"Da-deeee!" wailed Amy. Another bullet whizzed overhead. Anthony returned fire and then ducked back down to where Kazzan held the sick child. Her eyes were huge and swimming with fear and sickness. She reached toward Anthony and he felt as if his heart would shatter if he didn't take her back into his embrace. But he couldn't do that. Not now.

And maybe he would never get another chance.

"Quiet, honey," he said to her as he stroked her hair. "It's very important that you be real quiet for a while." She seemed too tired to make more of a fuss, so she just stared at him from the arms of the man he'd entrusted with her care. "I love you, Amy," he said, his voice came out raspy and uneven.

He tore his gaze from her, knowing he had no time for sentimentalities. Turning onto his stomach, he readied his weapon for rapid fire. "When I spray the area, go that way," he said to Kazzan as he pointed. "Send back whoever can be spared to help us."

And as soon as Anthony raised himself high enough to splatter the area with bullets, Kazzan and Amy were gone, running for the denser trees. God, if anything happened to them, he'd never forgive himself. Yet he knew he'd done his best. Nothing he could have done differently would have made things easier now.

He heard over his headset that the team members back at the camp had Kazzan and Amy on their heat-sensing computer screens. They also realized that Anthony had come under fire. Whatever help could be spared would arrive in due course. He couldn't wait. Bjornvik could order Kristen's bomb to be detonated at any time. He had to get her out of there now.

AFTER LONG SECONDS of listening to her own hammering heartbeat, punctuated with the faraway pops and booms of the war taking place outside, Kristen heard people right outside the booby-trapped door. They seemed to be arguing among themselves. Even without knowing the language, she could deduce that they weren't sure how to get inside without blowing themselves up. Yet they clearly wanted to get inside. With shards of cold anxiety slicing her insides, she realized that Anthony's rescue attempt had been discovered.

And terrible thoughts began to swim like circling sharks through her murky, sleep-deprived head. She wondered if he would come back for her. And even if he did come back, would he forgive her for overriding his wishes in regard to Amy's rescue? Had he said he would when they'd talked on the cell phone? She couldn't remember. But she recalled that their marriage had been teetering on the brink of failure. And surely this whole experience wouldn't help. If they survived.

The voices grew louder on the other side of the door and something about their urgency reminded her that Anthony would not leave a fellow soldier behind if there was any way to avoid it. He would be back, no matter how he felt about her as a wife. And then the terrorists would have nothing. That must be why they were so determined to get into the room.

The very thought of being recaptured and used as a tool against her husband and his team made her sick. She took in great gulps of air through her mouth and tried hard not to let her mind wander too far into despair.

At least Amy was away from here. Anthony would make sure she got to safety. She would be okay. But even these thoughts did little to chain the panic that snarled and gnashed at her as the seconds ticked by.

Just when her body began to quake with fear and tremble with fatigue, her husband appeared before her again. Relief made her vision blur and her sense of balance tilt. He turned on a light attached to his helmet, no longer caring to be stealthy, and she blinked against the sudden brightness. She could see him no better now than when he'd been a dark shadow, but his voice came to her, soothing and calm. The dizziness subsided.

"Amy?" she asked.

"Heading for the medevac. I'm going to cut your ropes, Kristen, but you have to try not to move too much. I'm not sure how this bomb is rigged. We need to do everything slowly.''

"Some of the terrorists want to get in through the door," she said as hope and dread tugged her in different directions. In another moment, her hands were freed and she could gently flex her fingers so blood began to circulate again. Then he cut through the ropes at her feet.

"I know. I can hear them, too. But we'll have you out of here before they figure out what they're doing." He wielded his blade confidently around the wires so that he cut through only the bindings that held her torso to the chair.

When she was free of the ropes but not the explosive material, he spent a precious second or two helping her relax her arms and legs into more normal positions, slowly so she didn't set anything off. Her fingers tingled and her legs ached as blood began to circulate through normal pathways once again.

While a louder argument broke out beyond the door, Anthony turned a little away and inquired into his headset, "Where's that expert we were talking about, Fang?" As he listened to the response, she saw his mouth go thin and felt the tension in his body ratchet up another notch. Yet when he faced her again, he forced a smile.

"We can't wait any longer, so we're going to get these explosive packs off you and bolt for the opening in the wall. I'm going to defuse the mechanism, but these things can't be trusted, so I need you to get out of here as fast as you can go the instant you're free. When you clear the building, enemy fire will be coming from the left. Duck and weave until you can take cover to the right. Don't look back. Just go. I'll be right behind you. Understand?"

"Yes," she said, hoping that her legs would work

well enough. She didn't want to hinder Anthony's escape by stumbling. "Do you know how to defuse bombs like this?"

He huffed in exasperation as he squatted to examine the connections and timing device. "You don't suppose your U.S. Government would spend millions of dollars on my training and not teach me something as vital as this, do you?" he asked conversationally while the voices on the other side of the door became interspersed with thuds and grunts. But Kristen saw the gleam of sweat on Anthony's brow and found herself closing her eyes against any other signs of the strain he was under. She needed to believe he was as calm and cool as he sounded. She wanted to delude herself that they would get out alive.

"So, let's see. We've got a red wire going this way and a blue wire here," he muttered as he held his knife ready to cut one. "Seems pretty simple. The red one should do it." He cut the wire. In the next instant, the timing device went "ping."

All at once, he stood up and slid the six-inch blade along the fastenings that held the explosives to her. The packs slid off of her, but she detected an ominous tick tick tick that made her blood run cold. She couldn't help but notice that the numbers on the timer were changing downward, second by second.

"Go, go, go!" he shouted. And she scrambled from the chair, heart hammering.

Her legs didn't want to obey. The opening in the wall, beyond which darkness yawned, appeared to be miles away. But she scrambled as fast as she could, half on her feet and half on her knees. Desperate not to hold Anthony back, she launched herself through the opening and into the cool night. The rat-a-tat of bullets began immediately, but as soon as her mind registered the sound and the need to take cover, the building she'd just left blew up.

She went deaf in that instant and heard nothing at all as her body sailed away from the explosion, borne on the violent wind that swept from the collapsing building. She had just enough time to cover her head with her hands and arms before she landed.

She had no time to lie dazed upon the damp ground. She couldn't hear whether the gunfire had resumed after the surprise of the blast, but she was sure it would any minute. Her survival instinct took over and lifted her to her hands and knees. She crawled behind a tree off to the right, as Anthony had ordered.

Anthony! Where was he? He'd said he'd be directly behind her! And he had been, she was sure of it. She remembered feeling the pressure of his palm on her lower back, urging her through the wall and away from the ticking bomb. She'd lost the sensation of him behind her when she'd been thrown and now nothing seemed as imperative as finding him again.

Oh, God! There he was, lying motionless on the ground, too close to the demolished building and with nothing between him and the enemy. Debris still sifted down on him, visible because of the light on his helmet that had somehow withstood the blast. That light made him an easy target. The terrorists would have him properly sighted along the barrels of their AK-47s any minute. She had to get him to safety before they recovered from the shock of the explosion and started shooting again.

Her brain seemed to shut down against the horror of her husband's danger, against the futility of any attempt to rescue him. Yet her body acted of its own accord, darting from tree to tree to get closer to his inert form. Then, without giving more than passing thought to her own danger, she dashed into the open to where he lay.

Somehow, her trembling fingers managed to shut off his light, shielding them in the limited security of darkness. Then she hoisted him quickly into a fireman's carry and headed for the relative safety of the wooded area. As she staggered along, she saw dirt and leaves spatter upward all around her as the gunfire she still couldn't hear began again.

Almost as soon as she reached cover behind the first substantial tree, her body gave out under the weight of her husband and she collapsed. It had been a miracle she'd lifted him at all.

She could make out some sounds now, shouting voices and renewed gunfire, as if they were all underwater. One shot splintered the bark from her refuge and sent shards flying toward her face. She winced and bent over Anthony, protecting him with her body.

She said a little prayer and may have even engaged in a bit of silent bargaining with God as she checked for his pulse. There it was, strong and steady. But her groping hands felt blood oozing from the back of his head. And there was something wrong with the back of his shirt, too. It felt torn and hot in places. But she had no time for a more thorough examination. She needed to focus on keeping them both alive.

More detonations resounded in the night, distant and muffled. She supposed Anthony's team members had their hands full. She couldn't expect the cavalry to come rescue her. And yet, she knew it would be only minutes before the terrorists came and got them. She had to *do* something, anything, to keep them at bay.

That's when her hand fell upon Anthony's M-4, still

strapped to his shoulder. Had the situation not been so desperate, she would have laughed. A Ranger is never parted from his weapon, even when he's nearly been blown up. Except when a wife unfastens it from his shoulder strap, as she did now. She'd trained on the M-16 and had never touched an M-4 in her life, but she figured it would fire pretty much the same. All she had to do was aim it toward the bad guys and keep on squeezing the trigger until help arrived.

What if she actually hit someone? As a healer, she loathed the possibility of killing. But the crunch of boots on dried vegetation, coming from the direction where the terrorists had been, erased everything from her mind except the need to protect the unconscious soldier at her side—the man she loved more than life itself.

She raised the weapon to her shoulder and fired.

ANTHONY CAME BACK to consciousness reluctantly. The empty, cold, black peace seemed infinitely more appealing than the throbbing pain that any attempt at wakefulness brought him. But he could hear Kristen's voice calling to him again. She kept telling him he needed to open his eyes now. She kept saying she needed him to come back to her.

He called on deep resources to lift his weighted eyelids. And he wished to God he hadn't made the effort when the overhead light pierced his brain like a laser. But Kristen called his name earnestly and he had to respond somehow. Fluttering his eyes open seemed far less work than forming a word.

"You're awake!" she said, the relief and joy in her voice made him smile without even trying. The flex of facial muscles tore at him, exacerbating the pain that seemed to surround his skull, but he was just so damned glad to see her, it didn't really matter.

"We made it, Anthony! We're all alive." Her face glowed with happiness and his heart brimmed with love for her. How could he have ever considered leaving her?

Another face appeared in his line of vision next to Kristen's, blotting out more of the awful light. Dave Batsin leaned over and looked at him critically. "Looks like you'll live after all, Major."

Had he been in peril of dying? Anthony wondered. He couldn't remember anything at all after seeing the timing device begin to tick away the seconds remaining of his life and Kristen's. But here he was, apparently in a hospital room, if the antiseptic scent and chirp of electronics were any indication. And these two babbling fools seemed to think his return to consciousness was only slightly short of a miracle.

"Amy?" he asked, and his voice scraped through his throat like hot shards.

"She's going to be fine. We got the antibiotics started in time and she's doing well. She's still in pediatrics, but she ought to be up and around soon."

He looked at his wife, who had tears streaming down her cheeks. "You look terrible," he croaked. It was true. She had dark circles under her eyes and a huge, purple bruise on the side of her face. Seeing that made the blood surge through his veins and he tried to sit up, saying, "He better be dead, or by God..."

"He's dead," said Batsin. Anthony allowed himself to ease back onto the pillows, recognizing that he couldn't have gotten to his feet anyway.

"Major Clark got him just before we arrived," Dave continued. "He'd decided to kill you more directly, once his bizarre plans were foiled. But your wife wasn't letting anyone near you. He got a little too close and well…'' He trailed off as he noted Kristen glaring at him. Clearly she didn't want her heroics discussed.

She returned her gaze to Anthony. "You can have all the details when you're recovered," she said, as if they were talking about the outcome of a softball match.

"Want details now," he whispered past his raw throat. He could hardly believe that his healer of a wife had managed to kill the terrorist herself. But then again, the deceased had kidnapped her daughter. Mothers didn't take well to having their kids swiped. Kristen would have been magnificent in her fury. He wished he'd been able to see it.

"No, you need to rest. The doctors said so. And you need to save your strength so I can bring Amy to see you soon. I know that neither one of you will feel settled until you see each other."

That was true. He needed to see his little girl. He wanted to look at her pink, chubby cheeks and gaze into her big eyes. If he could hear her laugh, or even gurgle and chatter, he might be able to concentrate on his recovery instead of thinking about all the things that could have happened to her and to Kristen.

God, he was tired. His eyelids threatened to close again. He wanted to stay awake, to keep Kristen in his line of vision, to assure himself that she could cope with the painful knowledge that she'd killed people. She was neither the hardened soldier he'd become, nor trained to do whatever was necessary to accomplish a mission. Taking a life was never easy, even for the most experienced among them. But for someone like Kristen, a nurse and caretaker, the event could be shattering.

He forced his eyes to remain open and squeezed his wife's fingers. "You okay?" he rasped.

She looked back steadily, but he caught a fleeting glimpse of the haunted soul within her. Then she forced a smile—a sad, determined one—and nodded. "I'm going to be fine. I have a new psychologist, a part-timer to whom Paul transferred my file. I have to stay with it and do the work, facing my emotions. I'll get past this." She spoke as though saying it out loud would make it so. He would not disabuse her of the notion. She might have more success than he'd ever had.

A nurse whom Kristen greeted as Laney bustled in just then with a tray for blood work. She was pleased to see him awake and said she'd send for the doctor. Then she shooed Kristen and Dave out of the room.

"I'm a nurse. I can stay," Kristen protested on the threshold.

"No, you can't," Laney insisted. "You need to go home and get some sleep. Or at least go down to the pediatric ward and sleep on the cot in your daughter's room." She looked to Dave with a lifted eyebrow as if to ask whether he could make himself useful in this situation.

Dave took the hint. "We'll come back to see you in a few hours," he said to Anthony. "C'mon, Major Clark. Your friend is right about you getting some rest." The man winked at Laney as he led Kristen away. From beneath drooping lids, Anthony saw the young nurse blush.

As soon as Laney finished drawing blood, Anthony let his eyes slide closed. He could feel the bruising all over his back that his Kevlar had not been able to protect him from. Still, the vest had clearly saved his life. The vest *and* Kristen, he amended.

He'd forgotten to ask what day it was, how long he'd been out, or when he'd be able to go home. Yet he couldn't muster much more than these fleeting thoughts before a healing sleep began to creep up on him. Just before he drifted away, he resolved that he would find a way to give something back to Kristen and Amy, who had loved him even in his darkest hours.

KRISTEN HAD BEEN GRANTED emergency medical leave to care for her rapidly recovering daughter and more slowly healing husband. For three days, she'd made the rounds to each of them several times a day, and she had even managed to bring Amy to visit Anthony briefly the previous morning. But today she wanted to see Anthony alone. If he seemed strong enough—emotionally and physically—perhaps she would find a way to broach the difficult subject of their marriage. Because one thing seemed clear to her now that the crisis was behind them—there would be no future for the two of them if her heart was the only one yearning for it.

Rounding the corner near Anthony's hospital room, she noticed his door stood ajar. As she approached, she heard conversation within. She would have gone forward anyway, on the assumption that he was conversing with his doctor, but she realized just in time that the speaker's voice was not one she could identify immediately. Hesitating, not wanting to intrude, she listened for a pause in the exchange and glanced through the small window set into the door.

What she saw froze her in place. Anthony's father— a man she had met only once, when she'd been introduced after her brief courthouse wedding—stood at his bedside. His mother waited quietly nearby. From the occasional phone calls Anthony had made and the rare stories of his childhood he'd shared, Kristen knew that

Mrs. Garitano's silence went completely against the woman's nature.

She didn't want to eavesdrop, but neither did she want to interrupt. And she wasn't sure she could move anyway, so stunned was she to discover that the Garitanos had come all the way to Germany to see their son without a word of warning. So she stood outside the door with her heart hammering, watching and listening to the unexpected scene unfold.

"I didn't join the Army to get away from you, Dad," she heard Anthony respond. From where she stood, she could see him sitting up in the hospital bed wearing an Army T-shirt and probably those hospital pants with the string tie. The sheet and blanket covered most of him from the waist down. He looked young and vulnerable as he said, "I joined because I wanted to become someone you could be proud of."

"I was already proud of you before you left," said his father gruffly. Mr. Garitano looked a good deal older than the photograph in Amy's room. From the shocked look on Anthony's face, Kristen could guess what he was feeling before he hesitantly spoke. "You never said so."

Kristen recalled that throughout Anthony's life, his father had rarely said much of anything. But in the short time she'd been in the Garitano family, she'd surmised that Anthony's dad must have had a hard time getting a word in edgewise, when Anthony's mother and sister were so talkative.

"You never asked. I figured you knew," said Mr. Garitano. "You're my son. My only son." This seemed to sum up everything for the older man.

Kristen saw Anthony's mouth compress and his eyes blink rapidly for a second or two, forcing back emotion as he so often did. "Maybe we should both work on speaking up a little more," Anthony conceded.

"That's what I keep trying to…" his mother began, but then she heeded Mr. Garitano's quelling look and stopped. When her husband turned back to his son in the hospital bed, Mrs. Garitano smiled behind him.

"I'll start," the older man offered. He cleared his throat and rubbed his nose. Then he said, "You scared me shitless when you got yourself blown up in that god-forsaken foreign country. And then I find out you went and got yourself blown up a second time! Well, I had to come over here and make sure you knew."

He stopped, and Kristen had to resist the urge to shout "Make sure he knew *what?*" Mrs. Garitano seemed to want to do the same thing, because she leaned toward her husband. Anthony, however, waited quietly, staring at his father.

Mr. Garitano coughed and scuffed his shoe on the clean linoleum floor. "I love you, Anthony," he said, and his voice caught on the last syllable and he closed his lips—exactly the way Anthony sometimes did when he held back a tide of feelings.

Kristen's glance shifted to Anthony and her heart went out to him. How many years had he waited to hear those words from his father? And what would he do with them, now that he had? If ever there was a time for her husband to say what he felt, this was it. She willed him not to let the moment pass.

He didn't let her down.

"I love you, too, Dad." And he reached out to grasp his father's hand, then pulled him down into an awkward hug.

Mrs. Garitano clasped her hands together and raised them to her lips, almost as if she were sending up a prayer of thanks. Tears spilled onto her cheeks even as her eyes danced with joy.

Kristen didn't have the luxury of letting any tears fall, no matter how they crowded into her throat and eyes. She couldn't let them know she'd been standing there all these minutes. So she sniffed hard and tugged on the shirt of her uniform. Composed once again, she breezed into the room as if she'd only just arrived. Feigning surprise, she gushed a welcome to her in-laws.

A full ten minutes of bubbling conversation between the two women followed as Mrs. Garitano explained that her husband had insisted on coming the instant Kristen's mother had called and told them what had happened to Anthony and Amy. They were staying at a nearby hotel that Corrine Clark had recommended—typical of her mother to be the catalyst for something so unexpected, Kristen thought. Kristen had sent her parents an e-mail expressing some of the sentiments from the note she'd written before going to meet Bjornvik. Her mother must have read between the lines about the close call they'd all had and shared the story.

The Garitanos were sorry that they hadn't warned anyone of their arrival, but they'd been in a rush and the trip had been bewildering. Kristen assured them that she was thrilled to see them and so glad that they were here for Anthony. She kept to herself how grateful she was that her father-in-law had come, too. This was exactly what Anthony needed in order to begin again, in whatever direction he chose.

"But he looks awful," his mother exclaimed. "And you look awful, too!" She eyed Kristen's fading facial bruise with consternation.

"I'm fine. Honestly. And Amy is doing well, too."

"Oh, I can't wait to see my granddaughter! Is she

really recovering? When can we see her? Will you take us to her today?"

Kristen hesitated. She didn't want to delay their first in-person meeting with Amy, but she dearly wanted to talk with her husband. Her gaze darted to Anthony and back to his parents as she tried to decide what to do.

Her salvation came from an unlikely source. Mr. Garitano stepped forward and took his wife's elbow. "We'll leave these two alone for a while," he said. Then he gave Kristen a small smile. "You can find us in the coffee shop when you're done here."

"Okay," she said to him as self-doubt skittered around inside her stomach. She'd never been sure what her father-in-law thought of her. But when his gaze met hers, an understanding seemed to pass between them. They both loved Anthony and wanted him to heal, body and soul. Perhaps they would find common ground during this unexpected visit.

"Take your time," the man added as the older couple headed for the door. "You two may have some things to say to each other, too." And wasn't *that* the truth?

In the blink of an eye, Kristen was alone with her husband. Uncertainty scrambled out of its dark hiding place and took center stage in her mind. Because, no matter how she tried to deny it, one thing remained certain—this man was very changed. She could only hope he'd let her come to know the person he'd become.

CHAPTER NINETEEN

ANTHONY LOOKED AT HIS WIFE and her tentative smile. She looked beautiful and capable, yet vulnerable at the same time. He realized that even though so much had changed between them in the last few days, one thing remained the same. He didn't know her very well anymore.

But he sure as hell hoped he'd get the chance to change that.

He wanted to say so many thing to his wife, but he didn't know where to start. Talking—really *talking* about things that mattered—was not a skill he'd ever mastered. But he knew he had to try. Look how many years he'd wasted thinking his father wasn't proud of him, believing he didn't really love him. He didn't want to repeat the same mistake with Kristen.

"Kristen," he began, but then his thoughts jumbled together with his doubts and insecurities and he closed his mouth and looked away, trying to sort out the right words from the ones that would ruin any chance he might still have with her.

"I know you must be angry that I disobeyed your orders and went with Bjornvik," she said. Her words added to his confusion.

"But you were right in the end," he admitted, not comprehending why she was the one apologizing. "Your medical background and the fact that Amy trusted you and took comfort from your presence made you the only one who could have kept her alive. You took an enormous risk, but you saved Amy's life. Doing something like that is considered the pinnacle of success among Rangers." He offered her a tentative grin with that last observation.

Her expression became hopeful. "I thought you'd think I...well, never mind."

"No, tell me what you thought," he urged, glad to have her talk so maybe he wouldn't have to. He reached for her hand and squeezed her fingers.

She hesitated, but then said, "I thought you'd think I betrayed you or something. Going behind your back the way I did."

These words stymied him. After a moment or two, he managed to say, "Does this have anything to do with Paul Farley?"

A blush crept over her cheeks, and she nodded as tears sprang to her eyes.

"He says it was a classic case of transference. When I...I...."

Anthony reached for her hand. "I know what happened and I understand. Stress and fear do terrible things to people."

"How will you ever trust me again?" A single tear dripped down her face.

"I'd trust you with my life. In fact, I think I did that already. Under fire. What's more, I'd trust you with my daughter's life. Come to think of it, I did that, too." How could she think this would be an issue of trust? She'd proven her love in so many ways. "And you did pretty damn well on both counts."

She squeezed his fingers. "I love you so much."

He couldn't help the surge of protectiveness that

welled inside him. "Please don't ever take chances like that again. I'd be lost without you."

With an effort, she regained her composure. "Not so long ago you seemed more than willing to be lost *and* without me." There was a question implied at the end of the statement.

He nodded. She'd articulated the whole thrust of the problems between them in one succinct sentence. "I don't want to be lost anymore. And I'm very sure I don't want to be without you." He said it as gently as he could, protecting this fragile honesty with the softness of his voice.

She said, "Neither Amy nor I would be alive today if you hadn't come for us. No one else would have gotten us out in time. You accomplished something nearly impossible." The light of hope had returned to her eyes and he liked seeing it there. Yet he felt she deserved more of an explanation. He struggled to find the words while she waited, obviously sensing he had more to say.

"Kristen, when I lost all the men in my team, I didn't feel that I deserved to live. I didn't want to recover—it seemed far too painful even to contemplate. But somewhere deep down, I was afraid that Bjornvik would come after you. Even when the doctors kept telling me that I'd imagined the sighting, I couldn't let go of the idea that you might need me. Just for a little while longer." His throat went tight and he stopped talking, trying to bring his rioting emotions under control. These memories still bled all over the inside of his heart. But they had to be spoken. Now was the moment.

Kristen gazed at him with tenderness but not pity. After what she'd been through in the last few days, he trusted that she understood him better than ever before. "I will always need you, Anthony," she assured him.

"Sometimes I may not act as if I do—I put on this strong, superior facade, especially when it comes to Amy. But the truth is, half the time I have no idea what I'm doing. I need you to help me figure it all out."

He nodded. Her confession had given him time to force away the thickness choking his speech. "That's what I like most about you. It's always been clear you could get along just fine without me, but you still need me anyway. It turns out I'm no different. I may be a Ranger, trained to succeed and survive against all odds, but I still need you, too."

She leaned forward and kissed him, a tender, gentle kiss. "I love you, Tiger," she whispered as she straightened. But Anthony couldn't bear to let her get away.

His arm snaked around her waist and tugged her gently toward him until, with a small laugh, she perched her hip on the edge of his mattress and hugged him close. His recovery suddenly took a leap forward as his blood surged and his heart pounded and his breathing became labored. He wanted her. Here. Now.

As he kissed her, he pulled her more fully into his embrace until she sprawled across him, pressed chest to toes against his body. She made a few halfhearted sounds of shock at what he was doing here in his hospital bed, but he just kissed her some more until she became melting wax beside him.

"We shouldn't," she murmured when he released her mouth to nibble beneath her earlobe.

"I know," he agreed. "But how often can we expect to be alone once all three of us are back home?"

"True," she conceded as she wrapped an arm around his neck and drew him closer. "You're sure you're sufficiently recovered?"

"Recovering more and more every second." If there

was an occasional twinge of discomfort where he'd been bruised during the bomb blast, he hardly noticed. He was with the woman he loved beyond all reason and his spirit demanded that he show her, without hesitation, without remorse, without guilt. "I love you, Kristen. Get ready to find out just how much," he warned.

"MOM, YOU KNOW I'M GLAD you came to help us with Amy, but you can't keep on giving in to her. She's not sick anymore and needs to be reminded of her boundaries." Kristen grasped one end of the cookie Amy struggled to retain and managed to wrestle it away. Toddler-size screams of outrage followed.

Over the din, Kristen's mother said, "Boundaries, shmoundaries, she's just a baby and a sick one, to boot. And I'm her grandmother. I can spoil her if I want to." With a defiant expression, she gave the child another cookie. The screaming stopped instantly and Amy stuffed the treat into her mouth as fast as she could to ward off any further parental interference.

Kristen threw her hands into the air and let them fall again. There was no talking to the woman. Corrine had left her husband in charge of their dogs and arrived on the doorstep two days after Anthony's parents had departed. She'd insisted that married couples needed time alone together, and what better way to get that than to have a grandmother around to look after the baby.

Her mom had been delighted to see Amy again, so grown up compared to the newborn she'd last seen. And from the instant the fully recovered Amy had met her grandmother, the two had been best friends. Unfortunately, Anthony had spent long hours coping with the inquiry that had followed his team's unauthorized rescue mission. Kristen had seen precious little of him, despite the live-in baby-sitter they had in her mother.

"You are not helping when you do this kind of thing, Mom. She's going to be impossible if you continue to give her every little thing she wants."

"You seem to have survived my child-rearing methods," her mother retorted with a chuckle.

"I joined the Army because I couldn't get any stability at home!" Kristen blurted. Then she covered her mouth as if she could somehow stop the hurtful words from getting out. Too late. Her mother had heard. The blush that rose to Corrine's cheeks made that all too clear. An answering heat suffused her own face.

But instead of weeping, as she might have done when Kristen had lived with her all those years ago, Corrine lifted her gaze to her daughter's and nodded. Wearily, she said, "And it all turned out fine, didn't it? I'm glad you found the Army, because there was no way I was ever going to measure up as a parent in your eyes."

"That's not true!" Kristen cried, contrite and suspicious at the same time. Was this a new side of her mother she had never known, or simply a different method of creating melodrama?

Corrine lifted an eyebrow. In that gesture, Kristen saw both herself and her young daughter. They each had a knack for raising one eyebrow to effect. "All right, maybe there's some truth in it. I might have been a little demanding and maybe a bit too critical," she admitted.

The older woman laughed. "You and your father are so much alike. You both always have all the answers."

Suddenly, it occurred to Kristen that her free-spirited mother must have been completely overwhelmed by the child she'd been. And having a husband like Master Sergeant Clifford Clark couldn't have been easy for a woman with a spirit as flighty and sweet as a butterfly's.

"You're so much like your father, it's almost appalling. But Amy will teach you a thing or two. She'll mellow you out, whether you like it or not." Corrine smiled at her granddaughter and handed over another cookie. At Kristen's scowl, Corrine added, "They're wholegrain carrot cookies. More like a meal than a treat. Try one." She slid the box forward.

Kristen glanced down at the wrapping and saw that they were, indeed, health food cookies, guaranteed to make for an interesting diaper change in a few hours. The thought brought a rueful smile to Kristen's face.

"How's Anthony doing these days?" Corrine asked.

"The bruises are gone. Thank God for Kevlar. His head injury seems to have healed and he hardly ever gets those headaches anymore."

Corrine put her hand gently on Kristen's arm. "I meant, how are the two of you doing? Together? As a married couple?"

Kristen looked up at her mother. Sometimes it was scary how her mother knew things she'd never been told. Kristen had been very careful not to wear her heart on her sleeve as she and Anthony made slow progress toward a normal life together.

"We're doing fine," she began, unsure how much she wanted to share. But something in the way her mother looked into her eyes, the warmth and kindness of her steady gaze made Kristen open like a blossom. She smiled. "Actually, I'm cautiously hopeful. We talked at the hospital just before he was released. We both realize we have to get to know each other again, but we're willing to do that. More than willing." And she found herself blushing at the memories.

"Oh, I'm so happy for you, sweetie. You deserve a good marriage."

"Is yours a good one?" she asked, shocked that she'd dared.

Corrine smiled and her focus seemed to drift inward. "Yes," she said.

Kristen found herself grinning. The unlikely commitment between Clifford and Corrine had lasted thirty years. A stiff, unyielding Sergeant and a meditating flower child had somehow made things work between them. So there had to be hope for the Ranger and the nurse.

"What are my favorite women so happy about?" asked Anthony from the doorway of the kitchen.

Love did a pirouette in her heart and other emotions filled her, dancing and spinning and singing as she looked at him wearing his dress blue uniform for the first time since their wedding. He was impossibly handsome—tall, broad, and decked out in all his medals and ribbons. She rejoiced that she could claim him as her own. "You're home!"

"Dave drove me home so you didn't have to come get me." He leaned a shoulder against the doorjamb. There was a letter in his hand. Kristen saw that it was the note she'd written before she'd gone with the terrorists. She'd asked Dave to give it to her husband when he got the chance.

"We're eating cookies and talking about good marriages," said her mother.

"Da, da, da!" Amy shouted as she bounced in her high chair so hard it jigged across the floor a few inches.

"There's my girl!" he said as he went to her with outstretched arms.

"No!" Kristen said. Anthony stopped in his tracks

and his smile wavered. "I mean, she's covered with cookie gunk and you're in your uniform," she tried to explain. "And you look pretty damn good, so let's not mess it up."

A small grin curved his mouth at one corner. The other side was still affected by jagged scars. "Do you hear that, pumpkin? Mommy likes how Daddy looks in his dress blues." He grabbed the pudgy little hands, cookie scum and all, and bent to kiss them until she wriggled and laughed. When he stood up straight, his face was smeared with disgusting brown goo. "How about a kiss for you, too?" he said, and he started after her.

Kristen chuckled, then saw that he wasn't going to stop as she'd expected. A laughing shriek escaped her as she bolted around the table and out the door. From behind her she heard her husband tell Amy that Grandma would watch her for a little while.

"Take your time," said Grandma, with amusement in her voice.

Kristen knew she didn't have time to get out the front door so she flew up the stairs, hoping to achieve the bathroom in time. She crossed into the confined space and almost had the door closed when Anthony's foot and hand appeared, preventing her from barricading herself within. All the while, laughter bubbled through her. "You can't come in!" she declared. "You're covered with carrot cookie goo!"

"The carrot cookie monster!" he said in a pretty good imitation of the Cookie Monster. Amy would have been delighted. For some reason, Kristen got a warm, sexy feeling instead. "I'm going to get you," he said in a sing-song voice.

She really hoped he would, but giving in now wouldn't

be any fun. She pushed harder on the door, bolstering her foot against the tub and leaning her whole weight on it. Inexorably, Anthony forced the door open until she saw an arm, then a shoulder, then his face. The sight of it covered with brown smudges brought on a new wave of laughter and she was helpless to hold the door another second. She gave up and the man stepped inside the tiled room with her.

He shut the door behind him.

The air went hot all at once. Kristen could hardly breathe as hilarity evolved into something much more sensual. Her insides began to melt. And he hadn't even touched her yet!

"You gonna let a little thing like baby spit keep us apart?" he asked. And somehow he made it sound like the sexiest invitation she'd ever heard.

"Not a chance," she answered as she glided into his arms and wrapped herself around him. In less than a second, his lips and tongue made her forget all about the cookie gunk.

But then he pulled a little away, grabbed a towel and swiped it over his face and then hers. "I really hadn't planned on being your Cookie Monster today, but it has possibilities. We'll have to give this role-playing game some serious consideration."

"What's wrong with now? I'll be the cookie," she offered, with a smile she hoped would make him groan.

He didn't disappoint her. He closed his eyes and a little sound murmured deep in his throat as he slid his hands to her butt and pulled her tightly against him. "I will have to take you up on that offer very soon. But I came home to tell you some things, and if we make love, I'm likely to forget half of them and…"

"Okay, okay," she interrupted, still grinning. "Tell

me. There might still be time afterward.'' She knew there might not be too many more opportunities like this, what with her mother having to fly back home so soon.

He laughed. Then he took a breath and turned serious. ''First, no charges will be brought against any of the Rangers who helped us,'' he said.

She went very still. ''What about you?'' The German authorities had not been happy about the interference of the American soldiers in what should have been a local concern. And there was the little issue of how they had blown up about an acre and a half of countryside and abandoned warehouses. Still, General Jetyko had been optimistic.

''No charges for me, either,'' he said, but there was a note of hesitation in his voice.

''But?'' she prodded.

''I won't be leading any more combat missions.'' His voice sounded so normal, given the import of his words.

Kristen's eyes instantly began to burn and her desire to make love to her husband turned into molten fury at the authorities who could do this to him—this man, this hero, this soldier! ''No! You can't let them do that!'' she blurted.

''It's already done. I agreed,'' he said in the same voice he used to mollify Amy when she had one of her little tantrums. But Kristen was too outraged by the injustice to be soothed. When she continued to shake her head in denial, he nuzzled the side of her neck and danced her in a tiny circle, calming her, distracting her. ''It's done. I'm okay with it. Really. And part of me knows it's time for this.''

''Wh-what do you mean?'' she asked, nearly overcome with sorrow for the loss of the career he'd worked so hard for.

He lifted his face from the hollow at her throat. "We have Amy now. And each other. I've had a lot of time to think while I cooled my heels waiting for the various investigators to get on with their inquiries. I realized a week ago that I wanted more time with both of you. We have so much catching up to do. And I'm not getting any younger. I was going to request a teaching position among the Rangers anyway. So when the General offered me this bargain to make peace with the Germans, I was happy. Of course, I had to pretend to be chagrined when we met with the German authorities so they would be appeased. In the end, it worked out perfectly for me. For us."

She stared into his brown eyes, and saw that he spoke the absolute truth. He was ready for this change, eager for it. Of course he'd miss the adrenaline rush of missions, but he seemed genuinely ready to trade that in for the less dramatic but no less difficult task of building a family and teaching younger recruits what they needed to know to stay alive under the worst of conditions.

"Oh, Anthony," she murmured as she fell in love with him all over again. Right there in the tiny bathroom. "I'm so glad for you. And for me and Amy, too. The truth is, everything I know about raising a child comes from books. And I'm finding out that books don't have much to do with reality. I could really use your help."

He looked at her as if this surprised him. Then a slow smile eased over his face. "I was a little worried you wouldn't want to give up any control."

"Control! You've seen your daughter in action. Does it look like I have any actual control?" Kristen had come to appreciate this even more in the time her mother had been in residence. Corrine had a way of easing Kristen past frustration and into a celebration of Amy's spirit.

Maybe Anthony could help with that after Corrine returned home.

"We'll probably be transferred back to the States," he said. "You don't mind, do you?"

"No. There are hospitals everywhere for me to work in."

"Which reminds me of one more thing," he said, holding her gaze with his own. "Before we go, there's this plastic surgeon on a fellowship here from New York. He thinks he can fix my face. We've had some discussions. I want you to meet him, too, so you can tell me what you think. It would be great if I could get this taken care of while we're still here and I have all this downtime. I'd like to go for a look that's maybe a little more sexy-pirate than the crazed-monster thing I'm currently sporting."

This, more than anything else he'd said to her since the end of their ordeal, moved her deeply. His agreement to plastic surgery demonstrated his desire to begin living his life to its fullest. Tears filled her eyes and spilled over. But her heart was smiling.

He leaned his forehead against hers. And he started slow dancing her in circles again. She saw that his eyes shimmered, too. "So what do you think?" he asked softly.

"I think I love you," she said.

"I think that's a good thing. Because I love you, too." Then he danced her against the shower door and kissed her breathless.

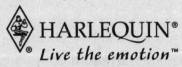

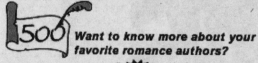

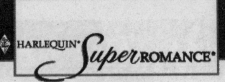

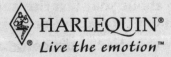

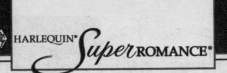

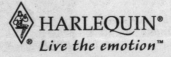

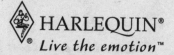

HARLEQUIN® _Super_ROMANCE®

Men of the True North—
Wilde and Free

The Wilde Men

Homecoming Wife
(Superromance #1212)
On-sale July 2004

Ten years ago Nate Wilde's wife, Angela, left and never came back. Nate is now quite happy to spend his days on the rugged trails of Whistler, British Columbia. When Angela returns to the resort town, the same old attraction flares to life between them. Will Nate be able to convince his wife to stay for good this time?

Family Matters
(Superromance #1224)
On-sale September 2004

Marc was the most reckless Wilde of the bunch. But when an accident forces him to reevaluate his life, he has trouble accepting his fate and even more trouble accepting help from Fiona Gordon. Marc is accustomed to knowing what he wants and going after it. But getting Fiona may be his most difficult challenge yet.

A Mom for Christmas
(Superromance #1236)
On-sale November 2004

Aidan Wilde is a member of the Whistler Mountain ski patrol, but he has never forgiven himself for being unable to save his wife's life. Six years after her death, Aidan and his young daughter still live under the shadow of suspicion. Travel photographer Nicola Bond comes to Whistler on an assignment and falls for Aidan. But she can never live up to his wife's memory…

Available wherever Harlequin books are sold.

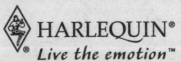

HARLEQUIN®
Live the emotion™

www.eHarlequin.com

HSRWM